Step inside th... ...se
for the annual y... ...er
Captain Treev... ...o
Cornwall, find a... ...the shadows from
enigmatic Emily Faulkner's eyes for good? And
watch out for the sparks flying between dashing
composer Cador Kitto and no-nonsense
Rosenwyn Treleven! With passion, newfound hope
and a dash of Christmas magic in the air, it promises
to be a celebration to remember...

Don't miss this delightfully romantic duet from

Marguerite Kaye and Bronwyn Scott

Read Emily and Treeve's story in
The Captain's Christmas Proposal
by Marguerite Kaye

and

Cador and Rosenwyn's story in
Unwrapping His Festive Temptation
by Bronwyn Scott

Marguerite Kaye writes hot historical romances from her home in cold and usually rainy Scotland, featuring Regency rakes, Highlanders and sheikhs. She has published over forty books and novellas. When she's not writing, she enjoys walking, cycling (but only on the level), gardening (but only what she can eat) and cooking. She also likes to knit and occasionally drink martinis (though not at the same time). Find out more on her website, margueritekaye.com.

Bronwyn Scott is a communications instructor at Pierce College in the United States, and is the proud mother of three wonderful children—one boy and two girls. When she's not teaching or writing, she enjoys playing the piano, traveling—especially to Florence, Italy—and studying history and foreign languages. Readers can stay in touch on Bronwyn's website, bronwynnscott.com, or at her blog, bronwynswriting.blogspot.com. She loves to hear from readers.

Invitation to a Cornish Christmas

MARGUERITE KAYE
BRONWYN SCOTT

HARLEQUIN®HISTORICAL

Recycling programs for this product may not exist in your area.

ISBN-13: 978-1-335-63539-6

Invitation to a Cornish Christmas

Copyright © 2019 by Harlequin Books S.A.

The Captain's Christmas Proposal © 2019 by Marguerite Kaye

Unwrapping His Festive Temptation © 2019 by Bronwyn Scott

This edition published by arrangement with Harlequin Books S.A.

For questions and comments about the quality of this book, please contact us at CustomerService@Harlequin.com.

www.Harlequin.com

Printed in U.S.A.

CONTENTS

THE CAPTAIN'S CHRISTMAS PROPOSAL

Marguerite Kaye

Chapter One

November 1822
—Porth Karrek, Cornwall

It was still dark when Emily Faulkner left her rented cottage on the estates of Karrek House, which sat on a bluff headland above the small fishing port after which it was named, the high cliffs and narrow entrance providing a safe harbour from the rough Cornish seas. Last night's sky had offered the prospect of a brief respite from the winter storms which had been raging interminably, and she was eager to take advantage of any break in the weather. She hated these bleak winter days which kept her indoors and restricted her ability to work, since the intricate nature of the tasks involved in producing her only source of income required natural light.

The permanently lowering skies which had so far defined November were one of the many aspects of life in Cornwall she hadn't anticipated when she'd fled here, back in April. Yet Porth Karrek was an ideal bolt-hole. Snuggled into a small inlet on the rugged south Cornwall coast, about four miles from the larger port of Penzance and a day's travel from Truro, the regional capital, it was a world away from London. The perfect place to disappear from view, which was what she had craved.

Her cottage stood on the periphery of the estate, in an exposed position, the low drystone wall which formed the boundary of her tiny garden providing little protection from the elements. The briny prevailing wind which blew in from the English Channel made gardening a challenge, just as Jago Bligh, the surly estate manager, had predicted. The cottage itself was almost impossible to keep warm, as the wind howled through every nook and cranny of the floorboards and window frames—something else Mr Bligh had pointed out when she had first viewed it. Emily had thought it odd at the time that he seemed so intent on discouraging her from taking up residence when it was obvious that the place had been lying empty for some time, but she reckoned now that her crime had simply been her lack of Cornish heritage. Like the proud Highlanders of her mother's native Lewis, the Cornish considered themselves a nation apart, isolated from the rest of Britain, with their own traditions and way of life— which, needless to say, they considered vastly superior to any other.

Emily, Mr Bligh had made clear, would be a grudgingly tolerated outsider, and once again he'd been proved right, but this too had suited her. Back in April, with her life in tatters, she had been happy to close the door of her cottage, turn her back on the world and lick her wounds. Weeks passed, and she had been barely conscious of life outside, spending the days at her workbench or tending her sparse garden, cursing the day she had met Andrew Macfarlane, and reliving every moment since she had, wondering if at any point she could have avoided her fate. If she hadn't been so blinded by her feelings for him, might she have spotted the signs before it was too late? A painful and ultimately pointless waste of time those weeks of recrimination had been, for she couldn't undo the past. All she could do was wipe the slate clean and start again.

Spring had passed, and summer had been making an early appearance in June when Emily had begun to emerge from the dark cloud she had been under since her world had collapsed around her at the start of the year. She had awoken just after dawn one morning to vibrant blue skies. In the garden, the earth had been warm beneath her bare feet, the rows of vegetables, which had appeared on the point of dying, had blossomed, seemingly overnight. The air had been heavy with the tang of salt, and when she had made her way down to Karrek Sands, the sea was turquoise, sparkling, the waves gentle, the rhythmic swish as they broke on the beach no longer a warning but an invitation.

She hadn't intended to swim, but she'd been unable to resist, wary at first of the undertow, the unfamiliar currents and her own neglected muscles. But the skills honed by years of swimming in the wild seas off Lewis had not deserted her. The familiar sensation of being cocooned in water soothed her. Pitting herself against the tow and pull of the waves invigorated her, cleared her mind and made her look anew at her life, forcing her to admit that she had been living under a cloud of fear for most of last year. Now the worst had happened and she had nothing more to lose, she need no longer be afraid.

She took to the sea every day after that, in the early

mornings when Karrek Sands were deserted, unaware that she had an audience until the two fascinated local children plucked up the courage to speak to her, so utterly strange it was to them, to see anyone swimming. Teaching them to swim, watching their initial fear turning to sheer joy as they grew in confidence had been a real pleasure, a balm to the raw pain caused by the humiliating and devastating nature of Andrew's revelations, if a bittersweet one. She missed their company at summer's end, when they returned to school.

Now, more than half a year after arriving in Cornwall, Emily had come to love her wild, rugged adopted home. She was mentally scarred but her heart was no longer bleeding. She had struck up no friendships with the villagers, but the hostility and suspicion which had greeted her arrival in Porth Karrek had given way to bland indifference. Emily was lonely but content.

The November storms forced her to settle for a paddle in the shallows, which was what she intended to do today. The narrow strip of her front garden led on to the main path which wound its way up to the gates of Karrek House—though it would be more accurate to say gate posts, for the gates themselves were long gone, only the vacant gatekeeper's cottage an indication that they had once functioned. From here the path forked. The broader path led through the estate cottages to St Piran's Church, which stood guard at the top of steep Budoc Lane, the hub of Porth Karrek village, leading down to the harbour. But it was the lesser-used path Emily took, which cut across the grassy headland to a point above the beach.

Grey dawn had given way to a fair morning. There were hints of pale blue sky peeking through the clouds, though how long it would last was another matter. The wind buffeted her skirts, sending her cloak flying out behind her as she hurried along, enjoying the salty breeze on her face, even though it made her eyes stream. Breathless but exhilarated, she arrived at the clifftop where the path narrowed significantly, cut like a staircase into the cliffs. Intent on keeping her footing, she didn't notice the solitary figure until she had reached the sands.

She felt an illogical spasm of resentment. Who was trespassing on her private domain? The man was standing at the water's edge with his back to her, and she knew even from this distance that he was a stranger. Yet there was something in his confident stance, feet planted firmly in the sands, shoulders set, back straight, that gave her the strong impression that he belonged here.

He appeared to be staring out at the outcrop of rocks known as The Beasts, the serrated tips of which were visible at low tide. For the rest of the time, The Beasts lurked just below the surface, waiting to trap the unwary sailor headed for the sanctuary of Porth Karrek harbour—or, if you listened to Jago Bligh, de facto harbourmaster, to ensure that only a native Porth Karrek boat might tie up there.

The male figure was standing stock-still, as yet unaware of her presence. She could not ignore him. She could either abandon her paddle, take a chance on the weather holding and return later, or she could walk down to the water's edge, bid him good morning, then leave him to his own devices. Shielding her eyes to gaze out at the horizon, Emily could see the first signs of clouds gathering. It wasn't worth holding off and the tide, in any case, would be against her later. If she stood here prevaricating for much longer, he would eventually spot her and assume she'd been spying on him.

For goodness sake, she had as much right to be here as he did! Perching on a rock, Emily took off her boots and unrolled her stockings. The sand was firm and damp. She set her bare feet down, closing her eyes in bliss at the feel of the soft, golden grains oozing between her toes. Tucking her stockings into her boots and placing them behind a rock, she made her way down the sands towards the lone figure. The waves were lapping just short of the tips of his brogues, though the sea was creeping ever closer now that the tide was on the turn.

He must have sensed her presence rather than heard her approach, muffled by the roar of the surf further out, for he turned around while she was still a few steps from him. He was dressed in a wide-skirted brown coat, buckskin breeches and thick woollen stockings. It was rough country garb, though not coarsely made, for his coat fitted perfectly across his shoulders, and he wore underneath it not only a white linen shirt and neckcloth but a waistcoat of fine wool. Country garb, made by a city tailor, and certainly not purchased from the Chegwins' store by the harbour. His skin was deeply tanned, with a fretwork of lines at the corners of his eyes as if he spent part of every day squinting at the horizon. His blue-black hair, slightly too long for current fashion, was tousled by the wind. The stubble, which was not quite a beard, not quite simply a matter of him having forgotten to shave, was the same coal-black colour.

His smile dawned slowly as she approached, the nascent beard accentuating the fullness of his bottom lip, the whiteness of his teeth, and Emily's insides responded in a positive lurch of attraction. He was not handsome, he was far too striking to be considered handsome, too unkempt—no, not unkempt, and not wild but—untamed, that was it.

'Good morning.' His voice was low but cultured, with no trace of the lilting Cornish accent.

'Good morning.' His eyes were hazel. He really did have a most beguiling smile. Emily smiled back. 'It's a lovely fresh day, isn't it?'

The man nodded at the massing bank of cloud on the horizon. 'For the moment. Allow me to introduce myself. Captain Treeve Penhaligon.'

'And I am Miss Faulkner, Emily Faulkner. How do you do, Captain—' She broke off, her eyes widening. 'Captain Penhaligon! The late Mr Austol Penhaligon's brother? I never met him,' she added when he nodded, 'for I came to Porth Karrek in April, three months after he was lost at sea, but I know he was both respected and very much loved around here. Please accept my condolences for your loss.'

'Thank you, I appreciate it, though in truth we were not close,' Captain Penhaligon said awkwardly. 'I have been travelling the high seas for nigh on twenty years and Austol was sure if he breathed anything other than Cornish air, he'd be poisoned, so our paths rarely crossed. To be perfectly honest, the officers and men of my ship are more family to me than a brother I barely knew as an adult. Still, it seemed very strange to me, arriving last night, not to find him in residence.'

'That must have been very difficult for you.'

'Of all the fates I've ever considered for myself, inheriting the Karrek estates wasn't one. If one of us was going to die prematurely, you'd have thought it would be me, captain of a warship, not a country landowner. I'm not sure what to make of the situation I find myself in now, and I'm sure the villagers are equally apprehensive.'

An understatement, Emily thought, though did not say. From what she could gather, the majority had hoped that Captain Penhaligon would never return to claim his inheritance, happy to continue under Jago Bligh's familiar stewardship. 'You're an unknown quantity, and people in these parts don't welcome change,' she equivocated. 'I'll leave you to your musings.'

'Please don't. I have leave of absence until the end of the year, and plenty of time to muse. Right now, I'm happy to be distracted, and, if you have no objection, I'd very much like to accompany you on your walk.' Captain Penhaligon glanced down at her bare feet, smiling quizzically. 'Or should that be paddle? Unless you have that rare talent, the ability to walk on water?'

Emily was surprised into a little huff of laughter. 'When it comes to water, I much prefer to swim.'

'I hope you weren't planning to swim today? At this time of year, the tides and currents are too strong. It's dangerous.'

'You needn't worry, I'm a very strong swimmer and I was raised to respect the sea in all its moods.'

'Round here, people respect the sea by staying out of it.'

'Round here, people believe that if you learn to swim your ship will sink.'

'An old wives' tale, adopted by mariners the world over.'

'It's true,' Emily said. 'I was born on the Isle of Lewis, in the Outer Hebrides, where the sands are every bit as golden, the surf just as high and the sea itself, not only every bit as wild and beautiful, but even colder than here. Lewis is very like Cornwall, where the people rely on fishing for a living, yet none of the fishermen will learn to swim for fear it will tempt the sea to take them for her own.'

'You don't share that particular superstition, then?'

'My grandmother taught me to swim. She was an extremely practical woman, who believed you make your own luck.'

'And you take after her?'

'I do think you make your own luck, both good and bad.'

Captain Penhaligon raised a brow. 'Now that sounds like the voice of experience talking.'

How little he knew! But Emily did not want to taint this surprisingly enjoyable conversation with her sordid past. 'If I am ever unfortunate enough to fall overboard, I shan't be trusting to luck to throw a helpful wave my way and cast me safely on the shore. Can you swim?'

'I confess I can't, though you've made see that I should learn,' he answered, looking somewhat shame-faced. 'Perhaps you will teach me?'

'Not in these winter seas. If you were staying until the summer, it would be another matter entirely. You could join my little class of two pupils.'

'You teach swimming! Here! Who are these rebels?'

'They are the niece and nephew of your estate manager, as a matter of fact, Kensa and Jack Bligh. They spied on me for days before they plucked up the courage to speak to me, and it took me a week before I could persuade them into the water.'

'And what did their parents have to say?'

'They were afraid they'd be told to stay away, so it remained our little secret. The two of them were like seal pups by the end of the summer, diving in and out of the waves, though of course the weather is far too rough for them now—and they are back at school.'

'You sound as if you miss them.'

'Oh, I do. They thought I was a mermaid, when they first saw me.'

'Oh, no, you are far too lovely to be a mermaid. They are ugly creatures, more fish than female, with seaweed for hair and scales all over their bodies.'

Lovely? He meant in comparison to a fish, Emily told herself sternly! 'Are you telling me you've seen one? Had you been at the ship's rum ration?'

'No, and no—I never drink on board, but I've heard enough tales from my men to believe there's something in it—as there is with all superstitions, I reckon. There's a place on the other side of Penzance known as Mermaid's Rock, where they are said to comb their hair, and sing a siren song to lure sailors to their doom.'

'In Lewis, it is not mermaids but selkies the sailors fear will lure them on to the rocks. Selkies are seals who can take the shape of a beautiful woman on land, and who are said to have certain *appetites*, according to my grandmother,' Emily said. 'I remember wondering what on earth she was talking about. I thought perhaps they liked porridge.'

Captain Penhaligon gave a bellow of laughter. 'She was not, then, quite lacking in superstition?'

'Oh, selkies are no myth. Ask any Lewisman or woman.'

'A seal who can take the shape of a beautiful woman,'

Captain Penhaligon mused. 'I wonder if that's what your pupils saw, a selkie looking to beguile a sailor?'

Emily chuckled. 'You will never know, their victims never do know, until it's too late.'

'I'm a sailor. Are you warning me off, Miss Faulkner? You don't look the siren type.'

'Ah, but that's why I'm so dangerous.'

'You are certainly intriguing. I am very glad that I decided to take a walk this morning. Not that we've done much walking yet. Or even paddling.'

Emily looked at the incoming tide in surprise. 'We must have been standing here for at least half an hour.'

'A very pleasant half-hour, as far as I am concerned, though perhaps I've intruded on your privacy too long?'

'When I saw you standing here this morning, I'll admit I was irked,' Emily confessed. 'I consider Karrek Sands my own personal beach, I'll have you know. But now—I am enjoying our conversation, Captain Penhaligon.'

'Will you call me Treeve?'

'If you will call me Emily.' There was a warmth in his smile that she could not resist. It seemed to her that fate had brought him to the beach, the perfect antidote to her loneliness for he was, in some ways, as much a stranger here as she. A very appealing stranger, who for whatever reason, seemed to find her appealing too. And whether that made her shallow or not she didn't care! It was a salve to her ravaged sense of self-worth. What harm could there be in enjoying the moment!

A wavelet, bolder than the rest, washed over Treeve's brogues, and she burst out laughing. 'If we are actually going to do any walking today, you'll need to take those shoes off or they'll get ruined.'

'And here was me thinking that you were going to teach me to walk on water too.' Treeve knelt down, divesting himself quickly of his brogues and stockings. 'There, now we can both enjoy the bite of the sea on our toes. Shall we?'

Chapter Two

The wind blew Miss Emily Faulkner's cloak and skirts around her legs, revealing tantalising glimpses of her slim ankles, her shapely calves. Her face was tanned. From the long hours she had spent in the Cornish sunshine this summer past, Treeve presumed, swimming here in the cove. He'd give a good deal to have watched her. Miss Emily Faulkner was one of the most attractive women he had ever met. Though it had never happened to him before, it would be no exaggeration to say that he was, in fact, well and truly smitten.

She was not in the first bloom of youth—thirty or so, would be his guess—for though she looked no more than five or six and twenty, her expression had none of the openness of a younger woman, and all the guarded-ness of one having lived long enough to have secrets to protect. Her hair was the colour of wet sand, dark blonde streaked with gold, and her eyes were the colour of a stormy ocean, grey-blue fringed with long dark lashes. Perhaps she was a sea nymph after all! Her nose was too strong to belong to an accredited beauty, her mouth too generous. Intelligence blazed in her eyes, something that many a man would find intimidating. He thought it merely added to her charm.

'What brings a Highland lass all the way to Cornwall?' he asked.

'I am renting that cottage up there, the one on the furthest point of the headland, which I suppose makes you my landlord.'

'Forgive me, I'm a rough sailor accustomed to speaking my mind, but frankly you neither look nor sound like a woman obliged to fend for herself.'

'Necessity, as they say, is the mother of invention. I do very well for myself, thank you. And while I know next to nothing about the Royal Navy, I am pretty sure they expect their officers to be gentlemen, not rough sailors.'

'Oh, I can play the gentleman if required, and the rough sailor too, if the situation demands it. Tell me, is the cottage in good order? If there is anything that can be done to improve it?'

She cast him a levelling look. 'It suits me very well, and if there was anything needing done, I am sure Mr Bligh, your estate manager, would attend to it.'

'I was merely thinking of your comfort.'

'Thank you, but it's more about how it would look. I've already stolen a march on all of Porth Karrek in meeting you this morning. Imagine the reaction if one of your first acts of generosity was towards an outsider like me.'

'You're right, it was naïve of me.'

Emily shook her head, smiling faintly. 'A lovely gesture nonetheless.'

The wind ruffled her hair, dragging thick tendrils free of her ribbon and whipping it around her face. He had been apprehensive about returning to his birthplace, even temporarily, but the prospect of spending the next few weeks in Cornwall suddenly seemed a lot more appealing. A *lot* more, Treeve thought, as she stooped to pick up an empty crab shell, and the wind tugged at her skirts, outlining her very shapely bottom.

'We used to boil these up in buckets of salt water on the beach,' Emily said, happily oblivious. 'The claw meat in particular is so sweet. The fishermen throw them back into the water in Lewis though, no one wants to buy them.'

'It's the same here. I must admit, I've never tasted crabmeat.'

'Oh, you should.' She cast the shell into the waves. 'There's nothing like it.'

'You have not the accent of a Highland woman,' he said, as they continued on.

'That's because I'm not really a Highland lass. I was born on Lewis, as was my mother, but my father was a Londoner and that's where we made our home. We visited my grandparents every summer, Mama and I, and when she died—I was only fifteen—I became even closer to them. I lost them both ten years ago.'

'That must have been difficult for you.'

'They were elderly—my mother was a late child—and they died as they'd have wished, in their own beds, only a few months apart.' Her voice wavered. 'I've never been back. Far too many ghosts.' She paused for a moment, her throat working, then gave a tiny shake of her head, as if to clear it of unpleasant thoughts.

Her words struck a chord. 'When they served dinner last night, I almost told the housekeeper we'd better wait for Austol. I feel like I'm trespassing. If I could have stayed away—ah, but then I'd never have met you, and that would have been a great pity.'

She glanced at him, coloured faintly, then looked away. 'I was fortunate to be spared the difficult task you face. My grandparents' estate was inherited by a rather distant cousin from my grandfather's side—though in actual fact I think he is now my nearest relative, since my father died. Mama was an only child, you see, as am I. It is the way of things up there, for lands to be passed down the male line. Besides, John-Angus had long acted as my grandfather's estate manager—as Mr Bligh does for you. And I know nothing about farming.'

'I pictured you holidaying in a small, whitewashed Highland croft,' Treeve said. 'I take it I was mistaken?'

'There were certainly a number of crofts on the lands. It was—is—a substantial estate. John-Angus will keep them it in good heart. And he has three sons. A good strong line to continue,' she said wistfully. 'My grandmother was an only child too. I think—I know, for Grandmama told me—that my grandfather brought John-Angus in as a sort of insurance policy. And he was wise to do so.'

'I understand that is how things are done, but it seems very arbitrary, to take no account of the possibility of your having a son. Ah, forgive me,' Treeve said, aghast at his own thoughtlessness, seeing Emily's stricken face. 'I meant only that you were so young when they died—not that I mean to imply that you are too old now, but I—' He broke off, cursing. 'I'm so very sorry. As I said, I'm a rough sailor, but I should not have spoken out of turn.'

She shook her head, turning away from him, though

not before he saw a sheen of tears in her eyes. 'I will never have a son,' she said flatly.

Was she set on spinsterhood? Or had she been badly hurt? Both questions were intriguing and impossible to ask. 'I apologise unreservedly,' Treeve said, 'for commenting on such a very personal matter, especially since we've just met. You don't know me well—or at all,' he added, with an embarrassed laugh. 'I'm not usually so forthright. It's partly the awkward position I find myself in, I expect—a position I never sought. I know I'm an outsider here in Porth Karrek, an unknown quantity at best. I'm in uncharted waters, and that's not something that sits well with me, after all these years in the navy, knowing precisely where my duty lay. I'm rambling on now, which is something else I never do. But it's not only the situation, it's you. I must confess I am very drawn to you, I feel there is an affinity between us. Have I got it completely wrong? If I have, tell me to go to the devil, I beg you.'

Emily frowned down at the sands, digging her toes in. He waited on tenterhooks for some long, painful moments. Seven waves' worth of waiting. Finally, she looked up, meeting his eyes, smiling faintly. 'I don't intend to tell you to go to the devil.'

'Thank you.' He followed her lead, walking on, forcing himself to remain silent for fear of saying anything that would make her reconsider. Who was she, this obviously beloved granddaughter and only grandchild, who had inherited nothing? She did not have the look of a woman who had spent the last ten years living in poverty. Her well-made clothes had the kind of quiet elegance that spoke of excellent cloth, and though they were not in the first style of fashion, nor were they

dated. Her figure was slim, but in a lithe way, and her
skin had none of the unhealthy pallor which he'd seen
in many a new recruit starved in the city of both sunshine and sustenance. Why had she avoided marriage?
He could not believe it was for want of any offers. There
could be any number of reasons—he'd avoided marriage
himself, hadn't he? Better to not risk asking for fear of
upsetting her again.

Their hands brushed as they walked, and each time it
happened, Emily felt her fingers tingle, as if they were
asking to be clasped, she thought fancifully to herself.
Though Treeve's words had startled her, in a way they'd
been a relief, for she'd felt it too, the instant attraction
between them. They did not know one another at all,
but she felt that they should, as if they were meant to.

It was decidedly not at all like her to be so fanci-
ful. She had been on her own too long, not only here
in Cornwall but before. For months before she had finally confronted Andrew, she had been lonely, a self-
imposed isolation, unable to confide her doubts and
fears to anyone. Not that there had been anyone, for
Jessie, who had known her since she was a bairn, and
had been Mama's maid before she was ever Emily's,
had finally been persuaded to retire. As for Beth, she
wouldn't have dreamed of polluting her happiness, even
if her oldest and closest friend had been close by, rather
than in distant Yorkshire with her beloved curate.

So the fates had been kind to her, to provide her with
a confidante. Not that she would ever dream of confid-
ing in him exactly, but to talk—yes. She liked the way
he listened to her, not simply waiting until she'd finished so that he could have his say as Andrew was wont

to, but really listening. And not just answering but responding. And she liked the way he looked at her, the frankness in his eyes that told her he found her attractive. She knew that the frisson she felt—there, just like that!—as their hands brushed again, was not one-sided.

Treeve had been quiet for some time now, for fear of upsetting her further, no doubt. The next time their hands brushed, Emily met his eyes and smiled. 'What would have happened to the Karrek estates if your brother had been an only son?' she asked.

'My cousin is next in line, by default, I suppose,' he answered, his relief at her breaking the silence obvious. 'That's another thing I must do, make my will. Austol's will left everything to me in the absence of a son, though I reckon he'd have preferred to hand it over to Jago Bligh. A true Cornishman, and one who, like your John-Angus, knows the lands. His would be a safer pair of hands than mine.'

'You don't consider yourself a true Cornishman then,' she quizzed. 'Though you are from Porth Karrek, born and bred as they say.'

'I doubt they do say that. In fact, I'm pretty sure that some would disagree most profoundly with you there. I was born here, that is true enough, but bred—no, the navy made me, not Porth Karrek. My one love,' he added with a wry smile, 'and my only mistress.'

'But your brother, being a true Cornishman, no doubt thought your career choice somewhat disloyal?'

Treeve rolled his eyes. 'He certainly did, as do the entire population of Porth Karrek and beyond, I'll wager. In Cornish eyes, there is not an iota of difference between a captain of the Royal Navy and an Exciseman. I'm only one step above being an informer.'

'I've only been here a short while, but it's long enough to know you're not exaggerating. You must have been very keen to join up, in the face of such opposition. And indeed, very determined, for one so young, if you've been twenty years in the navy.'

'I was sixteen, and the second son, so my father was largely indifferent to what I did. And before you pity me, let me reassure you that I consider myself fortunate, since it meant no obstacles were put in my way. In fact, if I'd not joined the navy of my own accord, it's likely that my father would have tried to push me towards the church, and in doing so deprived the parish of an excellent man in the form of Reverend Maddern.'

Emily raised her brows sceptically. 'I can't imagine that you would allow yourself to be pushed into anything by anyone.'

'It's been attempted, but none so far have succeeded.'

'Though now,' she ventured, 'you must be torn?'

'What do people here want to happen?'

'You've not been away so long as to imagine that anyone in Porth Karrek would share their thoughts with an incomer, surely?'

'No, I suppose not.'

They had come to the end of the beach, where the cliffs of the next headland protruded out to sea, preventing them from continuing. The wavelets washed over their toes, drenching the hems of her cloak and skirt. Emily frowned. 'There has been a good deal of speculation about you, I know that much.'

'I couldn't have come here any earlier—until last week I was at sea. I didn't even hear of Austol's death until a month after he was drowned. People will be wanting to know where they stand, and that's natural enough.' Treeve picked up a flat stone and skimmed it expertly into the surf. 'As far as I'm concerned, provided I can satisfy myself that Jago Bligh has been doing his job, they stand exactly where they do now. My leave of absence expires at the end of the year. I have no plans to extend it, and certainly no intention of making it permanent. Don't people get on with Bligh? Is that what you're hinting at?'

'I'm not hinting at anything. Mr Bligh, though not exactly loved by all, is certainly held in respect—and in some awe, since he wields quite a lot of power. But that's only an impression. You must make up your own mind.'

'Oh, I intend to, but it's always useful to have an independent view from someone with no vested interest.'

'Well, I can certainly provide that.'

Treeve sighed, digging his toes into the sand, in precisely the same way as she did. 'It's a damned mess, all the same. Karrek House shouldn't be left to lie empty. My brother's widow has moved back to Penzance to stay with her parents. I called on her yesterday, on my way here. It is a great shame that their union wasn't blessed with a son. She's a Hammett of Penzance, whose father would have been happy to look after the estate on behalf of his grandson.'

'And now it will fall to you, to marry and provide an heir.' Emily spoke lightly, but avoided his eyes all the same, for fear that he'd see the pain her words induced. All men wanted a son, didn't they!

But Treeve looked quite aghast. 'That is something I have not considered, nor intend to. I am at sea more often than I'm ashore. I would make a very poor husband and father.'

'Loyalty, a strong sense of duty, honour, and respect for those you command—the attributes which make you an excellent naval captain would surely also serve you very well as a husband.'

'Are you funning?'

'Only a little.'

'You don't think that love is the starting point? Surely if one loves, then the rest follow—save that I don't think a husband should *command* a wife.'

'That is very enlightened of you.'

'I know little of such matters, to be honest.'

'Ah, yes, the sea is your mistress, as you said.'

'Well, not precisely my only mistress, but the one I have always returned to.' Treeve cursed under his breath. 'That makes me sound like the archetypal sailor with a woman in every port. It's not what I meant at all.'

'You don't have to explain...'

'I meant only that I'm thirty-six years old. Of course there have been women. But I've never been a man to make any sort of false promises, Emily. That's what I meant. And now it sounds as if I'm propositioning you, which I'm not. I'm simply— I want us to be honest with each other, that's all.'

A very refreshing change indeed, if he meant it. All her instincts told her that he did, but her instincts had been catastrophically wrong before. Yet she did feel she could trust him. Was it then dishonest of her to keep her past to herself? No, she decided. All Treeve wanted was her honest opinions, and those she could give freely.

'I honestly think we should turn back,' Emily said teasingly. 'Before we're trapped by the rising tide.'

'I've said too much again, haven't I?' Treeve said,

making no move, pushing his hair, damp from the salt spray, back from his brow.

'We've only just met. You are only here until the end of the year.' She considered this. 'Though I suppose that is an argument for us to skip the conventional niceties.'

'I think we've already done that,' he replied, indicating their bare feet.

'Very true.'

They set off back through the lapping waves. The next time their hands brushed, their eyes met, and their fingers clasped. His hand was warm against her icy skin. The sun was bright now, making the sea glitter. Emily's blood tingled and fizzed in her veins. Any other day she would put it down to the exhilaration of walking on an unspoilt beach in fine weather. Today, it was a whole combination of things: this particular beach; this particular sun; this particular man.

'I'm a silversmith,' she said, wanting to surprise him, to give him the gift of an unsought confidence, wanting to trust him with it.

Treeve looked suitably startled. 'A silversmith?'

'That's how I earn my living.'

'How extraordinary. You don't look like a silversmith.'

'What do you imagine a silversmith looks like?'

'A wizened old man wearing spectacles, hunched over a workbench. How on earth did you learn such a trade? Doesn't it require some sort of apprenticeship?'

'My father was a silversmith of some repute. I lost him six years ago.'

'By the sounds of it, you were very close.'

'Very.' Emily blinked furiously. 'I worked with him from an early age, and through a friend of his, also learned the basics of jewellery making—the two are very distinct trades, usually. I combine them. My father made much bigger pieces on a grander scale than I could produce here. My work is not so profitable, but luckily for me, I've discovered that I'm most adept at cutting my cloth to suit my purse.'

'By moving to a tiny cottage at the ends of the earth,' Treeve said. 'Though you only arrived here in April.'

He wanted honesty. How to explain that honestly? Emily wondered. 'London is expensive and I also desperately wanted—needed a change. My resources have been dwindling.' Which was most certainly true. 'Though I am quite self-sufficient,' she added. 'You must not feel sorry for me.'

'I don't,' Treeve said, clearly confused by the challenge in her voice.

'Good. I won't be pitied, you know.'

'I can't imagine why you think I would do such a thing. If anything, I envy you your independence.'

She bit her lip. 'It has been hard earned, believe me.'

He eyed her for a moment, struggling, she thought, with whether or not to pursue the subject, whether to ask her the obvious question. 'All the best things are hard earned,' he said eventually, a platitude for which she was grateful.

'True. I like to be busy, though the short days at this time of year are problematic. My work requires daylight.'

'Is that a hint that I'm holding you back?'

'No, though I ought to get back to my workbench soon.'

'May I have the privilege of seeing some of your work?'

'You are very welcome to call, though I think you will find that your time is not your own, once it becomes known that you have arrived. Everyone will want to meet you, and you will wish to make yourself familiar enough with your new domain to be able to decide whether or not to entrust it to Mr Bligh.'

'True, but I think you in turn underestimate my determination to become better acquainted with you. Assuming, of course, that you have a similar wish?'

This time there was no mistaking the glow in his eyes. Emily's cheeks heated. 'I think I've made it plain that I do.'

They were back where they started on the sands. The tide had all but swallowed The Beasts. The surf was getting higher and the clouds lower. Treeve rescued his shoes and stockings from an incoming wave, and they headed up the beach to the foot of the cliff path, Treeve turning his back without being asked as Emily picked up her own shoes and stockings.

'Why is it,' she said when she had finished, 'that damp sand on bare feet feels so delightful, yet damp sand in wet wool is so unpleasant?'

He laughed. 'Perhaps every pleasure comes at a price.'

Now, what was one to make of that remark? He led the way up the path. She allowed herself to enjoy the view of him from behind, the athletic ease with which he negotiated the steep path, and the smile he gave her every time he turned around to check that he had not gone too far ahead.

When they reached the top, Emily was more breathless than she should be. 'Are you headed to the village? There's a path…'

'I know,' Treeve said.

'Of course you do!'

'Actually, I'm headed back to Karrek House. An appointment with my brother's lawyer. Or I should say mine, now. I am not looking forward to it, but there's no point in putting it off. The sooner I understand the extent of my obligations, the better. I've very much enjoyed our walk.'

'As have I. I walk on the sands most mornings. If you feel like company. I mean, you don't have to join me.'

'I'd like that, Emily.' He caught her hand, covering it with his own. 'I would very much like to say that I'll see you tomorrow, but I think you may be right, in the very short term at least. My time is not likely to be my own. Shall we say soon?'

'Soon.' Their fingers twined. 'I should go.'

He nodded. He stepped towards her. She thought he was going to kiss her. He would taste of salt. His hands tightened around hers. Then he let her go.

'Whatever happens with the rest of the day, it has begun very well. Until the next time, Emily.'

'Until the next time.'

She headed along the path towards her cottage. She could sense him watching her, telling herself she was being silly, resisting the urge to turn around. And then she thought, why not, turning around. And he waved. And though she couldn't see his face clearly, she was sure he smiled.

Chapter Three

For the next three mornings, Karrek Sands was once again Emily's exclusive domain. She was not surprised, but she was more disappointed than she cared to admit. Replaying her conversation with Treeve, she was astonished by her own frankness, not so much with facts but regarding her feelings. To admit, within such a tiny space of time, so much, seemed to her in retrospect utterly foolhardy. Yet she had done no more than he—had in fact followed his very frank lead. Had there really been the affinity that both of them had professed to feel? How could she be sure that he had not pretended, in order to gain her trust?

Opening the door of her cottage, Emily shook her head decidedly. Treeve was no dissembler, she simply knew it, in her bones. She had been nineteen when she met Andrew Macfarlane for the first time, a green girl with no experience of life. The second time, she had been grieving and vulnerable in a different way, and ripe for the plucking. Yes, she could admit that. But she was thirty-two now, an independent woman who knew her own mind, her strengths and more importantly her limitations.

She sat down at her workbench, pulled the bonbon dish she had been working on towards her and began to smooth the pierced silver with a wire brush. The light was good this morning. She ought to make the most of it, finish the decoration at the very least.

Treeve was drawn to her. She was drawn to him. Their attraction was one of the mind, but it was also physical. Yes, she could admit all of those things, and she could relish them too. Why not, when there was absolutely no risk of either of them becoming in any way embroiled. He was going back to sea at the end of the year. And she—well, her heart was well and truly locked away.

If it wasn't, or if Treeve ultimately decided to stay, then that would be a very different matter. If he were to remain as lord of the manor, she would have to keep him at arm's length, for she could not risk their feelings running deeper. She knew what heartbreak felt like. She would not inflict that on either of them.

Emily stared down at the bonbon dish in dismay. She had brushed so hard, she was in danger of wearing through the design. Was she still heartbroken? She must have loved Andrew, that other, gullible Emily. If she had not loved him, he would not have succeeded in his deception, and if she had not been so determined to turn a blind eye, he would not have continued to succeed. She most certainly didn't love him now. His betrayal had been so callous and the extent of it so shocking that he had destroyed not just her faith in him, but in human nature. She was determined to recover from that, despite the fact that a separate part of her was broken irreparably. But she couldn't blame Andrew for that. His only crime had been to inadvertently highlight an unpalatable but inescapable fact.

Casting her work in progress aside, Emily got to her feet. This morning's paddle had not eased the restlessness she'd woken with. She was tired of being cooped up here, alone. Pulling her cloak back on, she hurried out once more into the fresh air.

The gatehouse had been built at a later date than Karrek House, though in a sympathetic style, with a sharp pointed roof and mullioned windows. It had lain empty since Emily's arrival, but now the windows on the top floor were open, presumably to give the place an airing. Treeve's doing perhaps, or possibly a signal that a new tenant was imminent.

There were two stone lions standing guard just beyond the gatehouse on the path leading up to Karrek House. The salty Cornish air had eaten away their features, leaving the pair with bizarrely broad smiles, no noses, and manes that had long lost their shagginess. The Penhaligon family home was beautiful, an Elizabethan manor built of Cornish granite with five distinctive Dutch-style gables. Three narrow protruding wings formed an 'E' shape. Was Treeve inside, going through his estate account books? Or was he outside, making a tour of his inheritance in Jago Bligh's company, eager to be reassured, eager to get back to his ship, and the life he loved?

A seagull came to a squawking halt on one of the lions' heads, making Emily jump. The last thing she wanted was to be caught gazing forlornly up at Treeve's house. Emily turned on her heel and headed for the village.

* * *

Budoc Lane, the main street of Porth Karrek and the hub of village life was narrow, steep and cobblestoned, the whitewashed shops which lined both sides protecting those going about their business from the worst of the elements. The door to the butcher's shop stood ajar, but there was no sign of Phincas Bosanko. Phin, as he was known, though Emily never dared address him as such, was a very fine specimen of a man, if you valued brawn—and a fair few of the local maids certainly seemed to. As far as Emily had been able to deduce, the butcher dispensed his favours evenly, treading a fine line between flirtation and commitment to cannily keep all his options open. It amused her on one level, but on another, the idea of him assuming he had the right to break as many hearts as he wished made her hackles rise—though she knew she ought not allow her own pathetic history to colour her view.

The mouth-watering smell of fresh-baked bread wafted from the baker's yard at the rear of the shop. 'We've no pasties ready yet, if that's what you're after.' Eliza Menhenick eyed Emily with her customary reserve.

'Thank you, I would like a loaf of that delicious-smelling bread, Mrs Menhenick.'

'What size of loaf would suit you, Miss Faulkner?'

'The smallest one you have, as usual.' Emily forced a smile. She'd been buying her bread here for nigh on seven months, yet each time Eliza Menhenick asked the same question, determined to remind Emily that she was a stranger in Porth Karrek, and a solitary one at that. How long would it take, she wondered as she left the shop, the bread tucked into a fold in her

cloak, before she was accepted as one of the locals?
A lifetime most likely, and for the likes of Eliza Menhenick and Jago Bligh, even that probably wouldn't
be enough.

The village shop run by the Chegwin family was
at the bottom of Budoc Lane, facing directly on to the
harbour. Besides groceries, the shop stocked a bit of
everything, from rope, needles, cotton, and the rough-
spun, oiled wool used to knit fishermen's jumpers, to
nails, ink, pencils, herbs and spices, and cooking pots.
There were everyday candles of tallow, more expensive ones of beeswax, and the most beautiful carved
and scented candles made by Cloyd Bolitho, a melan-
choly candlemaker who looked as fragile as his cre-
ations. The Chegwins also stocked flagons of rough
cider, the strong fermented apple drink that Emily suspected would crack her head open with one taste. There
were other, unmarked barrels in the shop too, which it
didn't take a genius to work out contained contraband.
She had enjoyed a glass or two of Bordeaux in the past,
but she couldn't afford such a luxury now, and in any
case knew better, as an incomer, than to suggest to
the Chegwins that they would be able to sell her such
a thing. The shop smelled of a particularly pleasant
combination of tea leaves and coffee beans and cheese
and—for some reason—wood shavings, but Emily had
no purchases to make there today.

The harbour beach, a mixture of sand and stones,
sloped steeply down to the water. The tide was still
out, leaving the limpet-covered harbour wall exposed.
A number of the smaller boats were beached on the
sand, their moorings at full stretch, though the bigger
pilchard boat belonging to Jago Bligh was tied up close

to the wall, and still afloat on the water. The air was rich with the tang of the sea, the remnants of yesterday's catch, and that distinctive smell of brine-soaked nets and rope which Emily had never been able to put a name to, but which was another reminder of happier times, watching the catch come in on her grandfather's herring fleet at Stornaway harbour.

She wandered out along the harbour wall to stand at the furthest point gazing out beyond the headland to the sea, where The Beasts were only just visible, the waves cresting white as the incoming tide broke over them. Beyond the wall the sea was grey-blue, but inside it was calm, turquoise, the sandy seabed visible, shoals of tiny fish darting about in the seaweed.

Picking her way back through the ropes, creels and nets, she saw a tall figure striding down Budoc Lane, recognising him immediately. Treeve didn't get far before he was waylaid by the butcher. The two men struck up what looked from this distance like a friendly conversation.

Emily stood in the lee of the Ship Inn, curious to see what the other villagers would make of their new landlord. Phin was laughing at something Treeve had said. The two men shook hands. The butcher, in her view, had an inflated opinion of himself but there were no sides to him, from what Emily had seen, and she liked that about him. When she'd arrived in the village back in April, Phin had been openly curious rather than hostile, his blunt questions as to where she had come from and what she was doing in Cornwall a refreshing change from the mutterings and speculation of most of the others. She had, of course, answered none of his questions, and to his credit he'd not persisted either.

A man who liked plain dealing. He and Treeve would likely do well together.

How the Menhenicks received Treeve, she had no idea, for he disappeared into the shop for a good ten minutes. Several other villagers watched his progress towards the harbour front, some answering his ready smile with a doffed cap, a curtsy, a handshake, others a sullen look, one or two with a pointedly turned back. She could have avoided him altogether and headed back up Budoc Lane while he was in the Chegwins' shop, clearly on a mission to make himself known to one and all, but that would be to attach an importance to him she had decided she didn't want to encourage. So Emily waited, intending to bid him a polite good day, before heading home.

'Ah, the very person!' Treeve exclaimed, emerging from the shop. 'If I hadn't bumped into you here, I'd have called at your cottage. I'm afraid I haven't had a moment to call my own since I last saw you.'

'I did warn you that would be the case.'

'You're on your way home,' he said. 'I don't suppose you can wait for half an hour or so, then I can walk back with you? No, it's wrong of me to ask. The light is good. You'll be wanting to get back to your workbench, so I won't detain you.'

'I can spare half an hour,' Emily found herself saying, which she wouldn't have, had not Treeve acknowledged that she too had other claims on her time.

'Thank you,' he said, smiling. 'I appreciate that. I'm told I can get a decent cup of coffee at the Ship, will you join me?'

'I'm not sure that I'll be welcome there. As a female, I mean.'

'This is not London, Emily. The Ship has always been the hub of the village, a place for men, women and children to relax—not in the taproom, obviously, but there is a parlour.' Treeve pursed his lips. 'But you must know that, you've lived here long enough. What you mean is that you don't think you'd be welcome as an outsider. I'll let you into a secret. I am not convinced I'll be welcome either, and I own the place. Shall we step inside and find out?'

'Oh, what the devil,' Emily said, earning herself a raised brow and a conspiratorial smile.

The parlour of the Ship was empty. It was cosy and low ceilinged, a fire smouldering in the stone grate that took up most of one wall. The floors were bare boards, pitted and scarred from decades of contact with the customers' hobnail boots, the seating a combination of tall settles on two walls, and rickety chairs, with a scattering of small wooden tables, as scarred and pitted as the floor. The air was pungent with the smell of stale ale and the vinegar used to mop it up. The room was dark, lit only by a small window, and smoky, not only from the fire but the open hatch through which the taproom could be seen—and could likely be heard too, Emily presumed, were it not for the deathly silence which greeted their arrival.

Treeve pulled two chairs and one of the tables closer to the fire, stretching his long legs out to rest on the hearth. He was wearing buckskin breeches and boots today, another wide-skirted coat, dark blue, made of fine wool, with a waistcoat to match. His linen was pristine, making his beard seem more blue than black—not that it was quite a beard. Emily wondered how he managed to keep the bristle in trim, for he looked like a man who must shave at least twice a day, yet it was every bit as neat and tidy as it had been when she first saw him.

A low mutter had resumed in the taproom, but no one had yet appeared to serve them. Treeve, rolling his eyes, was just pushing back his chair to get up, when the door opened.

'Captain Penhaligon.' Derwa Nancarrow, the Ship's formidable landlady, was about the same age, Emily reckoned, as herself, with the black hair and very pale skin of the Celt so common in Cornwall. She was a handsome woman, with deep-set brown eyes and a mouth that was capable of producing a sultry smile, but today was decidedly sullen. 'How may I help you?'

'I see I have no need to introduce myself,' Treeve said, getting to his feet. 'How do you do, Mrs Nancarrow? I don't think we've met before.'

'I'm from Helston. You had left Porth Karrek for the navy before I married Ned. Your brother is much missed. He was a true Cornishman.'

If she had not been watching him closely, Emily would have missed the slight tightening of his mouth at this barb. 'None truer,' Treeve replied blandly enough, however. Not indifferent, but determined to be seen to be. She admired him for that.

'What can I get you?'

'I'm not your only customer. This is Miss Faulkner, who is renting one of the estate cottages,' Treeve said.

'I know who she is. I'm assuming it's coffee you're after?'

'If you could find it within yourself to bring us some,' he answered sardonically, 'that would be delightful.'

'I warned you,' Emily said as Mrs Nancarrow disappeared again, her entrance next door clearly marked by the sudden increase in voices.

'I wonder, if I'd asked her, if she'd have served me a fine French cognac.' Treeve sat down again beside her. 'No, she'd have told me they don't stock such things, even though they almost certainly do.'

'You think that is why she was so…'

'Sullen? Wary? Yes, because she doesn't want a navy man asking awkward questions as to whether it is contraband or not.'

'Especially since you own this inn now.'

'I wish to hell that I did not. Excuse my language.'

'Oh, for a rough sailor, your language is remarkably civilised.'

Treeve gave a snort of laughter. 'You have no idea.'

'If you came here in the hope of gaining acceptance,' Emily said, keeping her voice low, casting a wary glance at the open hatch, 'you'd have been better off in the taproom, taking a glass of rough cider and rubbing shoulders with the men.'

'I'm not sure I'm looking for acceptance. It might be different if I planned to remain here.'

'You've decided that Mr Bligh is trustworthy then?'

'He seems to have kept things ticking over very well since Austol died, but I've discovered in the last few days that there's a great deal more required than simply keeping things ticking over. A good many decisions have been put on hold. I had no idea. These last few days have been quite an eye-opener. If I told you…'

'Captain Penhaligon. Miss Faulkner.'

Ned Nancarrow set down a tray bearing two cups, a pewter coffee pot, and a sugar dish. A tall man of sparse build, with hair to match, he had a long face, and a way of looking sideways that gave the impression he was forever keeping a weather eye on his potential escape route.

'Thank you, Ned,' Treeve said, getting to his feet and holding out his hand. 'How are you?'

'Well enough.' The hand was taken, rather reluctantly. 'Jago tells me you're headed back to your ship at the turn of the year.'

'Does he?' Treeve sat down again, picking up the coffee pot. 'He knows more than me then.'

'Said you had leave until the end of December.'

'That's true enough.'

'So you'll be here for the Nadelik celebrations then— that's what we call Christmas, Miss Faulkner. You'll be hosting Gwav Gool up at the big house, as your father did, and your brother, too?'

'I had not thought that far ahead.'

'People expect it. No Gwav Gool festival means the harvest will fail, and the catch next year will be poor. You should know that, Captain. It's a tradition that goes back generations. Perhaps it might be best to leave it to Jago to organise. He's well versed in local customs.'

Treeve set the coffee pot down again. 'When you know me better, Ned, and I hope you will take the time to do that, you'll understand that I prefer to make my own mind up about local customs, both good and bad.'

He spoke quietly. He hadn't moved from his chair, but there was no doubting the steel in his voice. Emily sensed it, and so too did Ned Nancarrow, who narrowed his eyes. 'Not sure what you're getting at, but I sincerely hope you're not casting no aspersions. The

Ship has been run by my family for generations without any complaints from the authorities.'

'I'm aware of that, and I'm happy for it to stay that way.'

'I told Jago, you're a Cornishman, before you're a naval man.'

'The world is changing, Ned, and Porth Karrek is being left behind.' Treeve held up his hand to stall the other man's protests. 'I want only what is best for this place, I assure you. We all want that. We should all be on the same side.'

'Aye, you're right, we should. Can I get you anything else? Only I've some thirsty fishermen in the taproom.'

'Nothing, thank you.'

The door closed softly, and Treeve pushed a cup of coffee towards Emily. 'It seems I have my answer, with regards to the cognac at least.'

'Is smuggling really still a problem here, now that the war is over?'

'Locals would claim that it's the over-inquisitive Excisemen who are the problem, not the smugglers earning an illegal coin.' Treeve stirred sugar into his coffee. 'For me, it's not a question of right or wrong, it's a simple matter of the law. You can't pick and choose what laws to uphold and which ones to break with impunity, even if they do seem to be unjust, or the punishment seems to far outstrip the crime. I've seen that for myself Emily, at sea. I've been obliged to enforce ship's discipline, even when in my heart I wanted to be merciful.'

He finished his second cup of coffee, grimacing. 'I sound like a pompous ass, but I know what I'm talking about. Mutiny. Whether it's on board a ship on the high seas or here, in Cornwall where the likes of Bligh and Nancarrow think themselves above the law. I won't tolerate it.'

'But how can you stop it, if you are not planning to remain here?'

'Damned if I know!' Treeve groaned. 'Nancarrow's right about Gwav Gool though. As a man of the sea myself, I know that she has to be placated.'

'Are you teasing me?'

'Only a little. Your family are from a seafaring community, you know how superstitious such folk are. Gwav Gool is a very ancient Cornish tradition, celebrating the year gone past, and looking forward to an even better one to come. In Porth Karrek, it takes the form of a dance with a supper hosted, as Nancarrow pointed out, by my family two days before Christmas. What's more, there are a raft of other traditions, both pagan and religious, all tangled up together.' He frowned. 'The shopkeepers dispense gin and cake to their customers in December as a thank you for their custom. As I recall, there's usually a solstice bonfire on the beach which the Treleven family host a couple of days before Gwav Gool. Then Nadelik—Christmas Day—sees the Reverend Maddern's yuletide service.'

'Good heavens,' Emily exclaimed. 'It sounds as if the entire month of December is given over to some sort of celebration or another.'

'It's a hard life here, it's not surprising they celebrate with gusto. This will be your first Cornish Christmas. Are you looking forward to it? You'll be expected to join in, you know.'

'Oh, no, I'm not—all those things you describe, they are for local people.'

'Which, for the time being, includes you. Don't you like Christmas?'

'I'm simply— I don't mark Christmas. In Lewis, the New Year is more important, and so it was with my family, even after Mama died. And since Papa died...' She trailed off, appalled to discover her throat clogging. Not one Christmas in their whole five years together, had been spent with Andrew. How virtuous she had felt, surrendering him to his poor mad mother for the festive season. What a fool she had been to believe that barefaced lie.

'This year will be different,' Treeve said, so kindly that she felt herself on the brink of most unusual and unwelcome tears. 'Since I must host Gwav Gool, perhaps you'll help me out? On board ship, it's just another day, it will be quite a change for both of us.'

A radical change, and a refreshing one. Emily nodded gratefully. 'If you think it won't be resented—my helping you, I mean?'

'They'll get short shrift from me if anyone does. Anyway, it's a good few weeks away yet. I wish I'd thought about it last night, I could have discussed it with Sir Jock Treleven. It is his family who host the bonfire. I had dinner at the Trelevans' and met all six of his daughters.'

'Several of them are of marriageable age, I believe. Sir Jock was making hay.'

'Oh, no, I don't think—' Treeve broke off, looking aghast.

'Oh, come now, you are not so naïve. The new lord of a very wealthy manor, unattached, very far from his dotage—quite the opposite in fact. Sir Jock would have been signally failing in his duty, if he had not introduced you to his little stable of fillies.'

'I'm not in the market for a horse, far less a wife.'

'But if you were,' she persisted, 'then you would struggle to find anyone more appropriate than one of the Miss Trelevens. I have not met any of them, of course, but I have heard they are all very convivial, and have dowries as attractive as they are.'

'They are undoubtedly both pretty and convivial, though I'm not sure I could tell one from the other.' He eyed her coolly. 'I am not a thoroughbred to be put to stud, Emily. If I married, it would be because I had found a woman I didn't want to live without, not to provide Karrek House with an heir.'

'I was only teasing.'

'It didn't sound as if you were.'

Mortifyingly aware that he was right, that her words had been laced with an inexplicable and most unworthy envy, Emily pushed back her chair, but Treeve stayed her with a hand on her wrist. 'Why do you consider yourself so beneath them—the Trelevens, I mean? No, don't deny it. "I have not met them, of course", that's what you said. Why *of course*?'

'I'm a silversmith, the daughter of a silversmith, eking out a living in one of your cottages.' She tried to free her wrist, but his fingers tightened around it.

'Your mother was the only child of a clearly respectable and wealthy Lewis family. From what you've said, your father was no lowly artisan. Your accent and manners betray your roots and your education, the quality of your clothes, the fact that you need to eke out a living is a relatively recent development. The only thing that makes you an unlikely friend for the

Miss Trelevens is your age.' He smiled at her. 'Quite in your dotage as far as they are concerned, though I consider you the perfect age to make for interesting company.'

'A back-handed compliment if ever there was one,' Emily said drily. She was flattered, but wary too, for Treeve had garnered a great deal from the little she had told him of herself.

'A compliment, sincerely meant.' Treeve let go of her wrist, but only to cover her hand with his.

'I'm sorry. I'm not used to compliments.'

'You have been hiding yourself away for far too long.'

'I think you might be right.'

She smiled. Treeve smiled back. Their eyes locked. Her fingers tightened in his, and she felt a quivering response, saw a flare of heat in his eyes that she was sure was reflected in her own. She wanted to kiss him. He wanted to kiss her. The possibility drew them towards each other, then the grating opening of the door sent them jumping apart.

'Mr Penhaligon.' Jago Bligh entered the parlour, pulling up short when he saw Emily. 'Beg pardon if I'm disturbing you,' he said, drawing her a look that made it very clear he disapproved of her presence, 'but I believe we had an appointment.'

'As you can see, I am currently otherwise engaged.' Treeve eyed his estate manager with some hauteur. 'Why you felt it necessary to seek me out when there are, as you have told me several times now, not enough hours in the day for you to attend to your work—'

'We have important matters to discuss,' Jago interrupted truculently.

'I do hope, Mr Bligh, that you are not implying that my discussion with Miss Faulkner is of lesser importance?'

Treeve spoke with an air of quiet authority. His expression was bland, but his message was perfectly clear. Jago Bligh's jaw tightened. 'I shall await your convenience back at Karrek House,' he said finally.

'Good man. I will see you there once I have escorted Miss Faulkner back to her cottage.'

'There is no need.' Unwilling to be the cause of any other further tension, Emily got to her feet, pulling on her cloak. 'I've detained you long enough. In any case, I intend to walk the long way around the headland, get some fresh air while it lasts. Good day to you, Captain Penhaligon, Mr Bligh.'

Outside, the clouds were ominously black, the wind was up, and her cloak whirled around her as she climbed up to the cliff path. Looking back, she saw Treeve emerge from the tavern, striding ahead up Budoc Lane, his estate manager lagging slightly behind, gesticulating in a way that made it clear that whatever he was saying, he wasn't happy.

Mr Bligh was not unattractive, with craggy but regular features set under a thatch of thick dark hair, and a beard which he kept neatly trimmed. She reckoned he must be about ten years older than Treeve, though he was very fit and muscled, his bulky shoulders and barrel chest testament to the hours he spent at sea, skippering his pilchard boat. Both he and Treeve were captains—how odd that this hadn't occurred to her before—but they could not be more different.

Jago Bligh was very much respected in the village—though as she had observed for herself in a confrontation between Mr Bligh and Abel Menhenick, it was a respect bordering on fear. She did not like him, and it was not simply because he treated her with the contempt of a man who considered her beneath his notice. He looked to the right when he spoke, never quite avoiding her eyes, but never quite meeting them square on. And he was not confident, he was arrogant.

'Foolish man,' Emily muttered to herself, as the pair disappeared from view. 'In any conflict, I know who my money would be on.'

Chapter Four

'Of course, these are small-scale pieces compared to my father's,' Emily said, 'but the techniques are the same, whether you are making a tea urn or a snuffbox. The first task is to cut a shape from a sheet of metal, such as this, using a template. I make them myself, from practice pieces of brass or copper.'

Treeve watched, fascinated, as she demonstrated, seated at the long wooden bench which took up most of the living space in the cottage. He had planned to call on her yesterday morning, having reluctantly allocated Bligh the rest of the day before, once the blasted man had sought him out at the Ship Inn. But once again his best-laid plans had been holed below the waterline, this time by Austol's lawyer—correction, *his* lawyer, who had arrived unannounced with another wooden chest full of documents to be perused. This day, he was absolutely determined to claim for himself, and if he could persuade Emily to spend it with him, then all the better.

'Next,' she continued, 'I use a small hammer to beat out the shape I require.'

'You don't need to heat the metal then?'

'No, it is hammered cold, but as you work it, the silver hardens, so you do have to soften it now and then—we call that annealing. I have a small brazier which burns charcoal, which I keep outside, so you need not worry that I'll burn down your cottage by dropping hot coals. It's not big enough for me to do any casting, which is why everything I make is on a small scale.'

'What happens next?'

'The piece is soldered together, if required—if it is a box, for example. And of course if I'm making jewellery it requires extensive soldering, using silver wire. Then the last stage is the decoration, which is the part I enjoy the most. See, here are some samples which are complete, apart from final polishing. This is filigree, which is formed from fine silver wire.'

The trinket box was adorned with a delicate pattern of leaves and flowers. A central flower in each panel sent twining garlands out to each corner, and the four little feet were formed from leaves. 'It's beautiful,' Treeve said, tracing the design with his fingers.

'This one is made using a mixture of hammering and pierced work,' Emily said, swapping the box for a salt lined with dark blue glass. 'I buy the glass linings, obviously, and then make the framework to fit each exactly. And here,' she said, unrolling a piece of chamois leather, 'are some earrings which I've been working on. The stones are paste, I can't afford precious gems.'

'Bluebells?' Treeve asked, gazing down at the tiny flower-like earrings set with blue glass.

'They are, how clever of you to notice.'

'It is you who are clever. These are wonderful pieces. And so diverse.'

She beamed. 'Thank you. I must confess, I enjoy the variety.'

'Such craftsmanship, I would have thought it would have earned you your fortune.'

'Sadly not. If I wished to make my fortune, I'd have to set up on a much larger scale, and make much grander pieces too, as my father did. Dinner services, tea services, serving dishes, epergnes, that kind of thing. But aside from the fact that is simply not possible here, I prefer working on smaller, more modest pieces.'

Emily took the earrings from him, rolling them carefully back in the chamois leather before picking up a cloth. He watched her polishing the floral trinket box, a small frown furrowing her brow, her generous lips pursed in concentration. She was wearing a plain gown of soft wool the colour of a pale wintry sky. She had rolled the sleeves up to expose her forearms. Tanned and slender yet far from frail, he could see the ripple of the muscles under her skin as she worked, and dammit, he found it absurdly arousing. She wore her hair up in a knot. There was something arousing too, yet vulnerable, in the long line of her exposed neck as she bent over her work.

Looking up, she caught his eye and smiled faintly, offering him the little box. 'If you look closely, you'll see my hallmark.'

'"EF",' Treeve read. 'If your father was so well known, and you were his apprentice, couldn't you continue to use his mark?'

'No. It wouldn't have been permitted, I was never his official apprentice.' She got to her feet, retrieving a walnut tea caddy from a shelf, and took out the silver spoon inside. 'There, you see. "RF", for Robert Faulkner. That was my father's mark.'

'More flowers,' he said.

'He made it for my mother. It runs through the female line, the love of nature. There is a beautiful rose garden attached to the big house in Stornaway—that is the main town on the Isle of Lewis. It's a walled garden, to protect it from the harsh weather. I remember the scent on a sunny day—we did have them in Lewis, every now and then.' She closed her eyes. 'Perfume so strong it made you dizzy.'

'You are never tempted to go back? I do understand what you meant about ghosts, but—being here at Karrek House has also dredged up a plethora of happy memories for me. Things I had quite forgotten.'

'I can't possibly go back,' Emily said bleakly. 'My happy memories are now tainted for ever. Besides,' she added, before he could ask her what she meant, 'more than likely my cousin will have dug up the rose garden and planted potatoes. John-Angus never could see the point of flowers. Needless adornment, he'd have said of that spoon. It's one of the few of Papa's pieces I kept.'

Where had the rest gone? The obvious, painful answer, was that they were sold, so Treeve did not ask. He set the spoon down carefully. 'I can see you're busy, but I was hoping that I could persuade you to take a walk with me.'

'Don't you have other matters to attend to?'

'I'm beginning to realise that if I wanted to, I could tend to estate business twenty-four hours a day. But I don't want to. Bligh deprived me of a walk with you the other day, and legal business took up all of yesterday.

I've earned a break, but I know that your work must come first, I don't want to...'

'I work to eat, it's true, but I reckon I too have earned a break. Do you think the weather will be kind enough to us to allow us to go further than the beach?'

'I made a special plea to the weather gods,' Treeve said, 'in the hope that I could persuade you. The cliff-top path from here towards Porth Leven is beautiful.'

'I'll fetch my cloak,' Emily said.

Treeve's pleas to the weather gods had been answered, it seemed, for it was a lovely afternoon, the skies pale blue with a weak lemon sun, the breeze as gentle as it was possible to hope for at this time of year. Crossing the top of Budoc Lane by St Piran's church they avoided the village, making for the path that hugged the clifftops.

Emily was wearing one of her favourite dresses of russet-and-cream-striped wool. She had dressed carefully yesterday morning too, in another of her favourite gowns, telling herself that she was merely getting the use out of them, knowing perfectly well she was hoping Treeve would call.

'Are you immune to the cold?' she asked, hugging her cloak around her, for he was hatless and gloveless, without even a greatcoat.

'Try standing on the open deck of a ship in a storm,' he replied. 'The cold I never mind, it's being soaked to the skin that gets to you.'

'What about the heat? Have you been to the tropics?'

'I've been around the world several times over. I always laugh when I hear people in England complain about the weather. True enough, we have a bit of everything, sometimes all four of our seasons in a day, but it's all in moderation.'

'I'll try to remember that,' Emily said, smiling. 'The next day I'm confined to my cottage by the torrential rain, unable to work because it's as dark at midday as midnight.'

'What do you do, on those days?'

'It might sound stupid but sometimes, when it's really wild, I like to go outside. There's something so—so elemental about the storms here, you know? Standing on the headland, with nothing in front of you but the horizon, on days like that it can feel as if you're the only person left in the world.'

Treeve cocked an eyebrow. 'And that's a nice feeling, is it? Is that why no one even knows about your little cottage industry? I mentioned it at dinner to the eldest Miss Treleven and…'

She came to an abrupt halt, turning towards him angrily. 'You told her I was a silversmith!'

'Why wouldn't I?'

'I don't want people talking about me. I mean,' she amended, for her words had sounded disproportionately defensive, 'that I prefer not to be the subject of gossip.'

'I was expressing my admiration, not gossiping.'

'You hadn't even seen my work at that point.'

'My admiration was for your determination to make your own way in life, Emily, for the guts it must take, and the skill to make a living for yourself and, to use your own words, to "cut your cloth to suit your purse."'

Embarrassed, she felt her cheeks heating, but she could not keep the resentment from her voice. 'I also told you that I don't want to be pitied.'

'It seems to me, it is you who sees yourself as a

pitiful creature. I certainly don't, and nor did Miss Treleven.'

The truth of his words were like a punch in the stomach. 'I was too hasty,' she said stiffly. 'I apologise.'

'Don't look so stricken. Whatever travails you've endured since your father died…'

'Are my business, no one else's.'

Treeve put his hands on her shoulders, forcing her to meet his gaze. 'Don't be so defensive. I didn't ask you out here to interrogate you. Some polite conversation—you know, a little give and take.'

She smiled reluctantly. 'I've largely forgotten how to make conversation.'

'Would you like to put some practice in?'

'Yes, please.' She liked the way he met her eyes, so straight on, the way he looked at her, not through her, the way he listened to what she said, even if by listening he saw through her enough to tell her a home truth or two.

The wind had blown his hair across his face. Without thinking, she reached up to push it back. He caught her hand. She held her breath as desire flared unmistakably in his eyes, as her body responded, heat prickling her back, tingling deep inside her. He kissed her, but only by brushing his lips on her glove. When he let her go, she felt absurdly disappointed.

'Look at this.' Treeve made a sweeping gesture. 'On days like this, I can see why my brother always said there was nowhere like it in the whole world. Perhaps Cornwall is in my blood after all.'

He had turned them both to face towards Penzance. The tide was out, so the long crescent of beach which stretched almost all the way to Porth Karrek was revealed, and the cobbled causeway leading out to St

Michael's Mount, the tiny rocky island topped with a fortress, was clearly visible. 'I always think it is some sort of strange ship, moored to the mainland by a stone rope,' Emily said.

'There's another similar island just off the coast of Brittany you know, called Mont St Michel. They were both priories, up until about four hundred years ago or so. Shall we press on?'

They headed off along the path, just wide enough for them to walk two abreast as it hugged the clifftops, giving breathtaking views out to sea. Treeve pointed out a number of lethal-looking rocks similar to The Beasts, visible only because the tide was low. Little London, The Frenchman, The Bears, each had their own special name, and if they had any particular meaning, according to Treeve, it was long forgotten. What each was remembered for were the wrecks they had been responsible for, so many of them that Emily wondered why any fisherman would risk their life in these waters.

'It's true,' Treeve answered her, 'the Cornish coast is the most treacherous in all of England, the sea can turn from flat calm to a storm in the blink of an eye, but our fishermen must fish, or they will starve. They need to follow the shoals of pilchards wherever they go, regardless of the danger.'

'Did you ever sail here?'

'Of course I did. My father taught Austol and I to sail in the harbour when we were very young—he wouldn't allow us to venture out of Porth Karrek until he was happy we knew what we were doing, because of The Beasts. My father was an excellent sailor.'

'So it runs in the blood, your own affinity with ships and the sea?'

'It does, though my father, like my brother, had no interest in any sea beyond this one.'

'While you wanted to sail them all?'

'Something like that.' He frowned. 'It wasn't only a case of wanting to see the wider world though, I didn't relish the prospect of being constrained by the boundaries of their world.'

'And be obliged to become a vicar, to boot.'

He rolled his eyes. 'Heaven forfend. Truly.'

'You wanted to be your own man,' Emily said. 'I can understand that. I have worked very hard to become my own woman.'

'Yes, it's something we share, our refusal to be hidebound. Though it comes at a price. I am master of my own ship, but I still have to obey orders. What's more, the navy has a book of rules and regulations as thick as—I was going to say Jago Bligh's skull, but that would be unfair. He's not the least bit stupid, merely stubbornly attached to the old ways, like most of the village. You've experienced that, Emily. You had to swear Bligh's niece and nephew to silence about their swimming lessons, for heaven's sake.'

She wrinkled her nose. 'It's true, they don't like change, and they are wary of strangers. In that sense, Porth Karrek is very like Lewis.'

'And the scenery too, from what you've said.'

'Oh, yes. I came here because it was as far south from London as I could get, but I have stayed because it is quite simply beautiful. On days like this, who would want to be anywhere else? I love the sea, as much as you do.'

They stopped to admire the view back to Mount's Bay from Cudden Point. The causeway had disappeared under the incoming tide. A sudden gust of wind tugged a strand of Emily's hair free from its ribbon. The sea below was a deep blue, turning to turquoise in the shallower water back at Perranuthnoe where it met the sands, and further out, where the swell was rising, the water was almost midnight blue.

'But you have been lonely here.' Treeve turned to her.

'I have, but that's partly because I've chosen to be. I wasn't ready for company until you came along. Next April, I'll have been here a year. I have high hopes that by then, Eliza Menhenick will offer me a loaf of bread without asking me which size I want. Maybe next summer, Kensa and Jack will persuade the Nancarrow boys to join them to swim. In ten years' time, if I ask for a glass of cognac at the Ship, they might even serve it to me. You see,' Emily said awkwardly, for the revelation had only just occurred to her, 'unlike you, I'd like to make my home here. I don't have any family now, and I can't go back to Lewis, but this place is alike enough to remind me. I won't be a stranger for ever.'

'Shall I build a swimming pool in the rocks, so that you can give your lessons safely?'

'I know you're teasing, but I can't help but feel that the children here are missing out on so much, not enjoying the sea.'

'To say nothing of the fact that it's depriving some of them of the ability to save their own life.'

'Oh, Treeve, I'm so sorry. That was completely thoughtless of me.'

'No, but you're right. If Austol had learned to swim, there's a chance he may not have perished. I've resolved to learn, thanks to you, and see if I can persuade some of my men to do so. Perhaps one day we can swim together at Karrek Sands.'

'So you do intend to return?'

'Occasionally, my naval duties permitting. I'll have to. It's horribly clear to me that there are a good many things I can't delegate.'

'You know, it sounds to me as if being the lord of the manor and being a naval captain are more similar than you think. Both require a steady hand on the tiller, a man who is not afraid to make tough decisions, who can inspire loyalty and command respect.'

'What is demanded in Porth Karrek, is that the lord of the manor acts in the exact same way as his predecessors did. Austol essentially *became* my father, when he inherited. Acting the lord of the manor, is precisely what I'd have to do. I refuse to meekly follow in my father's and brother's footsteps.'

Emily dared to take his hand, pressing her lips to his knuckles. 'I, for one, applaud you for that.'

A gust of wind sent her staggering back. Her ribbon was torn from her hair, whirling up into the sky. Instinctively she lunged to catch it, only to be yanked back hard against Treeve as she stepped off the path and dizzyingly close to the edge.

'Thank you,' she said, clutching gratefully at him. He put his other arm around her, putting himself between her and the cliff edge. The wind suddenly dropped and the sun came out from behind a cloud, and Emily smiled up at him. His eyes were made golden by the sunlight, his close-cut beard coal-black. His bottom lip was full, his answering smile reflecting not only her own delight in the wild coastal scenery and the glorious freshness of the day, but the latent desire which had quivered between them earlier.

Treeve brushed her hair back from her face, his fingers warm on her cheek, on her neck as he tucked the long tress behind her ear. Her heart began to race. She took a step closer, and he slipped his other arm under her cloak, around her waist. She reached up to touch his hair and felt him exhale sharply as her fingers smoothed the silky soft damp curls away from his forehead. And then the sun was blotted out and the earth seemed to tilt on its axis as he lowered his head and their lips met.

He tasted of salt. His lips were gentle, his beard soft yet prickly, rasping just enough on her skin to delight rather than grate. She sighed, opening her mouth to his kiss, nestling closer into his reassuringly solid bulk, and he brushed his tongue along her bottom lip, making her quiver, her quiver made him sigh, his mouth covering hers, deepening the kiss, until another gust of wind made them stagger backwards.

'Are you all right?'

'Luckily the wind blew us away from the cliff.'

'You know that's not what I meant, Emily.' His eyes were lambent, heavy-lidded. It touched her that he needed reassurance. That he took nothing for granted.

'I'm fine.' Her words, so trite and so completely inadequate, made her shake her head at her own banality. 'I'm perfectly fine.' And free, she added silently to herself. Not that she'd tell Treeve, ever, but his kiss had freed her. 'Truly,' she said instead.

Treeve laughed, pulled her back into his arms and kissed her again. 'I feel like I've been waiting for months to do that.'

'Not even a week. I hope you're not disappointed.'

'You exceeded my very high expectations.' He wanted to kiss her again, but this was hardly the place! His body was thrumming with desire. For the love of the gods, it was just a few kisses. Extremely enjoyable, enough for him to want more, but dammit, he was not in the habit of going around kissing virgins. Not that Emily kissed like a virgin, though how the hell he thought he knew what a virgin kissed like when he'd never kissed one…

He cursed under his breath, scanning first the horizon and then his watch. 'I think we'd better turn back.'

Chapter Five

Emily dressed carefully, in a day gown of olive green taffeta silk embossed with pale pink roses. The tightly fitted sleeves were puffed at the shoulder, and the neckline was square-cut, without any adornment, for she had had it made to showcase a pink sapphire necklace she'd once owned, and had unfortunately been forced to sell. Today, she would have to make do with her only remaining piece of jewellery, her mother's gold locket. Just as well, she thought, for a pink sapphire necklace would be bound to raise a good many questions she'd prefer not to answer.

She stabbed another two pins into her hair before checking her chignon in the mirror. The smooth and simple style suited her thick, heavy tresses, which refused to co-operate with anything more elaborate. Turning and twisting in front of the small hand mirror, she assured herself that she had fastened all the buttons at the back of her gown. Ought she to have worn a simpler dress? Probably, but it was too late now. Besides, she liked this dress, and it suited her, and it suited the occasion, her first formal visit to Karrek House.

She was nervous. Which was silly of her. It wasn't as if she'd never paid a morning call before, had never crossed the portals of a country manor before. It wasn't as if she didn't know how to conduct herself in front of a butler or a housekeeper, or a houseful of liveried footmen. But still, she was nervous. It was one thing to meet Treeve on the beach every morning as they had done for the last week, to talk, to walk, even to paddle.

And to kiss. Such kisses. Salty, windswept kisses which punctuated their conversation. Moments when they stopped talking and looked, simply looked into each other's eyes, and saw desire reflected. Treeve's arms tight around her, his lips warm, his cheeks cold, the wavelets which rippled over their bare feet icy, their toes touching, though almost too numb to feel. She loved the graze of his beard on her cheek, the softness of his lips, the press of her breasts against his chest, the dragging, sweet ache inside her that the touch of his tongue roused.

She ought not to be nervous after sharing such kisses. But she was, all the same. On Karrek Sands they were Treeve and Emily, shielded from the prying eyes of the world. But at Karrek House she was a mere tenant calling on the lord of the manor, to be introduced to the eldest daughter of another of Cornwall's foremost families, not as an equal but as an artisan in search of a commission.

She didn't need the commission at this moment, but it would be very churlish of her to turn down the opportunity. Short-sighted too, for if Miss Treleven was happy, she would tell her friends and her relations and they might put other commissions Emily's way. What's more, she reminded herself as she donned her cloak and pulled on a pair of gloves, it was much easier to discuss commissions face-to-face than try to discern what a person required from a letter, as she had been obliged to do since moving to Cornwall. So she shouldn't be nervous, she should be excited, she told herself firmly, picking up the basket in which she had carefully wrapped a small selection of samples of her work.

A footman opened the door to Emily before she had a chance to pull the bell. Informing her that she was expected, he relieved her of her cloak and gloves before leading the way into a long narrow passage with a shallow domed ceiling decorated with a ribbon-like cornice painted plain white. The walls were a pleasing primrose yellow, the bare floorboards pitted and scrubbed. She felt as if she was walking through a tunnel, crying out with startled delight when it ended in a Great Hall, a massive double-height chamber with an ornately plastered ceiling and a minstrels' gallery featuring by one of the biggest stained-glass windows she had ever seen.

'It is made of almost six hundred individual panes of glass,' Treeve said, appearing from a doorway on the other side of the hall, 'some of them over two hundred years old. Welcome to Karrek House, Miss Faulkner. Thank you, John,' he added to the footman, 'we'll take tea as soon as Miss Treleven arrives.'

'This is a spectacular room,' Emily said, tilting her head back to look at the ceiling.

'Spectacularly cold, most of the time,' Treeve said.

'But imagine a ball held here. You could put the orchestra in the minstrels' gallery.'

'Do you like to dance?'

'I've never been to a formal ball, but there was a

ceilidh every year for Grandma's birthday. Everyone was invited, crofters, fishermen, villagers, the great and the good—such as they were. We'd dance reels— Scottish country dances—and people would take turns to entertain, reciting poetry, playing the fiddle, even telling jokes.'

'I've attended far too many balls,' Treeve said, grimacing, 'which involved escorting an ambassador's wife sedately round the floor, making polite conversation while wearing full dress uniform. Categorically not my idea of fun.'

'Then hold a ceilidh here for Gwav Gool,' Emily teased. 'Invite all of Porth Karrek and dance a hornpipe for them. They'll see their new lord and master in a very different light.'

He laughed sardonically. 'Different certainly, but still an unwelcome usurper.'

'I'm sure they don't view you like that.'

'And I am sure they are counting the days to the end of the year when they can wave me off, hopefully never to return.' There was an edge to his words which surprised her, but before she could say anything, he shook his head impatiently. 'It's not such a bad idea though, holding a ceilidh, rather than the dance Austol hosted, which I gather was always a rather sedate affair.'

'Tradition with your own twist?' Emily said.

'If you like.' Treeve smiled. 'Yes, exactly that. I think that's an excellent idea. We'd better go through to the drawing room. Miss Treleven will be here any moment, and before you say anything, the commission was her idea, I am simply the intermediary.'

'I'm very grateful all the same, Treeve, I...'

'You've no need to be,' he said brusquely. 'I have

seen your work and it's patently obvious even to a man who knows nothing of such things that you are extremely talented and in no need of patronage.'

'No, but a foothold here could prove extremely beneficial. It is much easier to do business face-to-face.'

'Really? I thought you preferred to avoid social encounters. Here was I, preening myself on being the only exception to your rule.'

His smile, the warmth in his eyes, the quirk of his mouth, sent a delightful little shiver down her back. She couldn't help but smile in return, and when she did, the air between them seemed to still and she felt as if she had stopped breathing, her skin prickled with awareness. 'You may preen yourself on being the exception that made me want to change my rule.'

'In that case,' Treeve said, 'I shall have to introduce you to the composer when he arrives.'

'Composer!'

'Aha, now I've surprised you. I thought I might. To be honest, I've surprised myself. He arrives on the first, I believe. The lawyer is making the arrangements. He'll be staying at the gatehouse.'

'I saw the windows open a few days ago, I had quite forgotten. I had no idea you had any interest in music.'

'I don't, but Austol's widow does. The idea was cooked up between her and Reverend Maddern, to offer the man a commission. She wants her piano moved there for him. A gift from Austol to her, apparently, not long before he died. She can't bear to touch the thing, but from the fuss she made about it, I gather it's special. Anyway, she wants the composer to have it. Cador Kitto, his name is, have you heard of him?'

'No, I'm afraid I'm not particularly musical either.

Do you know what sort of piece you have commissioned by proxy?'

Treeve grimaced. 'A Christmas cantata, whatever that is, to be played in St Piran's on Christmas Eve. Cador Kitto is a native of Porth Karrek. Reverend Maddern has known him since he was a child, and has been some sort of mentor to him. I've never met the man, he is a few years younger than I, and left the village when he was a lad, to attend a school of music. To my knowledge, he's never come back.'

'Until now. I wonder why.'

'Oh, that's an easy enough question to answer. He's rather down on his luck, and in need of work. Reverend Maddern spoke to my sister-in-law on his behalf. She wrote to me, and under the circumstances I could hardly refuse.'

'Is this Cador Kitto a famous composer? If it is an accomplished piece, you might acquire a name for yourself as a patron of music.'

'Not a particularly useful attribute for a ship's captain, though I suppose the commission will do me no harm with the local gentry, let them see that I'm not a complete heathen.' The doorbell clanged. 'That will be Miss Treleven, with a much more relevant commission for you, I hope,' Treeve said, ushering her ahead of him into a large drawing room. 'You can set your work out here, on the table by the fire. I'll make the introductions, then make myself scarce.'

Emily wrapped the little trinket box up in a soft cloth and set it carefully inside the basket. Miss Treleven— Rosenwyn, as she had insisted—had commissioned some silver hair ornaments as a Christmas present for her younger sister Marianne. Her admiration for Emily's work had been quite unfeigned, her delight in the sketches Emily had made for her most gratifying. She was going to make a point of delivering the finished pieces herself. It would make a very pleasant change, seeing Rosenwyn's reaction to her work, rather than simply dispatching them and receiving, at best, a thank you scrawled on the invoice returned with her payment.

Rosenwyn, more a redhead than a strawberry blonde, was no simpering country miss, but a decided, rather sophisticated young woman with several London Seasons behind her—glad to have them behind her, was what she had actually said, for she could not bear to be away from her beloved Cornwall. Beautiful, clever and kind, if Treeve *was* looking for a bride, Miss Treleven would be perfect.

Emily wandered over to one of the tall, narrow windows which flanked the marble fireplace. The view outside was of the knot garden, looking decidedly dreary in the rain, which drifted down from the sky like a gauzy veil, drops so small they seemed harmless, but so fine they seeped into your bones. Cornish rain, Emily called it, turning her back on it. The fire in the hearth blazed brightly in comparison to the dull exterior. The walls of the drawing room were painted a soft creamy mushroom colour, a few shades lighter than the stained floorboards. The rugs and the curtains, the sofa coverings, were in complementary muted tones, the other furnishings minimal, drawing attention to the beauty of the ceiling which, like the others, was white-painted and ornately corniced. It was a lovely room, understated, tasteful and tranquil.

Fortunate Treeve, to have inherited such a delightful house. Save that he didn't think himself fortunate at all. Was he in the least bit tempted to remain here? A house like this should be lived in, not left cold, unloved and neglected, as it would surely be, when Treeve left to sail the high seas again.

She would miss him. Though it was not quite two weeks since she had first encountered him, she had grown used to his company, looked forward to their conversations. When he was gone, she'd be alone once more. Ought she to pursue a friendship with Rosenwyn? Or make friends with Derwa Nancarrow, perhaps, a woman nearer her age and station—and with two children who could be taught to swim! Emily smiled wryly, trying to imagine how any such overtures would be received, but her smile quickly faded. When Treeve left, she would feel even more isolated than ever. She'd have to make more of an effort. Perhaps the Chegwins would sell some of her plainer pieces in their shop.

Of course, she wasn't obliged to remain in Porth Karrek herself. But she didn't want to move. Turning restlessly back to the window, Emily watched the Cornish rain fall. She liked the rain. And the wind. And the sun. She liked that they came one after the other in quick succession, sometimes. She loved the sea here, and the clifftop walks. And the village. She had come here to hide and lick her wounds. She hadn't expected to find contentment, but she had. And she hadn't expected to change, but she had. She was a very different person from the woman who had arrived here in April. With a bit of effort—and a lot of time, she added wryly to herself—she could find a niche for herself here. She would be part of the scenery. She might even come to be seen as a useful part, whether it was teaching swimming or silverwork.

It would take time, but she had time, and more importantly, she had the inclination. Thanks to Treeve, she had rediscovered her confidence. In her work—because she could admit it now, she had been extremely nervous, showing Rosenwyn her wares—but more than anything in herself. Talking to Rosenwyn had been—well, easy, natural, fun. Yes, fun. It made her realise how much she missed Beth. She'd been forced to lie to her best friend about her reasons for leaving London. She would write to her, Emily resolved. A long letter, telling her the truth. And she'd finally make good on her promise to visit too, she was able now, to see Beth's little brood again with pleasure rather than pain. After Treeve was gone. There were about six weeks of the year left. He would not leave for ever, he had already decided that he'd have to visit, that it was not possible to abdicate his new duties entirely.

Here Emily firmly reined in her musings. Treeve was an interesting man. He was an extremely attractive man. But for heaven's sake, Andrew Macfarlane was an interesting and attractive man. He was also a blackguard and a scoundrel! She was pretty sure that Treeve was neither of those things, but then she'd been pretty sure that Andrew wasn't either, and look how wrong she had been proved.

'Devil take it, Emily!' she muttered, irked with herself. Why on earth had she allowed her mind to wander down this pointless track? The situation was straightforward enough. She should make the most of Treeve's company while she could. If she wished—yes, she wished!—and if he wished—which he seemed to!—then they could also indulge in a little harmless dalliance. And it would be harmless because they were both perfectly well aware that it would end, because Treeve was leaving. The sea was his one true love. He couldn't have made that any clearer. And as if that wasn't enough, then there was also the fact that Emily would rather cut her heart out than give it to anyone ever again. And if that *still* wasn't enough, if she was ever so unbelievably stupid as to fall in love again, and if Treeve decided to upend his own world, and choose Emily over the navy, then there was the fact that she could never, ever allow him to marry her, for one over-whelming reason which he must never be privy to.

But it would never come to that. The odds were heavily stacked against it. She crossed her arms, leaning back against the window panes and nodded firmly to herself. 'When all is said and done,' she muttered, 'it can't be anything other than harmless.'

'What can't?' Treeve said, smiling as he re-entered the drawing room.

Emily coloured. 'Nothing. I was talking to myself.'

'Is that why you like your own company so much, because you always win the argument?'

'And I'm never wrong either! I wasn't sure whether or not you expected me to wait.'

'I'm very glad you did. I was up in the attics and saw Miss Treleven leaving. There is a panoramic view from the windows, all the way over to the Lizard, and out into the Channel for miles I thought you might like to see. It's a bit dusty up there though, I don't want you to ruin your lovely gown.'

'Oh,' Emily said, colouring even more, 'this old thing! A little dust won't harm it.'

'Silk. French, if I'm not mistaken. And though I'm no expert in lady's fashion, not so very old.'

'I had it made for my birthday two years ago.'

Two years ago, she had been well enough off to have a silk gown made, to celebrate a birthday. With whom? Perhaps no one. And if there had been some man? It was two years ago. He had no reason, nor any right to feel jealous, devil take it!

'The colour suits you,' Treeve said, though he wasn't looking at the gown, but into her eyes.

What was it about Emily that drew him? Less than two weeks, he'd known her. It felt like a lifetime, and also a matter of hours. He desired her, but not in the way he had desired women before. It was not her stormy-sea eyes, or her sensual mouth, or even the curve of her bottom or her breasts that kept him awake at night. It was the clearness of her gaze when she looked at him, the little frown that pulled her brows together when she was thinking, the way she closed her eyes, the little quiver running through her, when the first wave rippled over her bare feet, the little half-smile she wore when she dug her toes into the sands.

He felt as if he knew her, but at the same time, he felt that there was a great deal more she wouldn't let him know. She fascinated him and intrigued him. It worried him that their time together was fated to be so fleeting, for he must return to his ship at the end of next month. He would miss her. So he'd better make the most of the time they did have!

Treeve shook his head, for Emily's brows were raised in a silent question. 'It's nothing,' he said. 'I was trying to recall whether there was a shawl or something I could lend you. It's cold up in the attics.'

'I'm a hardy soul, Treeve, us Hebridean women are made of stern stuff.'

He led the way up the central staircase, slightly bemused by Emily's obvious admiration for the house. He had never really looked at the cornicing as anything other than a ceiling, never thought of the staircase as anything other than a means of getting from one floor to another.

'You really think it beautiful?' he asked, as they gazed down into the Great Hall from the minstrels' gallery.

'You don't?'

'I've never considered it at all. It was my father's house. Then my brother's. Now—it does seem a shame that it will lie empty.'

'Perhaps you should think about installing some tenants.'

'Oh, no,' Treeve exclaimed, horrified by the idea. 'There have been Penhaligons living here since the main house was built back in Elizabeth's reign—' He broke off, disconcerted by his own reaction. 'I will not be at sea for ever. And there will be times, when I am between ships, or when my ship is being refitted, when I'll want to return.'

Even to his own ears, he sounded unsure. Emily looked at him quizzically. 'You left twenty years ago, and have been home how many times?'

Treeve shrugged. 'My ship has always been home.' He ushered Emily from the minstrels' gallery. 'The attics are reached by the back stairs. Take care when you climb, the treads are a little uneven.'

In the attic, she seemed to be completely distracted by the view as he pointed out the various landmarks, but he was aware of her studying him. Indeed she made no attempt to disguise the fact, mulling over his words, turning them over in her mind, as if they were one of her silver boxes, to be inspected from every angle before she arrived at a judgement.

'Did your brother make any significant changes to the house when he inherited?' she asked.

'Austol, like my father, thought Karrek House should be preserved rather than improved. Personally, I think there's quite a lot of room for improvement. I'd do something about the plumbing for a start, and I'd have the chimneys seen to, they all billow smoke.' Treeve frowned, taking a mental tour of the house. 'The kitchens need to be ripped out and modernised. The stairs we've just climbed need attending to and this place...' He studied the attics with a fresh eye. 'If it were partitioned, I think this could make a very comfortable sitting room or study—it has the best view in the house.'

'But apart from that,' Emily said, smiling, 'you wouldn't make any changes.'

Treeve was forced to laugh. 'Actually, I think there's a perfect place to build a walled garden over there, do you see? It faces south, and with a bit of protection from the winds—in fact a succession house or two would be perfectly placed there.'

'Why not have a lake dug while you're at it!'

'Oh, no, if I were to spend my money on a water feature, it would be to have a pool built in the rocks at Karrek Sands. There's a perfect place, you know it—it would be filled at high tide. And if we're talking substantial building projects—well, that's easy, it would be a lighthouse on The Beasts. I'd try to persuade Robert Stevenson to build it—his lighthouse at Bell Rock is a remarkable piece of engineering. And to make the harbour truly safe, we'd need to strengthen the walls, which could be done at the same time.'

'Good heavens Treeve, that would surely cost a fortune. And it would take—I don't know, months?'

'Depending on the weather, perhaps longer. We'd need to bring in expert craftsmen—not just Stevenson, but engineers, if the harbour walls were to be reinforced. There's a man I know, who has overseen a great deal of work in Plymouth. And the fact that we're relatively close to Falmouth docks, too—there's a good pool of experienced men there we could use. It would be difficult—the logistics would be complicated—but I've actually been involved in something similar before. You need—' He broke off, taken aback by what sounded oddly like enthusiasm in his voice. 'Of course, I'm just speculating.'

Emily raised her brows. 'But if it wasn't only speculation?'

'Oh, then Porth Karrek could rival Penzance, or even Newquay, as the biggest pilchard port in Cornwall.'

'New fishermen and their families coming to live at Porth Karrek! Mr Bligh would have something to say about that.'

'Would it be so wrong?' Treeve frowned. 'It's very clear to me that Porth Karrek desperately needs some fresh blood, whether the people here will admit it or not. I can't fault Bligh as an estate manager, but he values traditions over all else, and despises change, even when it is much needed. The soil on many of my farms is good enough only to produce what is needed for survival, and there seems to be no understanding of modern farming methods. There are always pilchards to be harvested from the sea, but fishing is hardly the most reliable of occupations, and there can be weeks here in the winter when the boats can't be launched, which means there's no money to put food on the tables of the villagers unless they have another occupation. Many of them combine fishing and farming, but on such a small scale it is a hand-to-mouth existence.'

'Just like the crofters on Lewis.'

'Exactly. I suspect if you went back there, you'd find a number of the younger people have left in search of better lives, Emily. It will be the same here, if things don't change, and who can blame them?'

''What about tin mining? Are there any deposits on your lands?'

Treeve shook his head. 'Some small seams, but not sufficient to justify the cost of a steam pump and the building to house it.'

'Then what is the answer?'

'I have no idea, save that it's not to carry on regardless.'

'Though that is what Mr Bligh will do, in your absence. You say that what is needed here is fresh blood, has it occurred to you that might be you?'

'You think I should stay here, give up the navy? I know no more about modern farming methods than the people here. I'm a sea captain. Modernisation for me, is all about steamships. Besides, people here don't want modernisation. My brother and my father would be turning in their graves, to hear me.'

'People here want to stay here, first and foremost. Your ideas—they would change things for the better, wouldn't they? If they understood that, they'd see you very differently. A lord of the manor, but a benefactor, with people's welfare at heart.'

Treeve gazed out of the window. A customs cutter was heading out into the Channel from Penzance. '"A steady hand at the tiller. A man who isn't afraid to make tough decisions, who can inspire loyalty and command respect." That's more or less what you said, isn't it? You know me better than anyone else here—indeed, I think sometimes you can see inside my head. Do you really think I could be happy here?'

Emily looked uncomfortable. 'All I know is that you came here very certain that you would not stay and now you seem more ambivalent.'

'You're right, it's been keeping me awake at nights.' He sighed. 'Perhaps I should have left well alone, and stayed away completely. If I'd refrained from spending so much time these last few days trying to come to terms with my inheritance, left it in Bligh's capable hands, then I wouldn't be so worried. Ignorance is supposed to be bliss, after all.'

To his surprise she flinched. 'Trust me, you could not be more wrong. Far better to know the truth, no matter how unpalatable. Then at least you know what you have to face up to.'

'That sounds to me like the bitter voice of experience. Emily?' he added, when she shook her head.

'You could bring your telescope up here,' she said, ignoring the question.

'Someone already has, I found a tripod stand behind an offcut of carpet over in the corner. Please, don't turn the subject. Didn't we promise to be honest with each other?'

'I came here to escape from—from my life. I'm happy here, Treeve. I don't want to talk about the past.'

'Someone hurt you,' he said, gently. 'The man you wore this dress for, on your birthday, perhaps?'

She nodded, her eyes fixed on the floor.

'Emily, I don't want to reopen old wounds.'

'Oh, I am not still in love with him, if that's what you're thinking,' she said fervently. 'He killed any feelings I had for him when he— I promise you, Treeve, he is well and truly in the past.'

Feelings! The word caused something that was unmistakably jealousy to stab him in the gut. Feelings that this unknown man had killed. Jealousy gave way to a fierce, protective anger.

'You must not be thinking that I am broken-hearted,' she said, with that knack she had of reading his mind. 'I'm a very different person now. I was thinking that, only a few moments ago downstairs. Which is why I don't want to talk about it.'

But she had been hurt. And there was the question of her money too, Treeve thought. Had that man—he caught himself short. 'You're right,' he said, for she was eyeing him askance. 'I've no business asking. To be perfectly honest, I'd rather not know.'

'Treeve, you should know that I'm not— It was a— It was not an *innocent* relationship. Do you understand?'

'He took advantage of…'

'No! At least—no, not in that way.' Emily's cheeks were dark red, though she met his gaze directly. 'You said we should be honest. I am trying to be. As far as I can.'

He was momentarily overcome, not with the disgust or condemnation she seemed to expect, but with admiration at her courage. 'Emily.' He couldn't resist pulling her into his arms, kissing the top of her head. 'You shouldn't be ashamed to admit such a thing. It's the most natural thing in the world, to want to—to make love, though by the stars, the world makes it difficult enough for women to admit to wanting, never mind indulging! You're thirty-two years old. It would be a bigger crime if— I mean, if you had not— Dammit! I mean if you had denied yourself something so natural.'

He felt her laughter, soft against his chest. 'That's a rather unorthodox way of looking at it.'

He set her back, forcing her to meet his eyes. 'I'm aware of that. But I'm a rather unorthodox man, in that regard! You don't imagine I'm an innocent, so why should I assume you are? It doesn't make you a floosie—excuse my rough sailor's language—it simply makes you human.'

'You really mean that?'

'Honestly? I don't like to think of you with another man, any more than I want to think of myself with another woman, but I can't erase the past. But if you are a new woman since you came to Cornwall, why cannot I be a new man?'

'More evidence of your unorthodox thinking. I like it.'

Treeve grinned. 'So do I.'

She flattened her hand over his cheek, smoothing it down his chin. She liked the feel of his beard, he'd noticed that before. Her eyes fluttered closed when she touched him like that. She did not wear perfume. He could smell the lemon of her soap. Close up, he

could see that the tiny pink flowers embroidered on
her gown were roses. Though she had taken extra care
with her hair, still a thick strand the colour of wet sand
had escaped its pins. He brushed it back lightly from
her cheek, and her eyes flew open, locking on to his.

He trailed his fingers down the warm skin at her
nape, and she shivered. 'Emily,' he said softly as she
smoothed her hand over his cheek again. 'Oh, Emily.'

Their lips barely touched, and his heart began to
thud, his breathing becoming shallow. Her lips were
warm, no salty taste this time. He curled his fingers
into her hair, forcing himself to keep the tiny distance
between them. Their lips clung, moved, clung, small
kisses, kisses that were just enough to make him crave
more. He curled his arm more tightly around her waist.
She nestled closer. He could hear her breathing, feel
her breathing, was acutely aware of her breasts brushing his waistcoat, of her toes against his boots. He ran
his tongue along her full bottom lip, hearing himself
groan, hearing her breath catch. Her mouth opened to
his. Their tongues touched. Deeper kisses. Her hand
was on his backside now. He felt himself harden. He
angled himself away from her. It was a kiss. Just a
kiss. Such a kiss. His hand sliding from her waist to
the curve of her bottom, resisting the desire to pull her
against him, just about. More kisses. A tiny, strangled
moaning sound from her that set his blood alight. And
yet more kisses. Tongues. He was so hard. Just a kiss?
This wasn't just a kiss.

It took far more effort than it should have taken to
stop, and even then, dragging his mouth from hers was
as much as he could manage. He held on to her, gazing
into her eyes, hazy with desire, her cheeks not bright

but pale. She stroked her hand along his jaw. Then she gave her head a tiny shake, and the movement made him smile, as if she was trying to wake up, because that was what he felt, then she stepped back and he let her go.

'I don't want you to think I'm taking advantage of you,' Treeve said. 'What you told me in confidence— you know I would not...'

'I know. I do know that.'

'Emily...'

'I'd better go,' she said abruptly, stooping down to pick up a couple of hairpins.

'Emily, don't run off. I got carried away. I did not mean...'

She stopped, halfway to the door. 'We both rather lost our heads. But it was you who came to your senses. I'm leaving before we forget ourselves again, that's all. Stay here, enjoy the view. I'll see you for our walk to-morrow, if the weather holds.'

Treeve waited at the window, wondering if she would look up from the drive, but she did not. He watched until she turned into her cottage, trying to make sense of his feelings. Frustration—that was obvious enough! Not that he'd for a moment imagined that Emily would make love to him—or had he thought that, after what she'd told him?

He examined his conscience scrupulously. He was not a prig. What Emily called his unorthodox views *were* his views. He'd always thought it unfair that the world assumed unmarried women of a certain upbring-ing must be without either desire or experience, when the world assumed it was perfectly natural for an un-married man from a similar background to have an abundance of both. And he'd had both, in the past, though the desire had never lasted beyond a few kisses or a few torrid nights' lovemaking. Delightful enough, but quickly forgotten.

But Emily—oh, Emily was like no woman he'd met before. From the first he'd known that. Smitten, he'd thought. Beguiled, he was, the more he knew her. He had never been in love, was not such a fool to imagine that a man could fall in love in two weeks, but he could get in deep. Treeve cursed. He wasn't going to be in Cornwall long enough to get in deep. And yet…

And yet what? Devil take it, Emily was different! She was not a passing fancy. He wanted more. More of her company and her conversation, more insights into her mind, more of her history and yes, dammit, more of her kisses too. And he wanted to be more to *her*. Which made no sense at all, given that he was set on going back to his ship.

He *was* set on that, wasn't he? The window in front of him, where someone had placed a telescope, had been cleaned. Bligh was the obvious culprit. What would he do if he couldn't trust Bligh? And even if he could, did he really want to allow his inheritance to sink into a slow decline? Emily didn't think so. Emily, clever, insightful Emily, had encouraged him to paint a very different picture of his future than the one he'd always imagined. It would be a challenge, and Treeve loved a challenge. But lord of the manor? Not in his father's image or in Austol's shoes, but as Emily said, in his own style. Making his future here, turning the people around to his way of thinking, building a new Porth Karrek for their children, and for his own? But he had no son. And no intentions of settling down to get one either.

Chapter Six

Emily tested the strings were tied tightly round each of her parcels, even though she had already checked them several times this morning, before placing them carefully in her basket. Outside, it was a foul day, with the rain flying past her window in horizontal sheets, the wind gusting through the frames, rattling the panes and whistling under the gap at the bottom of the door. She was going to have to speak to Jago Bligh, else the next few months would be unendurable, for she knew enough of the Cornish weather, from the villagers, to be aware that winter was only just getting started.

She tucked a piece of oilskin over the contents of her basket to keep her precious work safe from the elements. If she complained to Mr Bligh, he'd mention the fact to Treeve, and Treeve would most likely order immediate remedial work. So she would hold off until after Treeve had left. When he was gone, she wanted her memories of this time to be unclouded by any hint that she might have taken advantage of his fondness for her.

Fondness? A now familiar heat prickled her skin as she thought of him. Though their histories were worlds apart, there was an affinity in the way their minds worked that made conversation flow, one minute serious, the next funning. She never had to explain herself to him. Were they friends? Yes, but it was more than that.

She sat down at the table, cupping her hands around the still-warm teapot. In the week since she had fled the attics at Karrek House, they had continued to meet for their morning walk. There had been more kisses on the beach. And here, in the cottage too, when they pretended to take a warming cup of tea. Those kisses were more languorous. At first. There would come a point when savouring would turn to hunger, when it would not be enough simply to kiss, when the need to touch became irresistible. Then, their kisses deepened and their hands roamed, smoothing and stroking and shaping each other's bodies. And then there was a moment when that was not enough either. When Treeve cupped her breast and her nipples ached for a more intimate caress, or when she pressed herself against him and felt the rigid length of his arousal, when they both caught their breath and sprang apart and stared at each other hungrily. And then Treeve would leave.

They did not discuss the situation. There was a tacit agreement between them that they would not risk more, but they did not talk of it, afraid to upset the fragile balance between simmering desire and conflagration—at least that's what Emily assumed. As long as they resisted that final step, there was no need to discuss their feelings or what those feelings might mean. And Emily could continue to pretend that nothing had changed. Even though she knew perfectly well that it had, utterly.

She no longer compared Treeve to Andrew, because

the comparison was odious, and because what she felt for Treeve was stars and planets away from what she'd felt for Andrew. Treeve was an honourable man. He was an honest man. She could trust him. He was a man she could very easily fall in love with. But she dare not. She must not. She absolutely must not.

Sometimes she could persuade herself she was safe. Only one week left of November, just over four weeks in December, and Treeve would be gone. But his leaving seemed no longer certain, and that was partly down to her. It had been she who had encouraged him to consider his duty to Porth Karrek, and his ability to improve its lot. She who had pointed out to him that he could be a very different lord of the manor. She who had also pointed out to him that he possessed the qualities to make an excellent fist of it. She would never have spoken up if she hadn't believed that all he needed to do was to look at his inheritance from a different angle, if she hadn't been so certain that Treeve was exactly what Porth Karrek needed, and vice versa. And he wouldn't have listened, if there had not been truth in her words, if he hadn't felt what she had, in his gut. But he had listened. And he was considering acting on it. Which was wonderful for everyone but Emily, because if he remained in this place she had come to love, then she would be obliged to leave.

She didn't love him, but she could. He didn't love her, but he might. She could tell him why that would be a huge mistake for them both, but she daren't. She had accepted the hand that fate had dealt her. It had been painful, but she no longer railed at the injustice of it. But she couldn't bear the thought of Treeve's pity. It had been difficult enough, confessing to having her heart broken, even though that was well and truly mended! But to confess to the devastating revelation which had caused it? And it had been devastating, even though she'd suspected for some time. A tear trickled down her cheek. Five years of living a lie. Of course she'd suspected something was not right, but that! There was a world of difference though, between wondering and knowing.

Enough! Emily sniffed, blew her nose, gave herself a shake. More than enough. The matter was straightforward. If Treeve returned to the navy, she would stay in Porth Karrek. If he stayed here, she would go. She could start again. She would have to. But until the end of the year, she wanted to make the most of the time they had together. Starting right now. She checked the little brass-cased clock on the mantel. Treeve would be here in a few moments. Their walk to Penzance was going to be a soggy one. She hoped the wind would be behind them on the cliff path.

They did not walk the coastal path, but arrived in Penzance dry and warm in Treeve's coach, an extremely smart affair with two horses and a box containing charcoal to heat Emily's feet. Treeve had dressed more formally today, even conceding that the weather required a greatcoat, which Emily had teased him about. While he sought out the coastguard, she quickly transacted her business, posting her commissions off, purchasing new supplies which she left at the coaching inn, leaving them free to explore the town.

The weather had lifted, the wind abating, the skies clearing, as they walked down to the bustling harbour, where the luggers used for pilchard fishing were crowded together in the harbour mouth, waiting on high tide.

'There must be fierce competition for space to land the catch,' Emily said. 'If you built your lighthouse at Porth Karrek, I reckon some of these skippers would be delighted to use the harbour.'

'We have no smokery at Porth Karrek,' Treeve said, 'nor even a fish cellar for salting.'

'If you can build a lighthouse, then surely a smokery or a fish cellar would not be beyond you. How long would it take to build your lighthouse?'

'*My* lighthouse, is it? I've no firm plans, you know.'

'Why then did you correspond with Mr Stevenson, as you told me?'

'Curiosity.' He met her sceptical gaze sheepishly. 'You're right, it's more than that. It may come to nothing. He might not be available. It might cost too much. But I feel I have to do something. I never wanted the Karrek Estate, but it's mine now, and I have a duty to make something of it.' He took her arm. 'Shall we walk on a bit, now that the weather has cleared? We can head out along the seafront. I don't think it will rain.'

'I'd like that.'

They made their way away from the port towards Newlyn, the fishing port on the other side of Mount's Bay, continuing on past the village in the direction of Mousehole. They stopped at the harbour, where another flotilla of pilchard boats awaited the tide.

'You keep asking me about my intentions, Emily. Do *you* plan to stay in Porth Karrek?' Treeve asked.

'I haven't decided yet,' she said, which was the truth.

'You can't live in that cottage for ever. The blasted thing is liable to blow into the sea in the next storm, apart from anything else. When the composer is gone, you could move into the gatehouse, rent-free.'

'He's not even arrived yet, and I don't want to live in your gatehouse on a grace-and-favour basis. People would talk.'

'You're right. That was a stupid suggestion.'

'Let's not wish our time away worrying about the future. Let's concentrate on the here and now and what little time we have together. I thought that's what we both wanted.'

There was a charged silence. What Emily wanted, suddenly, fervently, was for her slate to be wiped clean. She wished she had met Treeve and not Andrew Macfarlane six years ago. But six years ago, Treeve would have been at sea, on the other side of the world, perhaps, and not a man in search of a wife with a fortune to appropriate. Nor would Treeve ever have considered her fortune relevant, whether he'd been reliant on his naval salary or the vast wealth he had inherited, she knew that in her bones. But what was the point in wishing what could not be. Even if she could change history, she could not change the woman she was, and she would never wish that barren woman on Treeve.

They had resumed walking, though he no longer clasped her hand on his arm, and the gap between them felt like a gulf. 'Truly,' she said tentatively, 'I have no idea how long I will remain in Porth Karrek, but I know I will never return to London. It is not so much what I have left behind, Treeve, but what I have discovered here in Cornwall.' She risked putting her hand on his arm, giving his sleeve a slight tug to draw his attention. 'I am not Cornish, but the sea is in my heart and my soul, just as it is in yours. If I had been a man, perhaps I would have become a sailor, like you.'

He laughed softly, as she had hoped he would. 'I am eternally grateful you're not a man.'

'So am I.'

He stopped. Their eyes met. And just like that, it was there between them, the connection, almost tangible, like a rope twined from desire and understanding, tightening around them, making them oblivious of their surroundings, of everything save themselves.

'Emily, I've never felt like this about any other woman before. Whatever is going on between us, it is no mere passing fancy.'

His words brought a lump to her throat. She swallowed it, hard. 'Then let us not give it a name.'

There was a plaintive note in Emily's voice that set him on edge. Why was she so desperate to belittle their feelings? Or was it only he who had these feelings? Was she trying to let him down gently? The idea appalled him. He let his hand fall. 'It's getting a bit late to carry on to Mousehole, and I think the weather might catch up with us in any case. Shall we head back?'

'Don't be angry with me, Treeve.'

'Why should I be angry? What you say makes perfect sense.' He caught himself before he marched off, forced himself to laugh at his own contrariness. 'I'm not angry,' he said, meaning it this time. 'Not with you, at any rate. I suspect that Jago has been using the house as a base for smuggling. When we were in the attics I noticed that the window had recently been cleaned.'

'Of course, you said yourself, the view is second to none.'

'He denied it when I confronted him. Not that I thought for a moment he would do anything else. I could find no evidence of actual contraband in the cellars, thank heavens, but he's had months to clear those out.'

'Perhaps it wasn't him.'

Treeve pursed his lips. 'No, I'm pretty sure it was. He's not a very good liar and he looked decidedly uncomfortable.'

'Which leaves you in a quandary. But I'm guessing you'd rather not talk about it any more today?'

'No,' Treeve said gratefully, pressing her hand. 'Let us talk of another Cornish tradition. Have you heard of Stargazy pie? It originated here, in Mousehole. Legend has it that one winter, two hundred years ago, the weather was so stormy that none of the boats could leave harbour and the villagers faced starvation, with no food to put on the table for Christmas. So one bold fisherman sailed out alone in the storms, and caught enough fish to feed everyone in Mousehole. They made it into a huge pie to eke it out, with the pilchard heads and tails poking up from the pastry as if emerging from the sea.'

'That sounds revolting!'

Treeve laughed. 'Anyway, every year they honour the fisherman who saved the village with a festival on the twenty-third of December, which just happens to be Gwav Gool. I was wondering if we could have our own Porth Karrek version and serve it at the ceilidh. What do you think?'

'You could have Abel Menhenick come up with something. He's a very good baker.'

'Excellent idea. And I'll serve a punch made with cider. There will be dancing of course, Cornish reels and country dances—I'm sure Bligh will be able to educate me on those.'

'You realise if your ceilidh is a success, then you'll have to return to Porth Karrek at Christmas every year.'

'Aye, I'll ask the Admiral of the Fleet to make sure my ship's back in Portsmouth each December. I'm sure he'll be happy to arrange the manoeuvres of the entire Royal Navy to suit my convenience.' He frowned. 'Perhaps it's wrong of me to create an expectation I can't fulfil.'

'But you can't do nothing, can you? If you are set on involving everyone from the village, why not have them decorate the Great Hall together, a greening I think it is known as.'

'Another excellent idea, Miss Faulkner. We could combine it with the hanging of the kissing bough.'

'I'm sure I'm going to regret asking...'

'It's a wreath made of holly, mistletoe and ivy, sometimes with apples, and there's a candle. They are hung in every house five days before Christmas. It's said that dancing in circles underneath it when the candle is lit welcomes in the God of Light, but it's also said that if you kiss your true love beneath the candle, the flame burns brighter.'

'And if it goes out?'

'Ah then, you have kissed the wrong person! My mother and father used to kiss under it every year when it was hung. How odd that I'd forgotten.'

'Was Christmas a big celebration when you were younger, then?'

'You mean the day itself?' Treeve wrinkled his nose, trying to remember. 'There were food baskets for the tenants, I must make sure that these are made up and handed out. But most of the celebrating is done before Nadelik—the bonfire, the gin and cake progression, Gwav Gool. Christmas Day is celebrated in church. You will come to dinner at Karrek House, won't you, after church? I won't have you spend Christmas alone.' He pressed her hand. 'You have been far too much alone, since your father died. Six years. And in London too, isn't it rather unusual for a young woman to do so?'

'I was twenty-six, not a girl.' Emily avoided his eyes. 'And I didn't live alone.'

'You had a companion?'

'Yes.' She started walking faster. 'But not on Christmas Day.'

'She had her own family?'

'A family,' Emily said, with a strange edge to her voice. 'Yes. There was a family.'

He did not know what to make of her tone. Was she lying? He could not believe it of her, but she was certainly prevaricating. He decided not to press her further. Whatever the truth, he wanted her to tell him of her own free will. 'Then it sounds as if both of us are overdue a bit of a celebration this Christmas,' Treeve said. 'It will be the start of December next week. We'll need to put our heads together to organise Gwav Gool.'

'A Cornish ceilidh.' Emily's smile seemed to him tinged with gratitude at his forbearance. 'Are you sure you need my help?'

'I can't do it alone. And if Porth Karrek refuses my

invitation to celebrate, then at least I can be assured I'll have a dance partner.'

She laughed faintly. 'I don't think you'll lack guests. Or dance partners.'

They dined in Penzance, in a private room at the inn, with a low-timbered ceiling propped up by dark-stained oak beams set at odd angles, and a flagstoned floor with a distinct slope towards the sea. Soft candlelight, a roaring fire, and an excellent dinner of Cornish sole cooked in butter and parsley, left them both mellow, content to sit opposite each other at the table sipping their claret. It was an intimate, domestic and bittersweet meal. The sort of meal a husband and wife could have every night. Emily persuaded herself she was content to enjoy it this one time.

It was dark by the time they arrived back at Karrek House. Treeve insisted on walking back with her to the cottage. The night was clear. The stars hung low and bright in the inky sky. The waves were a distant murmur. They kissed in the doorway, their arms wrapped around each other, clinging to the dying embers of the most perfect day, not wanting it to end.

'Emily,' Treeve whispered, in that way of his that made her want to melt, nibbling on her earlobe, pushing back the hood of her cloak to kiss his way down her neck.

She tangled her fingers in his hair. Then she pulled his face down towards hers, hungry for his mouth again. Their kisses tasted of wine. Her head was woozy with the combination of wine and sea air and wanting. She pushed the door open, and they staggered across the threshold, still locked together.

They kissed. She undid her cloak, dropping it to the floor. He cast off his greatcoat. They kissed again, tugging each other closer, and kissed again. They fell on to the chair by the fire. She was straddled on top of him, the hard length of him pressed against her, making her moan, making her arch her back, and still they kissed. His hands on her breasts through her gown, her nipples aching for his touch. And there were still more kisses, ceasing only for them to draw breath before they kissed again.

Her hair was down. She was so aroused she thought she would combust. Treeve's breath was fast, shallow. Their kisses slowed. They gazed raptly at each other in the near darkness. Emily slid to her feet. Treeve picked up his coat. One last kiss at the door. No need for words. That was what shook her. The fact that they had no need for words.

She was in love. Lying in bed, she tried out the words. *I love you, Treeve*, finding not a trace of doubt, only a calm acceptance. She had been travelling towards this moment from the first time their eyes met, on the beach. All her precautions, all the warnings she'd given herself, had simply delayed the inevitable. She loved him. She was meant to love him. Made to love him. No wonder her feelings for Andrew paled in comparison! They were a shadow of her love for Treeve, so solid, so—so rooted inside her.

Did Treeve love her? From the beginning, he'd seen what she had refused to, the way they complemented each other, like two halves of a whole, the way they knew each other. Did he love her? Not yet. She couldn't let him. Even though it was what she longed for.

Wrapping her arms around herself, Emily closed her eyes. She wouldn't think about it any more. The clock was ticking towards Christmas. Let them have these few weeks together. She would keep her love to herself. And then—and then the fates would decide.

Chapter Seven

The storm swept in late on Saturday night, the last day of November, rattling the window panes of Emily's cottage, waking her up with a start. Wrapping a shawl around her, she gazed out of the window, but her view was restricted by the driving rain. There had been no talk of a storm in the village today. The boats which lay inside the harbour wall had not been moved higher up. But even the saltiest sea dogs were sometimes wrong-footed by the Cornish weather.

The windows rattled ever louder. Emily loved storms, she found witnessing nature at its most elemental exhilarating. She threw on stockings and shoes, wrapped her cloak around her and battled her way out to the headland. The tide was still low, though coming in. It was not the waves so much as the swell which was treacherous. The wind howled, the sea crashed and roared, and the rain drove. Keeping a safe distance from the cliff edge, she held her arms wide, lifting her face to the skies. If anyone could see her they would think her crazy, but no one else would be mad enough to be out in this extreme weather.

Except someone was, it seemed. Was that a light out there beyond The Beasts? Peering through the darkness, she thought she must have been mistaken, but there it was again, a faint gleam, disappearing into the swell, appearing again a few moments later. It was a boat, making for the harbour and in danger of being blown on to the rocks. It could be a fishing boat, but coming back to harbour at this time of night with the tide coming in—that didn't make sense. Bligh on a smuggling trip? It had been set reasonably fair this morning. If it was him, if he had set out for the Scillies, the stopping-off point that Treeve was convinced he must be using, he'd be desperate to get back before the Sabbath. The light bobbed into view once more. They were about half a mile from The Beasts, but the wind was blowing them steadily in that direction and the tide was coming in. The boat was too far away to make out how many were on board, but assuming it was the one Bligh used for fishing, she reckoned there would be six, maybe eight crew.

Emily took to her heels, running with the wind at her back as fast as she could towards Karrek House, tugging so violently on the bell without stopping that she summoned both Treeve, still dressed, and several bewildered-looking servants.

'A boat,' Emily said, panting. 'Heading for the harbour. I don't know what we can do, but the tide—The Beasts.'

'Bligh, damn him! Go back to your cottage, Emily, I'll sound the alert down in the village.'

'I'm coming with you.'

'It's wild. You'll be soaked.'

'I'm already soaked, and I'm coming with you.'

There was no time for argument. The full force of the storm hit them on the headland by St Piran's, driving rain, a southerly wind blowing directly in from the Channel, blowing the boat straight at The Beasts. On the harbour, a small group of people had already gathered.

'Bligh,' Treeve said again, his fists clenched as he made his way towards them. 'They know he was out. Look, Ned Nancarrow and Ezerah Chegwin right at the front.'

Both men eyed Treeve fearfully, shrugging when he demanded to know how many were on board. 'Six, I reckon Captain Penhaligon.' Phin stepped out of the shadows. 'They'll be on to The Beasts in minutes, and the tide is against them. Even if they can cling on, the rocks will be under water in less than an hour. What are we to do?'

'Nothing to be done now,' Nancarrow said.

A round curse greeted this, and Emily stared in astonishment as Jago Bligh appeared on the harbour wall. 'You see,' he said, addressing Treeve, who looked every bit as astounded, directly, 'I didn't lie. That's my brother out there. I'll launch my boat out. Who's with me?'

'The wind is against us, Jago. No, wait,' Treeve added, grabbing the man by the sleeve. 'I don't mean we should do nothing, but it would be madness to try to take a boat out in these conditions.'

'But not one of them can swim,' Jago said desperately.

'It's not so far at the moment, with the tide still low. If one of us could swim out with a rope? Tie it to the rocks, somehow? Is anyone fit for it?' Treeve looked around, but every man looked either helpless or shamefaced. Not one stepped forward. 'Fetch me a stout rope,' he shouted to Phin, bracing himself, and stripping off his coat. 'Knot one end to one of the rings on the harbour wall, give me the rest, I'll put it around my waist.'

'No! Wait! Let me!' Galvanised into action, Emily pulled off her cloak.

'Emily! No!'

'You can't swim, it looks like no one here can swim, but I can.'

'I can't let you do this. The waves—look at them. And the tide is coming in fast.'

'I know how to swim against it.' Emily handed her cloak to an astonished Ned Nancarrow, then kicked off her shoes and stockings, leaving her in her nightgown. 'Give me the rope, Treeve.'

'No, it's far too dangerous.'

'Yet you were going to risk it.'

'These are my people, Emily.'

'They're mine too.' She pulled him to one side, speaking urgently. 'Treeve, that's Kensa and Jack's father out there. And who knows what other husbands and fathers.'

'But...'

'Your brother drowned out there, on those rocks,' she said desperately. 'Do you want to take the risk of going the same way? Listen to me! These are your people, you said it yourself. They need you to be here for them in the future.'

'I can't let you risk your neck, Emily, I can't...'

'I won't drown,' she said, turning her back on the swelling sea, refusing to allow her fears to show in her voice or on her face. 'I'm not a fool, you know that I've been raised to respect the sea, I wouldn't be doing this if I didn't think I could pull it off. Treeve,' she said again, urgently, 'I *have* to do this, because no one else can. Give me the damned rope.'

'Emily...'

'This is your home now. You know it, even if you haven't admitted it to yourself yet. Do you want your tenure to begin with six deaths? I can do this. I *can.*'

Out at sea, a wail was heard, a thud and a crack, and the boat was on The Beasts. Treeve knew in his heart that he wouldn't make it, but to allow Emily to try— every fibre of his being rebelled. Yet if she did not try, they would lose all six men. 'Tie it around your waist, so we can pull you back in if you get into trouble. If you do make it, as soon as you're on the rocks, pray that some of the crew have made it too, get them to hold it taut and I'll follow you out.' It was the best he could do. He had to trust her confidence in her ability. 'Phin, make damned sure that rope holds firm.'

Stripping to his breeches and shirt, he forced himself to smile grimly at Emily.

'Trust me,' she said.

He caught her to him in a fierce hug. 'I don't want to lose you.'

Emily touched his face briefly, the strangest of expressions on her face. Then she turned away. His heart in his mouth, Treeve watched her wade into the sea, making steady progress as far as the harbour wall, where the waters were calmer. But the moment she was beyond a wave hit her. She dived under it, disappearing from view for a long, terrifying moment. He saw her head bob up, then watched, terrified to take his eyes off the receding figure, lest he lose sight of her for ever.

Around him, the crowd had grown, it seemed like the whole village had turned out. He could hear the shouts of the crew, hear Phin's running commentary as figures appeared on the emerging rocks, speculation as to who was safe, who was in the water, but he kept his eyes fixed on Emily. She knew what she was doing, he very quickly realised from her stop-start progress, not fighting the waves but waiting on them passing, then using the gap between to swim out. Fifty yards, sixty at the most, it felt like a lifetime before she made it to The Beasts, but he was in the water the moment he saw her tiny figure being hauled up, holding on to the rope, feeling it tauten as the sailors pulled it tight, allowing him to battle out to join her.

It took less than half an hour for the crew to haul themselves along the rope to safety, but by then the tide was already covering The Beasts. Treeve was the last out of the water, following closely behind Emily, who also clung to the rope now, exhausted by her efforts. As the pair of them staggered out, Derwa Nancarrow hurried over to Emily, shrouding her in her abandoned cloak before her slight figure in the tatters of her translucent nightgown could be seen.

'I'll take her back to her cottage,' she said to Treeve, gently coaxing Emily to take a sip of hot rum.

'Thank you. Go with Derwa,' he said, when Emily demurred, desperate to have her warm and dry, and out of earshot. Now that everyone was safe he was furious with the villagers. 'Please,' he added softly, for her ears only. 'I can't let the events of the evening pass without comment.'

He watched her go, making her way slowly up Budoc Lane, a frail, fragile figure, fading into the darkness of the night. Yet she had been a tower of strength and fortitude out there on the rocks, encouraging the more reluctant men into the sea, who would have clung to The Beasts despite the fact that they were fast being swallowed by the waters. A lump rose in his throat. If he had lost her—it didn't bear thinking of. His heart felt as if it was being squeezed. He would not lose her. Never.

The urge to run after her, to abandon the crowd and postpone his unpleasant duty was nigh on irresistible, but he knew from long years of experience, that his words would have a strength, here in the immediate emotional aftermath, that they would lose in the cold light of day. So he turned around, and an expectant hush fell as he surveyed the circle of men and woman around him in the lantern light.

'Now that you are safe, gentlemen,' Treeve said, 'I think it's time for me to lay my cards on the table. This will be the last cargo of contraband which you will attempt to land at Porth Karrek. That so-called tradition is now at an end, and if I discover that any of you have failed to heed this command, let me assure you that I will not hesitate to bring the full weight of the law to bear on you.'

He waited, but no one had anything to say, none but Jago and Phin, saturated from his role as the anchor man on the end of the rope, meeting his eye. The wind had died down, the hushing of the waves against the harbour wall counting out the silence in the salty night air. Ironically, if they had set sail an hour later, the crew would have landed safely.

'I don't give a damn how you dispose of the cargo when it is washed ashore. I don't give a damn what you do with the existing supplies in the Ship, Nancarrow, or in that shop of yours, Chegwin, but I want all of it out of Porth Karrek by the end of the week. Do I make myself clear?'

'It's all very well for you, Captain Penhaligon, but you don't understand how things are here.' Ned Nancarrow finally spoke up. 'You have your fine job in the Royal Navy, you don't have to worry about putting bread on the table, and when you go back to sea at the end of the year, you won't care a damn about this place. What difference does it make to you, whether I pay duty on the brandy I sell, you won't be here to know any different.'

'I'll know,' Jago said, to Treeve's surprise. 'And I'll make sure that the captain knows. I owe him that, after tonight.'

'Thank you, Jago, but there's no need. I won't be rejoining my ship at the end of the year.'

He had not intended to say any such thing, but Emily was right. These were his people. They needed him. They needed *him*, not another version of his father, or Austol. Emily had been right about that too. 'I've decided to stay here in Porth Karrek,' Treeve said, smiling at the villagers now, 'and I warn you now, there are going to be some changes, positive changes. I intend to build a lighthouse on The Beasts, and a stronger harbour wall for a start.'

There was a collective gasp of astonishment, then a cheer, then a volley of questions. He spoke. He had no idea what he said, but he was aware of his hand being shaken, his back pummelled. He was, belatedly, being made extremely welcome, but he had no time to savour the moment. The most important person in the world was not here, and he had to be with her. Now!

'Reverend Maddern,' he exclaimed, as the minister arrived breathlessly. 'Your timing is excellent. I think a prayer for the safe delivery of these men is in order.'

As heads were bowed, Treeve made his escape, passing Derwa Nancarrow return from tending to Emily on the way. He had forgotten all about the woman. Nodding at her, hurrying on his way, he wondered wryly what she would have told her husband, if he had come bursting in on Emily while she was still there. But what the devil did it matter! Soon, everyone would know.

Shivering, he became aware of his sodden clothes, the sting of the cuts and grazes on his arms and legs, the rope burns on his hands. He should go home, have a bath, wait until the morning. But he couldn't wait. Out there, at the mercy of the elements, with life and death on a knife's edge, he had seen quite clearly what he had known in his bones from the day he first set eyes on Emily. Tonight was a turning point. He had faced danger before, had battled the sea countless times, never fearlessly for only fools were fearless, but heedless of his own safety, putting his ship and his men first, always. But this was different. It was not a matter of duty to save Emily. It was a matter of love.

As he approached her cottage, he wondered if he was being precipitate. But when the world could change in the blink of an eye, why wait to say what was in your heart? He simply couldn't bear to waste another second.

* * *

Emily, shivering and wrapped in a blanket, watched impassively while Derwa Nancarrow stoked the fire, filled the kettle and set it to boil. She was aware of the woman eying her possessions, her work table, her tea caddy, the clothes in the closet which she rummaged through to find a clean nightgown, but she was too stunned and shaken by events to care. Now that she was safe, now that it was over, she was astounded by what she had done, amazed at her calm, the reserves of strength she had been able to summon. In the face of the sailors' terror she had been confident, reassuring, fooling herself as well as them into believing that all would be well, everyone would be safe. And they were, every last one of them, but it could so easily have been otherwise. Closing her eyes, she could see the waves crashing on the rocks, feel the undertow and fierce tug of the current, the thick taste of salt in her throat.

She shivered violently. They were safe. All of them, the sailors, herself and Treeve. Treeve, who had been at her side, fighting for every life despite the fact that he couldn't swim, despite the fact that his brother had drowned on those very rocks. She had thrown herself into the water for the sake of the men in the boat and their wives and children. But most of all, she had risked her life for Treeve, and he had risked his life to keep her safe. His faith in her had been the rock on which she had relied. Treeve, who said he couldn't bear to lose her. Any more than she could bear to lose him. She shivered again, violently. They were safe. Safe. Safe.

'Drink this, Miss Faulkner.'

A cup of tea was pressed into her trembling hands.

It rattled in the saucer as she took it. It burned her lips. 'Emily,' she croaked.

'Then you must call me Derwa. Is this your handiwork?' she asked, indicating the table. 'It's very beautiful. I had no idea. You're a deep one, aren't you? I knew you could swim. Kensa and Jack Bligh let slip to my two that you'd taught them. But it took real guts to go into the sea tonight. You must have been terrified.'

Emily shuddered. 'There was no one else.'

'But there should have been. I've two boys, Miss Faulkner, and they'll be old enough to go to sea before I know it. I won't let them go without learning to swim. Will you teach them?'

Tears burned in Emily's eyes. She had longed for this olive branch. 'When it's warmer, they can learn,' she said.

Derwa nodded, giving her a tight-lipped smile. 'What we need to do right now is get you warm. Kettle's boiling again. Shall I help you to wash?'

'No, please. I'm fine, thank you. It's very late, you should return home.'

'If you're sure?' Derwa pulled on her shawl, hesitating at the door. 'What you did, Miss Faulkner— Emily—it proves you're one of us. We won't forget it. Thank you.'

The door closed behind her. *One of us!* Chilled to the bone as she was, Derwa's words warmed her. If she made Porth Karrek her home, she would be one of them. She would have friends. She would teach the children to swim. When she walked into the baker's, Eliza Menhenick would bid her good morning and wrap her loaf without having to ask what she wanted. It felt good.

Casting off her blanket, Emily poured hot water into

the basin and set about washing the salt, sand, grit and blood away. Where was Treeve? *'I can't let the events of the evening pass without comment,'* he'd said. He intended to take the villagers to task. Was he still down at the harbour or had he returned to Karrek House? Was he feeling as she was now, giddy with relief, suddenly full of energy? Euphoric, that was the word, the result of having been so close to *not* being alive, of having survived what she now saw as a terrifying ordeal. Was he thinking of her, wondering what she was feeling?

Her skin tingling as it thawed from the hot water and the blaze of the fire, she had just pulled on a fresh nightgown when there was a knock at the door. Telling herself it was most likely Derwa coming back to check on her, she opened it hoping that it would be only one person, the person she most wanted to see.

'Treeve!'

'Emily!' He kicked the door shut and pulled her into his arms. 'Emily, Emily, Emily.'

'Treeve.' She wrapped her arms around his neck, pressing herself closer. 'Oh, Treeve.'

'Emily. I can't believe…'

'Nor can I. If it was not for you…'

'No, you. The credit is all yours. You were incredibly brave.'

'Because of you. Afterwards, when I realised what might have happened…'

He tightened his arms around her waist. 'It was only afterwards, I realised just how close we had come…'

She buried her cheek against his chest, relishing the reassuringly steady beat of his heart. 'You're soaking wet.'

'I should have changed clothes, but I was desperate

to see you. I needed to be here. With you.' He touched her cheek. He bent his head. 'You're more important than anything else.'

Their lips met. Salt and soap. Heat and cold. The bristle of his beard on her raw skin. It was a survivors' kiss, lips clinging, bodies pressed tight against one another, hands stroking arms, shoulders, backs, seeking to reassure, to satisfy themselves that they were flesh and blood, safe, together. A survivors' kiss that deepened into the desire to prove that they were flesh and blood, an irresistible, instinctive urge, to be each other's flesh and blood. Their kisses became feverish, their breath shallow, as they lost themselves, muttering each other's name over and over, like an incantation.

There was no moment when they stopped to think, no moment when they considered what they were doing, no point when either of them called a halt. Emily had only an urgent, driving need, to touch, to kiss, to stroke, to be touched, to be kissed, to be stroked, to eliminate every space between them.

She didn't know how they moved from the door to her bed, tucked in the recess at the back of the room, she didn't care, save that in the course of the short journey, she had torn the remnants of Treeve's shirt from him, and he had lost his boots and stockings. She smoothed her hands over his chest, pressed wild kisses to the grazes there, flicked her tongue over his nipples, rubbed her cheek against the coarse hair of his chest. Taste, touch, feel, she wanted it all. She eyed him hungrily, the way his muscles flexed, the dip of his belly, and she tasted him just as voraciously.

She spoke his name, and he spoke hers. He touched her, urgently, covetously, as if she might disappear at any moment, as if he couldn't believe she was real. Her nightgown fell to the floor, and she was glad to see it go, for it meant he could cup her breasts, take her nipples into his mouth, draw out such sweet, delightful, aching pleasure from her. A tiny ripple of air between them as he released her to remove the last of his clothing, and she could gaze at him blatantly, her belly clenching in response to the thick, jutting length of his arousal.

This was what she needed, but as she reached for him, for the first time he hesitated. 'You want this, Emily, as much as I do?'

'Oh, yes. Every bit as much.'

She kissed him, and her kisses convinced him, and she lost herself again, as he laid her down on the bed and entered her, slowly, slowly, slowly, and she wrapped her legs around his waist, and he pushed higher. And then…

Heat, friction, pulsing, throbbing, tension. He thrust. Emily moaned, holding him tight inside her. He thrust higher. She held on tight, tighter, and he thrust harder, and she dug her heels into his rear and urged him on, higher, faster. She clutched at his back, and she cried out wildly as his thrusts sent her over the edge, spinning, throbbing, wave after wave, urging him on, until he cried out too, spilling himself on to the sheet, collapsing panting over her, and she clung to him, wrapping her arms and legs around him. Safe.

'Emily,' Treeve murmured, kissing her tenderly. 'I didn't intend this tonight but—oh, Emily, I can't regret it.' He rolled on to his side, propping himself up on his elbow. 'Tell me you don't either.'

'No.' She smiled at him, her mouth softened with

kisses, her lids heavy, her skin rosy. 'After tonight, I *needed* you.'

His heart lifted. 'It was the same for me. I know we should have waited, but after tonight, I thought, why wait, when we *know.* I love you so much, so very much, and the very idea that I could have lost you. My love, my darling, I can't wait to call you my wife. You will marry me, won't you, Emily?'

She stared at him blankly for a long moment. Then she pushed herself up, grabbing the sheet, looking utterly horrified. 'No!'

'I'm leaving the navy. I've decided to stay in Porth Karrek,' he said urgently, thinking she must have misunderstood. 'I announced it down at the harbour tonight. You were right, I belong here, they need me. And I need you, Emily. I know it's sudden, but tonight made me see that I don't want to miss another second of our lives together.' Her expression had not softened. He took her hand. 'I've known from the moment I met you that what I felt was different and tonight—it took tonight to make me realise that it was love. And you said you felt the same.'

'No!' Emily shook herself free, jumped out of bed, grabbing her nightgown and pulling it on in a wild tangle of arms and sleeves. 'No, no, no. I said I needed you, I didn't say I loved you.'

'But we made love.' He felt as if she had punched him in the stomach, as if she had knocked the breath out of him. 'You must have known that I would never have made love with you if I had not thought that…'

'I can't marry you, Treeve, it's out of the question. I'm so sorry, I had no idea—but I won't. I can't.'

His body was still heavy with sated desire. His head

was spinning. He had been so sure. And they had made love. But Emily didn't love him. No, that simply didn't feel right! 'I've spooked you,' Treeve said, getting out of bed and covering himself with a blanket. 'I should have realised it's too much to absorb in one night. What happened out there. Then my deciding to stay here. And then proposing. It felt right to me, but I've been too hasty, I haven't explained myself properly. Deciding to stay here, it's a huge change for me, and I know I've not thought it through but I also know I won't change my mind, Emily. What I feel for you—what we feel for each other...'

'Please don't.' She was pale, her arms wrapped around herself, her eyes wide.

A huge shudder made her stagger, and Treeve caught her as her legs gave way, cursing himself. 'My poor darling, you're exhausted. What was I thinking, allowing myself to get so carried away when what you need is sleep! I'm so sorry.'

He picked her up, carrying her back to the rumpled bed and pulling the blankets over her. She watched him silently as he put on what was left of his clothes. 'We are both overwrought. I'll come back later this morning. Emily?'

'Yes. We need to talk, Treeve. I can't—'

'In the morning,' he interrupted her. Her tone was flat, but it was exhaustion, he told himself, she was physically and emotionally drained. Still he hesitated, not in the least inclined to leave her. But that was clearly what she wanted, for she had already closed her eyes, so he banked up the fire, then left.

Outside it was strangely light. It took him a moment to realise that it had been snowing. He plodded back to Karrek House, his body heavier, wearier with each step, the efforts of holding the rope, fighting the sea, finally taking their toll. He felt deflated, his exuberant mood quite lost in a vague depression. He loved Emily. She loved him. They belonged together. Their future lay here, in Porth Karrek. These things were irrefutable. When she had rested, she'd see it too.

Chapter Eight

Against her expectations, Emily slept deeply, waking unrefreshed several hours later, with an aching head and aching body, but with her mind quite resolved. There was a strange light coming through the window. A light dusting of snow covered the ground. Opening her front door, she took large gulps of icy air, and found a pail of milk and a fresh loaf wrapped in a cloth on the door-step. The gesture brought a lump to her throat. Finally, she had found a place she wanted to call home, and the events of last night meant she would be welcome here. But those same events had been decisive for Treeve too. He had decided to stay. And so she must go. She loved Porth Karrek, but she loved Treeve more. She could not remain here, so deeply in love, but unable to be his wife. He'd be here soon, hoping to persuade her, unaware that their conversation would be about how impossible any notion of their marrying was.

Picking up the loaf and milk, she closed the door, stoked the fire and set the kettle to boil. She was in love with Treeve, but it brought her no joy. Treeve was in love with her, and what should have made her heart soar made it ache. A tear trickled down her cheek, as she anticipated the pain she was about to inflict on him. But it was the only way. It would be over quickly, a ruthless cut such as a surgeon would make, and the love he felt for her would be gone. As she would be too, soon.

Another tear trickled down her cheek. There would be no Gwav Gool for her. She wouldn't see the bonfire on the beach, or hear the Christmas cantata Treeve had commissioned from the composer who would be arriving in Porth Karrek this very day. When Treeve knew her sad, tragic history, he'd want her gone, before she could taint his new beginning here. She would spend another Christmas alone. No different from the last five Christmases. So it was very, very stupid of her to cry over something she'd never had. But it was a great deal easier to cry over the loss of Christmas than to think about the huge chasm that the loss of Treeve would create.

She dressed carefully, her arms and shoulders screaming in protest as she pulled her dress on and struggled with the fastenings. She'd barely noticed her aches and pains last night, when Treeve arrived at her door. When she had thrown herself at him like a wanton. Her cheeks burned. She had never felt such an elemental passion as she had felt last night, making love to Treeve. Last night, the need to make love to him had been an irresistible force, a need to be part of him, body and mind. They were made for each other. Treeve, so honest and open with his feelings, had sensed it from the start, had seen what she too had been forced to admit.

The kettle was boiling. Emily made herself a cup of

tea. She made herself to eat a slice of fresh bread. And prepared to deny the truth in her heart, to protect the man she loved.

The snow was already melting when Treeve set out the morning after the storm dressed, not in his usual garb but in town clothes, a tailcoat, a high, starched cravat, tightly fitting pantaloons, gleaming boots. Cador Kitto, the composer, would arrive later that day, he reminded himself as he passed the gatehouse. He'd have to find time to make the man welcome.

Emily opened the door before he had time to knock. She too had dressed with care, in a pale blue gown he hadn't seen before, her hair pinned into a heavy chignon at her nape, rather than tied loosely back. Her face was pale, her eyes huge, her smile quite absent. She looked determined and apprehensive. The knot in his stomach tightened. Despite his best attempts to feel optimistic, he had not been able to rid himself of the sense of dread he'd woken with.

'Emily.' He took her hands between his, in their usual greeting. Her skin was icy. 'Did you sleep?'

'Do you want tea?' She pulled her hands away, not meeting his eyes, waving him to a seat, not at the fire, but at her work table, which she had cleared. 'There's fresh bread too, someone left it on my doorstep, though I expect you've already breakfasted.'

'I'm not hungry. Emily, I...'

'I've got something I must tell you.'

It was the way she said it. Baldly, almost ruthlessly, in a cold, taut tone so unlike her. It choked his own words of love and persuasion in his throat, and clutched

like icy fingers in his belly. He took the tea he didn't
want from her and waited.

'When I was nineteen, visiting my grandparents in
Lewis, I met a young man. Andrew Macfarlane. A distant relative, also visiting the island, he was handsome
and charming. It was one of those summers where the
sun shone every day—or so it seemed to me at the time.
I ended up half in love with him. But at the end of summer we went our separate ways. I went back to London, and thought no more of him, save as an innocent
holiday romance.'

Emily took a shaky drink of tea. Treeve simply
waited, with no idea where this unexpected story would
lead.

'Three years later,' she continued, 'my grandparents
died. The estate went to John-Angus, as I told you, but
my inheritance was still substantial. I had no idea of
how substantial. Papa called it my nest egg. He invested
it for me. We lived comfortably enough, but modestly.
Then Papa died, and I discovered that Papa had left
me another fortune on top of my original inheritance.
I was—well, I suppose you would call me an heiress.'

'An heiress! And you had no idea?'

Emily's expression hardened. 'None at all, nor any
idea, when I discovered the extent of my inheritance,
of the attention it would generate. How people came to
know, I have no idea, but I was inundated with begging
letters. And with invitations.'

'The press,' Treeve said, struggling to make sense of
what she was saying. 'I believe it is the practice to pub-
lish details of substantial estates in the press.'

'I didn't know that. That must have been how Andrew Macfarlane found me. He turned up at my door a

week after the funeral, offering his condolences. I can see by your face that you have guessed what happened.'

'He was a fraud,' he said flatly, for now the point of the story did seem clear enough. 'He cheated you out of your inheritance.'

'He was certainly a fraud, but I'm not sure—is it cheating, for a husband to take all his wife's money?'

He had been readying himself to assure her that he didn't give a damn how poor she was. He thought he must have misheard. 'What did you say?'

'I married him,' Emily replied, stony-faced. 'We were married for five years, during which time he took every penny of my inheritance without my knowledge, and mortgaged our home up to the hilt to boot. I finally confronted him in January this year. You cannot know how deeply I regret not doing so sooner.'

Treeve pushed back his chair so violently that it clattered to the floor. 'You're married?' He clutched at his hair, staring at her aghast. 'All this time, I've been falling in love with you, planning a future with you, and you were married to someone else. What the hell were you playing at?'

He was at the door when she caught him, grabbing him by the arm. 'Wait, I haven't finished.'

'I don't want to know any more.'

'I'm not married, Treeve. I thought I was, but I'm not. Though it makes no difference. I'm telling this all wrong. I'm so sorry.'

She pulled his arm. He let himself be dragged back inside. Picking up his toppled chair, he dropped into it, incapable of speaking.

'He told me he had never forgotten our summer in Lewis, couldn't get me out of his head but didn't know where I lived. He told me that when he read the notice of Papa's death, he'd taken it for a sign. I believed him. I believed all of it. So we were married.' She held up her hand to stay him when he made to speak. 'From the start there were absences. Long periods when he was away. On business, he said, some of the time, and at others he—he told me that his mother was deranged, and kept in a quiet house in Yorkshire.' Emily's mouth twisted. 'I fell for that too. Of course his mother was long dead.

'Last year, the holes in his story began to show, though I refused to examine them too closely. Creditors appeared at the door. He explained them away. More appeared. The bank would not discuss matters with me, because a wife has no authority over her own money, it seems, so I finally turned to Papa's solicitor and he uncovered the truth.'

A tear splashed down her cheek, but she scrubbed it furiously away. 'Andrew was married—is married—has been married to another woman for twelve years. He was married, in fact, the year I met him. He has four children. He admitted all of it quite freely, when I confronted him. He loves his wife and his children very much. Well, of course he does, he must do, for he's spent the last five years appropriating funds from me to provide for them. And now he can, he has no need of me.'

'Emily...'

'Please, hear me out. I could take him to court for bigamy. It's what Papa's solicitor recommended, but can you imagine what that would do to his wife and children—because they don't know, you see. All the times he spent with me, they thought he was abroad on business. And he was always home for the important things too—birthdays, anniversaries, Christmas. I worked it all out, afterwards. The dates.'

'But your fortune…'

'I don't care about the money,' she snapped. 'I don't deserve to have it back.'

'You can't possibly blame yourself for any of this?'

'Who else is there to blame? I allowed him to dupe me. A few simple enquiries, that was all it took in the end, but I didn't make them. Not at the start, when he appeared as if by magic, not when he disappeared, not when the creditors appeared. I went on burying my head in the sand until it was too late. And then, when it was over, I ran.'

'To Cornwall.'

'To Cornwall.'

Treeve was shocked. Appalled. Angry on her behalf. No, furious. And, dammit, he was touched by her bravery. Her spirit. 'It doesn't alter the fact that I love you, Emily.'

'Please don't.'

'I love you,' he persisted, 'and I know you love me. You wouldn't have made love to me last night otherwise, no matter what you say. We got carried away in the moment, it's true, but it was because of what we feel for each other. I know you love me.'

She gazed at him helplessly. 'I can't marry you. You couldn't find a more unsuitable wife. As far as the world is concerned, my reputation is ruined. I lived with another man for five years…'

'Thinking you were married!'

Emily reached her hand over to clasp his fingers. 'Five years, I lived with him, Treeve. As his wife.' She spoke gently now, carefully, her eyes fearful not for her-

self but for him. 'And I did not once conceive. I hoped.
You have no idea how much I hoped, but the discovery
that his wife has four children could mean only one
thing. Now do you see?'

And finally, he did. 'You can't have children,' he said
softly, heartsore for her.

'And you must have children,' Emily said. 'To carry
on your work at Porth Karrek. A future generation...'

'Stop!' He shook himself free of her clasp, running
his hand through his hair. 'We promised to be honest
with each other. Right from the start, we promised.
Why didn't you tell me?'

'Because I'm ashamed. Because I didn't want you to
know me as that pathetic woman. I wanted to be *whole*!
You admired me. You thought me brave.'

'I don't know anyone braver. Last night...'

'But I'm not brave. I was afraid to confront Andrew. I
was afraid to confront the fact that I couldn't have children. I closed my eyes and hoped against all odds—
how is that brave?'

'You didn't trust me! Right from the start, I couldn't
understand what it was—why it was that you wouldn't
talk about your past.'

'I wanted to wipe the slate clean.'

'He betrayed you, so you betrayed me, Emily.'

'No! Please don't say that.'

He clutched at his brow again. 'Do I know you in
the slightest?'

She gazed at him helplessly. 'Better than I know myself. I could lie to you, tell you that I don't love you...'

'I wouldn't believe you. You know that. It's why you
have finally told me this.' He cursed again, looking at
her helplessly. 'What am I to do? I don't want to think

about life without you. You're part of me, Emily. I can't lose you.'

'I can't be your wife. Think about it, Treeve, you're giving up your surrogate family by leaving the navy. It's natural, it's right that you should then want a real family of your own. Isn't that what marriage is all about?'

'I love you, dammit!'

'But you need more than just me in your life. And Porth Karrek deserves better too. An heir to carry on with all the improvements you're about to make. To pick up your legacy. That's not possible if you marry me.'

'I have come to love this place, but I'm not going to marry just to secure an heir. Emily, I love you, dammit, and you love me! I want to share my life with you.' He ached with the pain of her childlessness, he couldn't begin to imagine how she must have suffered. 'If we were blessed with children, I would be delighted, but I would rather do without them than without you. Can't you see?'

But he could see by the look on her face that she could not. 'I know what it's like,' she said, wringing her hands, 'to endure a childless marriage. I *know* the heartache that's involved, the disappointments. You love me now, but in time that would change. No, listen to me,' she said when he made to protest again. 'If the situation was reversed, if you could not have children, Treeve, what would you do?'

'I'd tell you. I'd offer *you* the choice.'

'And I would choose you. Just as you are choosing me—for now. In time though, my darling...' Her voice cracked. She drew herself up. 'You'd regret it. I couldn't bear you growing to resent me. I won't marry you. My mind is quite made up. I love you too much.

I'll leave Porth Karrek as soon as I can. It is best for all concerned.'

'No.' He was not giving up, but he knew better than to try to persuade her. He didn't want to persuade her, he wanted her to see that she was wrong. She wasn't the only one of them who wanted a future based on a solid footing, without any regrets. 'Stay for Christmas, Emily. Do this much for me, please? Promise you'll stay, just until the end of the year. Four weeks, that's all I ask. And if your mind is still made up to leave, then I won't put any obstacles in your way.'

The snow had melted by late afternoon when Emily made her way out of the cottage in search of fresh air. There was no trace of last night's storm as she reached the headland overlooking Karrek Sands. The sky was pale grey, through which a weak afternoon sun filtered, the sea a gentle swell, the wind no more than a breeze. She had expected her confession to herald an irrevocable ending. She had not foreseen Treeve's request that she stay till Christmas, but she had agreed to consider it. She had, for hours after he left, scrupulously questioned her conscience, agonisingly reviewing a list of reasons for her to leave now, a clean, brutal break, and possible reasons for her to remain.

Seeing the lone figure on the beach, gazing out at the spot where The Beasts lurked, her heart leapt. Months of practice had made her sure-footed on the descent to Karrek Sands. He sensed her arrival as she jumped down from the path, waiting for her to approach. She remembered the first time, not so many weeks ago, when she hadn't known who he was, hadn't guessed that he was actually the love of her life. She crossed the sands quickly.

'I'm worried that you feel sorry for me,' she said, resuming the conversation which she had terminated a few hours before. 'If you'd known the truth about me before you proposed, you wouldn't have asked me to marry you, and now you have...'

'You're offering me an escape route? I truly hope you know how insulting that is.'

She flinched. 'I had to tell you what I've been thinking. I can't have children. I wish it was otherwise, but that's the hand nature has dealt me. I've learned to accept that. Mostly.'

'I love you, Emily. For what you are. Who you are. I don't pity you. I admire you. I wouldn't change a hair on your head.'

'You've only just realised you love me, and I've only just told you that I am—what I am.'

'Which is why I want you to stay, at least for the time being. The rest of our lives are at stake, Emily, it's not a decision to be made lightly.'

'You can't persuade me to change my mind.'

'I don't want to. I want you to see that this is where you belong, with me. You shocked me to the core with what you told me this morning, but even while my head was reeling, I knew what I wanted. I didn't doubt my feelings.' He held up his hands when she made to speak. 'I know that what you believe is that I'll come to see that you're right over the next few weeks. Perhaps I will. I feel in my gut that I won't change my mind but I'll try, I promise you, to see things from your point of view. I'll ask myself, is she right? Will I come to resent our childless marriage? Will I stop loving you because you can't give me a child, or Porth Karrek an heir?'

She clutched his hand, pressing a kiss to his knuckles. 'I know you love me, Treeve, as much as I love you, which is why I cannot—you deserve more.'

'Isn't that for me to say? You are all I want, Emily. We can be everything to each other.' He sighed, freeing his hand.

'If I stay, I'm worried that it will be more painful for you when I eventually leave.'

'I think you're afraid that staying will make it harder for you to leave at all. Ask yourself why. If leaving is the right thing to do, won't staying entrench that certainty rather than weaken it?'

'You've only just decided to stay yourself. You need time to consider what that means…'

'You're right about that. It's a huge change, but an exciting one, don't you think? Don't you want to be part of it?' He pulled her into his arms, holding her tight against him. 'I'm sorry, of course you want to be part of it. You love this place. I love you. I'm desperate for you to see things my way, but I'll say no more. Only stay and take part in the village Christmas celebrations. Not because I want you to, but because you want to.'

'It would be my first proper Christmas for years.'

He held her at arm's length. 'That's settled then. And if it is to be the end, at least let's fill it with happy memories. You can help me with Gwav Gool as planned.' He kissed her brow, then he let her go. 'And after Nadelik, then you'll decide.'

Chapter Nine

The next day, the Monday after the storm, Treeve and Emily resumed their morning walks. They talked. They laughed. They stopped, eyes meeting, gazes locked. But where before there were kisses, now there was unfulfilled longing. Treeve held himself apart. His hands didn't brush hers. He didn't tuck her hair out of her eyes. She missed his touch like a physical ache. She yearned for his kisses. But they had reached a tacit understanding that there could be no more of those.

After their walk, Treeve left her to meet with Miss Treleven, who had offered to accompany him on his belated welcoming call on Mr Kitto, his composer, leaving Emily to head for the village. The welcome she received took her breath away. Her progress down Budoc Lane was punctuated by villagers stopping to pass the time of day, to ask her if she had recovered from her ordeal, to take her hand and simply thank her. Three mothers asked if their children could join Derwa Nancarrow's boys in their swimming lessons next summer. Phin came out of his shop to shake her hand.

At the baker's, Eliza Menhenick gave her a piece of

cake and a steaming mug of something that looked like coffee, but which made Emily cough when she took a sip. 'Mahogany,' the baker's wife explained, 'made with gin and treacle. And that's a saffron bun. It's the custom in these parts for us shopkeepers to reward our customers at Christmas. We usually wait until the week before Nadelik, but we got together this morning, and decided to bring it forward. We've a lot to celebrate, thanks to you, and a lot to look forward to, thanks to Captain Penhaligon.'

The cake was delicious. The mahogany went to Emily's head. She declined a second glass from Mrs Chegwin, who had been chatting to Derwa, she informed her, and wondered if Emily would consider selling some of her work in the shop. 'Modest pieces, candlesticks, perhaps, to match Cloyd's fancier candles,' she suggested. 'Or, getting ahead of myself a bit, what about salts in the shape of the new lighthouse Captain Penhaligon has promised us?'

It was bittersweet, this new friendliness, a glimpse of how Emily's life might have unfolded here, and a constant reminder of what she was giving up. Every day brought a fresh overture, a fresh possibility, and every day she had to smile and prevaricate, reluctant to disappoint.

Towards the end of the second week of that unusually mild December, Rosenwyn had called at her cottage to collect the hairclips Emily had made.

'She offered me another commission, and promised several introductions,' Emily told Treeve later that day, when they met in the Great Hall to discuss the food to be served at Gwav Gool. 'She was extolling Mr Kitto's talent. Unlike you or I, she is apparently very musical.'

'I wonder if she knows of any musicians who might be available to play at Gwav Gool then. I've promised to pay a call on Jock Treleven to discuss the various celebrations, I must make a point of asking him. Jago tells me that there's a tradition of dancing a six-hand reel in some parts of Cornwall. It sounds to me very much like one of your Scottish country dances. What do you think, shall we have him put together a six to demonstrate?'

Emily giggled. 'Why not, and ask Mr Kitto to provide the accompaniment.'

'If I wished to dance a waltz, perhaps.'

'Wouldn't a hornpipe be more appropriate for a naval captain?'

Treeve laughed. 'I would much rather waltz.' He eyed her speculatively. 'Do you waltz, Miss Faulkner?'

'No, I do not, Captain Penhaligon.'

His smile softened. 'Would you like to learn, Emily?' Without waiting for her to reply, he circled her waist, clasping her other hand in his.

It was such a blessed relief, such a sheer delight to be in his arms, that she made no attempt to escape. 'We have no music,' she murmured.

'We don't need it, we have each other.' He pulled her closer. 'Just follow me.'

Their waltz made little use of the floor. They danced slowly, pressed tightly together, more closely with each slow step, each turn. Her face was burrowed into his chest. Her hand crept from his shoulder to his nape, then her fingers curled into his hair. They danced, more and more slowly until they drifted to a halt, and she lifted her face, and he gazed at her with such tenderness she wanted to weep. His lips brushed hers.

And then he let her go. Her first and last waltz was over.

Half the village turned out to help decorate the Great Hall for Gwav Gool, which would be in two days' time. It was another bittersweet day for Emily, as Treeve's home echoed with the wild, whooping cries of children who had eaten far too much cake and sweetmeats. Several of the adults made pointed remarks about the racket being a taste of things to come.

'I'm sorry,' she said to Treeve when they had a rare moment together. 'They seem to assume that we—that you and I...'

'Will get married and have a family,' he finished for her. 'You've come a long way these last few weeks, from considering yourself an outcast, to being the hot favourite to become my wife. Quite a feat, considering you aren't even Cornish, don't you think?'

She knew he was trying to tease her, but she winced all the same. 'You promised you would not...'

'I am only pointing out the obvious, since you are determined to blind yourself to it. Open your eyes, Emily. Look at all these people. Aren't they our family?'

She looked. At the children. The villagers. The farmers and estate workers. Then she looked at Treeve, and saw in his eyes such a sadness that her heart twisted. It was one thing to break her own heart, but his?

Her hand fluttered to his cheek, but he removed it. 'I can endure almost anything, save you trying to console me.'

* * *

It was late afternoon and dusk was falling by the time they had finished decorating the Great Hall. It looked quite beautiful, hung with garlands of greenery woven with pine cones, holly and mistletoe.

Instead of going back to her cottage, on impulse Emily made for St Piran's, seating herself in the most forward of the uncovered pews, where she could see the advent wreath, where three of the four candles had been lit. Two days to Gwav Gool. The day after that, Mr Kitto's cantata would be performed here, on Christmas Eve. Then it would be Nadelik, and dinner at Karrek House. And after that, she would leave Porth Karrek for ever.

She didn't want to leave. Was it possible to fall more in love with someone every day? It must be, for that's what she was doing. But what difference did it make, how much she loved Treeve, when she couldn't give him a child?

Treeve loved her too. She didn't doubt that. He loved her enough to say that he would sacrifice any hope of children to spend his life with her. She'd say the same, if the situation was reversed, but would she mean it? She had married Andrew in haste because she wanted a family. It seemed obvious to her now. She'd married him because he was a connection to the family she had lost, and because he had presented himself at a time when she was alone and vulnerable. She had blithely assumed that children would follow in due course. When they did not, she had refused to despair. For five years, she had clung to her receding hopes. Five years! She had resented Andrew's extended absences as missed opportunities. She had affected an ardour she had long stopped feeling when he returned, making love not because she loved him, but because she could not bear to contemplate a future in which there was only him. She'd thought her inability to conceive was a punishment for this, and so she'd tried, she really had tried, to love him again. To love him more. All for nothing. If Andrew had told her he couldn't have children, she would not have married him. But Treeve...

She loved Treeve with all her heart and her soul. Their child would be the most wonderful gift she could imagine. But if Treeve had declared himself unable to father a child—oh, yes, she would still want Treeve. He'd been hurt when she implied that his love would fade because she couldn't give him a child. She'd said it, without realising at the time, because that's exactly what had happened to her love for Andrew. It was an unworthy comparison. Treeve wasn't Andrew. What she felt for Treeve was not what she had felt for Andrew. What Treeve felt for her...

'If you could not have children, Treeve, what would you do?' she'd asked him, the morning after the storm.

'I'd offer you the choice,' he had answered.

They had not spoken of any of it since, but she knew he hadn't changed his mind. He loved her for who she was, for all that she had done and for all that she couldn't do. Just exactly as she loved him. He would choose her, just as she would choose him, over anyone else.

Treeve was right. Porth Karrek could be her home. Treeve's people could be her people. Her family. Their family. If she left, would she ever forgive herself for not taking a chance on what they both felt in their hearts and their bones about each other, that they were made for each other, that they belonged together? They could be everything to each other. Being together was surely all that mattered.

She didn't want to leave. She wanted to stay. Was it really that simple? Emily closed her eyes and said a little prayer. There was only one way to find out.

Treeve eyed the kissing bough despondently. He had hung it himself, after everyone had left, in the doorway between the Great Hall and the drawing room. He had hoped that Emily would have changed her mind by now. He had hoped to propose to her under it. So much for that! It had taken all his resolve, these last three weeks, to stand by his promise not to attempt to persuade her to stay. Why couldn't she see what seemed so clear to him? If it came to it, would he really be able to let her go without a fight?

But he knew himself too well. He had never loved before, not even come close. He loved Emily with his heart and soul. He'd never love another woman in this way, but he was damned if he'd settle for anything less than her unequivocal love in return. He didn't want half-measures or compromises. He didn't want her to stay here out of a sense of obligation or worse, pity. And he didn't want her to be watching him every day, waiting for him to fall out of love, to resent her, to want what she couldn't give. He wanted them both to embrace life, dammit! He wanted them to savour every minute of it.

The doorbell clanged. Recalling that he'd given his household the evening off to attend the Trelevens' bonfire on the beach tonight, Treeve answered it himself.

'Emily!'

She threw herself into his arms. 'I was wrong. You were right. I don't want to go.'

'Emily, my love.' He tried to calm himself as he wrapped his arms around her. 'Come in out of the cold,' he said, ushering her through to the drawing room.

'I've been to the church,' she said. 'I didn't go home after leaving here. I've been thinking. A lot. Not only today but especially today. All this,' she said, waving at the garlanded Great Hall, 'it helped me see properly. You were right, Treeve. Being here. Being part of it all. It's more than I ever hoped for. And if it's enough for me...' She stopped, swallowing convulsively, pushing her damp hair back from her face. 'I shouldn't have doubted that it was enough for you.'

His heart leapt, but it was clear from her expression that she needed to unburden herself, so he unfastened her cloak, draping it over a chair, and urged her closer to the fire. 'Why did you doubt me, Emily?'

She flinched, but met his eyes bravely. 'Because it wasn't enough for me, before. With Andrew, I mean. He married me for my money. He committed bigamy in order to give his real family a better future. But I didn't marry him because I loved him, Treeve. I married him because I wanted to have a family. What I feel for you—it's not the same. It's—so very different. I love you with all my heart. So if you still want me...'

'Emily!' He could wait no longer, sweeping her into his arms. 'I will want you until the ends of time. Or at the very least, until the end of our time. Always. How could you doubt it?'

'I didn't doubt you, I doubted myself. I love you so much.'

'And I love you. If you knew how difficult it's been, to say nothing these last three weeks!'

'But you didn't. And I love you all the more for that.

I needed to see for myself, didn't I? I do understand, my darling. I'm not staying here for your sake, or indeed only for mine. But for ours.'

'Ours.' He thought he might burst with happiness. 'Ours,' Treeve said, pulling her tighter against him. 'Two becoming one. I never understood that until now,' he said sheepishly, 'but we were meant to be together.' He kissed her tenderly. 'Always.'

'Always,' Emily said, smoothing her hand over his beard. 'Do you think—starting right now?'

It took him a moment to understand her meaning. But only a moment. For an answer, he scooped her up against his chest, making for the stairs.

'Treeve!' Laughing, clutching her arm around his neck, Emily protested. 'Your staff...'

'All at the bonfire.'

'Won't they expect us to be there too?'

'We'll be a tad late.' He nudged his bedroom door open, setting her down.

Emily smiled up at him, a slow, sensual smile that lit a fire in his belly, twining her arms around his neck. 'Don't rush on my account.'

But in their excitement they did rush, making love urgently, fervently, too desperate to be one to care about finesse, their kisses sending their passion soaring, a conflagration that had to be sated without any further delay. Emily tumbled headlong into her climax almost as soon as he entered her, digging her heels into his buttocks, holding him fiercely inside her, tightening around him as he pushed higher inside her, their skin slick, hot, so that when he cried out his release, she truly felt as if they were one.

Afterwards, they lay together, her head on his chest, her hand on his heart, murmuring 'I love you' over and over. And long after that, guiltily remembering the bonfire, Emily made to get out of bed, but Treeve covered her body again, kissing her slowly, shaking his head. 'We've waited a lifetime for this, let them wait a few moments more.'

But it took more than a moment. She lost count of time as he kissed her. Her mouth. Her neck. The valley between her breasts. Then each breast, taking sweet, delightful aeons of time, licking, kissing, sucking. Then her belly. And then down, licking his way inside her, his tongue, his mouth taking her to new, dizzying heights that left her gasping, spinning, floating. And just when she thought she was spent, he entered her again, slow, deliberate thrusts that roused her anew, becoming faster, harder at her urging. Until they tumbled over the precipice, this time together.

Chapter Ten

Two days later, on Monday, the day of Gwav Gool, the snow began to fall steadily, carpeting everything in a sparkling white blanket, muffling sound so that even the sea seemed muted.

Fizzing with excitement, Emily dressed with care for the party, in a green gown of twisted silk and cotton with long sleeves—for the huge fire that Treeve had had burning in the Great Hall for the last two days had only just taken the chill off the air. She arrived early at Karrek House, anxious to ensure there were no last-minute hitches, but the small army of staff which Jago Bligh had marshalled, had matters well in hand. The garlands which had been hung two days before were adorned with fresh holly, the berries gleaming red in the candlelight. Bunches of mistletoe were hung on mirrors, on picture frames, in every doorway. The trestle tables which had been set up under the window were groaning with food: there were pies of every size and description, courtesy of Abel Menhenick's bakery, including a version of Stargazy pie bereft of star-gazing pilchards; there were three whole cheeses; there was a positive mountain of bread; there were jellies in jewel colours, and quivering syllabubs; turning on a spit over the fire, there was a whole roast suckling pig; resting on side tables were massive tureens of punch, some made with fruit, some laced with brandy; and in the centre of the table a huge cake proudly sat, featuring a model of the lighthouse perched on The Beasts, made of almond paste and sugar.

'What do you think?'

Emily spun around at the sound of Treeve's voice. 'Oh, my goodness!' He was wearing his uniform, a navy blue single-breasted coat with gold braid and buttons, white silk waistcoat and breeches, also with gold buttons, black shoes with gold buckles. 'I think you look absolutely magnificent. Should I make a curtsy, or perhaps salute, Captain Penhaligon?'

He caught her hand, pulling her underneath the nearest sprig of mistletoe, kissing her soundly. 'You look absolutely delicious,' he said, kissing her again.

Emily giggled. 'You make me sound like a cake.'

'A cake I would like to devour.'

This kiss was deeper, interrupted only by the arrival of a flustered footman bearing a tray stacked with crockery. 'Treeve,' Emily remonstrated, her face burning at the man's rapid exit.

But he was unrepentant, pulling her into his arms again. 'They'll get used to it. I intend to do a good deal of this, when we are married.'

'Yes, but your guests will be arriving any minute. And the musicians. And the children's choir are coming early for a final practice. And...'

'And I love you, Emily. I don't think I've told you nearly enough today.'

This time, their kiss was interrupted by the clanging of the bell, as the four Cornishmen from nearby Helston recommended by Jock Treleven arrived with their musical instruments, followed hotfoot by the children's choir, their teacher and the Reverend Maddern. This small crowd were joined by Jago, his brother and his cousin with their wives, to practise their reels. Very soon the bell was ringing non-stop as the villagers and a host of local gentry arrived, including the Trelevens and all six of their daughters. Mr Kitto, whose cantata was to be played in the church the next night, seemed glued to Rosenwyn's side, Emily noted without surprise, for that young lady was looking extremely fetching in a rose silk gown precisely suited to her name.

For the next hour, Treeve was kept busy at the front door welcoming the latest arrival, while Emily busied herself making sure that everyone was fed and watered. The children sang, sweetly and only slightly out of tune, a selection of carols leading into some sea shanties, which caused everyone to join in. At the end of the performance, amid the cheering and the shedding of a few sentimental tears, Treeve handed the large basket of wooden toys which the Chegwins had procured for him, to Emily to distribute.

'Ladies and gentlemen, boys and girls,' he said, when this was complete. 'Happy Gwav Gool. And a happy Nadelik to everyone too, when it arrives. I know you're all anxious to sample this magnificent cake—a masterpiece worthy of Mr Stevenson himself, if I may say so, Abel. But if you'll indulge me for a moment, I have something which is to me, at any rate, even more important than putting a lighthouse on The Beasts. Emily?'

He held out his hand. Blushing, she came forward, aware of a sea of faces, all eyes on her, but she had eyes only for Treeve. Who smiled at her, reassuring, loving, not giving a damn who saw how much he cared for her. Her heart soared. She smiled back.

'My love,' he said, clasping her hands between his, 'my one and only true love. Will you marry me?'

She couldn't speak. Her eyes filled with tears. She nodded her head. 'Yes,' she whispered, so quietly only he could hear, but a cheer went up all the same, and glasses were raised. He edged them away from the crowd, to the doorway where the kissing bough hung, and then he kissed her gently. 'Look up, Emily.'

She did. The candle flame in the centre of the bough of mistletoe and holly, which had been flickering in the draught, was burning straight and strong and true. Just like their love for each other. A love that would never be extinguished.

* * * * *

UNWRAPPING HIS FESTIVE TEMPTATION

Bronwyn Scott

For George and Elaine. Thanks for making us part of your community group and inviting us into your home. Merry Christmas.

Author Note

Nadelik Lowen!

Marguerite and I are excited to be doing another anthology together, especially a Christmas one. This anthology gives us the rich backdrop of Christmas in Cornwall. There were so many traditions to pick from. I centered my story around the tradition of Advent since Cador Kitto is a composer and the Christmas season is a time full of music, with all the cantatas and oratorios. I filled in with other specific Cornish traditions like the gin and cake practiced by the merchants. Throughout the book you will see mentions of the kissing bush, the solstice bonfire and Gwav Gool.

These traditions provide a homey holiday context for the story of Cador and Rosenwyn, which centers around the theme of coming home—something both of them have come to terms with in very different ways. Cador is resentful of his homecoming. Coming home denotes failure to him, while to Rosenwyn coming home is a safe harbor, a place to hide. Together, they challenge one another to redefine what home means.

Chapter One

December 1st, 1822, the first Sunday in Advent
—Porth Karrek, Cornwall

The Christmas season had come again to St Piran's in all its green-boughed, red-bowed glory, as it had every year on the first of December since Cador Kitto could remember. All the parts and players were in their places, from the evergreen swags decorating the pews to the candles on the altar. Nadelik. This was Cornish Christmas at its best.

Cade fought the urge to squirm like a child in the hard wooden pew against the uncomfortable memories the word conjured. He didn't want to be here, home again in Porth Karrek. He never thought he would be. He wanted no part of Nadelik. Apparently, his wishes held no sway with fate.

The Reverend Maddern, his friend and mentor, took the pulpit and intoned the familiar words of the Advent liturgy. *Today we light the candle of hope.* One wasn't supposed to tell lies in church and that was the biggest lie of all. There was no hope here although no one else seemed to notice. An altar boy dressed in a spotless white smock came forward reverent and slow, carrying a long wood taper, the sacred flame dancing at its end.

An uncharitable thought whispered through Cade's mind: perhaps the flame would go out before the boy could complete his duty. Where would the Candle of Hope be then? In the dark with the rest of them. The boy dipped the taper towards the wick of the candle and Cade's wicked wish became a fervent command, uttered silently in his mind. *'Don't light it. It's a trick to make people think the world is good.'* But the candle was lit, and with the flicker of flame Nadelik began, a celebration Porth Karrek was determined to make last all month. Much to Cade's dismay.

Reverend Maddern's kindly eyes landed on him from the great heights of the pulpit draped in Advent purple, scolding him for his disbelief, for bringing his pessimism into the House of God on this beautiful, snow-touched Sunday morning when there was so much to celebrate, so much to give thanks for after the storm last night. But Cade would not apologise. He tolerated Christmas. He'd never forgive it.

The Reverend's gaze moved on to sweep the congregation as he spoke, his voice still powerful after three decades in St Piran's pulpit. 'Today's verses come from the Book of Isaiah, Chapter Nine. "The people who walk in darkness have seen a great light…"'

It wasn't a hard message to sell this morning after a stormy night of desperation that had seen a boat wrecked upon The Beasts and six sailors in jeopardy of their lives. All six men were alive, thanks to Captain Penhaligon's daring. Reverend Maddern cheerfully reminded the congregation such fortune was a good omen on which to begin Advent—a season of hope and expectation.

Reverend Maddern gestured for him to rise. 'Today, we celebrate many things, among them the return of our own native son, Mr Cador Kitto, who is here by the invitation of our brave Captain Penhaligon to compose a Christmas Eve cantata.' That was his cue to face the congregation and make a small bow so everyone could stop wondering who the new arrival was and start focusing on the Reverend's carefully considered first message of the Christmas season.

Cade stood, his eyes skimming the congregation with disappointment. Nothing had changed. Twenty years later and it was all still the same right down to the Christmas decorations: fresh-cut green swags and red bows that were frugally stored year after year in the cupboard off the baptistery. Cornwall was still a broken, craggy, desolate land with broken, craggy, desolate people. He might not know these people by name—he'd been so very young when he'd left. But he knew their stories, their tragedies. The eyes of tired mothers looked back at him, their features so much like his own mother's, old before their time, worn out with birthing and grief, crying over the children who'd died and worrying over the children who'd lived; grey-pallored men, physically broken from the sea, or exhausted like his father from working mines that never paid enough for the risks they took, all for a little tin. There was no hope here except for the hope the good Reverend spun for them on Sunday mornings.

There were the landowners and gentry, too, sitting closer to the front. The Penhaligon pew was empty, the Captain recovering from his rescue efforts of the prior evening. But across the aisle the Treleven pew was burgeoning; Sir Jock Treleven, his wife and six pretty strawberry-blonde-headed daughters were all present, some of them a little bolder than the rest, judging from the lingering looks they cast his direction. Behind them sat four well-dressed young gentlemen who reeked of London, the *haut ton*, good health and wealth, stark reminders of the chasm between them and the downtrodden citizens of Porth Karrek.

Cade took his seat, letting his mind absorb the realisation. It was a powerful reminder that there was nothing for him here except this commission. The quicker he finished, the sooner he could get on to other things, whatever they were, wherever they were, as long as they weren't here. What had he been thinking? That somehow things would be different? That Porth Karrek had become civilised in his absence? He might as well as have never gone. The last part made him shudder. He couldn't imagine having stayed here or what his life would have become if he had, more specifically, what *he* would have become. He was right to have left. He'd traded Porth Karrek for a conservatory in London, a scared eight-year-old boy with nothing more than a single valise clutched in his hand and a voracious appetite for music. The Reverend Maddern had arranged it through a cousin. Thanks to that kindness, Cade had got out.

Twenty years ago, he'd left Porth Karrek on a crowded coach, sitting cheek to jowl between an old woman who'd smelled of garlic and a fat man who'd snored. Now, he was returning, a man of renown. He'd rubbed elbows with Europe's greatest leaders and nobles, written music for the most esteemed cathedrals and rulers the Continent had to offer. He'd been invited home by Captain Penhaligon, the type of man who would never have looked twice at the grubby boy he'd been. He'd arrived in the man's own carriage—a luxury the Kitto family could never have imagined. There were accommodations waiting for him, two meals a day and two servants to provide his every need. All at no charge. All he had to do was produce a Christmas cantata for his new patron.

How hard could it be? Hard enough, considering he hadn't written anything worthwhile in three years. Hard enough considering it had to be a *Christmas* cantata. Those two factors alone made it the thirteenth labour of Hercules. Throw in the fact that he had to come home to Cornwall to do it and it became a task that transcended even the might of Hercules in the scope of what it asked of him. *A little over three weeks.* To make a miracle.

He surreptitiously rubbed his palms on his breeches as clammy panic threatened to claim him. He should not have made this deal with the devil. But that was how desperate he was. He could talk of moving on to other things once he was done here, but in truth he had no other commission waiting for him. He could not afford the rent on his London rooms and he'd be damned if he'd move into squalor just to satisfy his finances. His critics would crow if they saw him living so meanly, proof that they were right—he *was* washed up, good for nothing but composing cheap drivel for the masses, that Cador Kitto was not a serious composer after all, that he would not live up to the promise he'd shown as a child prodigy. He would not give them the pleasure.

Slowly, Cade forced his thoughts to be still, aware that someone was watching him. He let his gaze slide

across the aisle to the overpopulated Treleven pew and
found the source; the bold one next to the aisle was pre-
tending to study her prayer book while she really studied him. She was younger than his usual preference
and far less married. She smiled at him and he smiled
back. Why not? There was no harm in it and it served
to keep his present wolves at bay. He wouldn't pursue
her. He wasn't here in Porth Karrek for romance. He
was here to do a job.

The girl's smile widened and she tilted her head,
a pretty, practised gesture. The sister beside her, an
older, sterner version of herself, scolded her with a sharp
elbow in her side. She dropped her gaze, immediately
contrite, but not before her sister speared *him* with a
look that said this was somehow *his* fault. *His fault?*
All he'd done was smile back. Oh, the audacity of those
sharp green eyes and the superior tilt of her chin! If this
wasn't church, Cade would make the Scold accountable
for that look. Apparently, audacity ran in the family.

As it was, he settled for a raised eyebrow of interest cocked her way and a polite nod of his head, just
enough to let her know he'd intercepted her look and
wasn't bothered in the least by her fine opinion of him.
She quickly looked away, but not before a hot rosy flush
tinted her cheeks, assuring him he'd hit his target. But
he might pay for it. *Red sky at morning, sailor take
warning.* The old proverb of the sea flitted through his
thoughts at the sight of her blush. He'd be on alert in
case a storm of another sort was brewing.

Cador Kitto, Cornwall's most renowned composer,
had come at last, blown in last night with the storm.
Rosenwyn Treleven lowered her gaze, her pride smart-

ing at having been caught and reprimanded for a scolding she'd rightly deserved. She'd done nothing wrong but bring Marianne's high spirits into line. Whether he'd started that little flirtation or not was irrelevant. He should *know* better than to encourage such behaviour with a young girl.

That he *did* know better, and hadn't, spoke loudly of his character. He was every bit as rakish as his reputation made him out to be and unfortunately just as handsome. His legendary gold waves skimmed his shoulders, his artist's face with its dramatic angles was shown to advantage in the winter sunlight streaming through Reverend Maddern's prized glass windows, and those blue eyes, the colour of a Cornish sea in summer, danced with mischief across the aisle. He was stunning and absolutely not for her. She'd learned her lesson in London about handsome men. She would keep her distance from Cador Kitto and see to it that her sisters did the same. One disgraced girl in the Treleven house was enough.

'We're inviting him to Sunday dinner,' Marianne whispered excitedly as they all rose to file out after church. 'Papa is asking him right now.'

No, not now. Not ever. What was her father thinking to invite him into a house with six unmarried girls? Rosenwyn watched in sinking disappointment as her father crossed the aisle and shook Cador Kitto's hand, acting as the nominal welcoming committee in the absence of Captain Penhaligon. Her father gestured for them to join him and the last of her hopes to maintain distance faded.

'This is my wife, Lady Treleven, and these are my

lovely daughters, Ayleth, Violet, Marianne, the twins, Catherine and Isabella, and my oldest, Rosenwyn.'

'*Enchanté*, Miss Treleven.' He bowed over her hand as if they were at a formal ball, his eyes meeting hers, still full of mischief over their previous exchange. 'I see you are recovered. Something seemed to bother you during the service.'

'Recovered?' Her mother swooped in with concern upon hearing the word. 'Are you not feeling well, Rose?'

'I'm fine.' Rose smiled tightly, shooting Kitto a warning glance. 'I had just got some dust in my eye, it was *nothing* of *consequence*.' He was a speck to her, nothing more despite his handsome face, well-tailored clothes and the fact that he was more attractive close up than he had been from across the aisle.

Her father had a friendly hand on Kitto's shoulder, far too familiar with the newly arrived composer than Rosenwyn liked. 'Mr Kitto, allow me to introduce you to the gentlemen sitting behind us, they're friends of the family and will be joining us for dinner as well. This is Eaton Falmage, Cassian Truscott, Inigo Vellanoweth and Vennor Penlerick.' He winked at Kitto. 'You needn't worry you'll be the only man at the table this afternoon. The Reverend will join us as well, although Penhaligon sends his regrets. Shall we be off?'

Rosenwyn tried, truly she did, to impose some distance between her and Kitto. She meant to walk back to Treleven House with Eaton, but Ayleth and he were already deep in discussion about their shared passion for truffles. Marianne was shamelessly practising her flirtation with Inigo and Vennor, one on each arm, while they egged her on with brotherly advice. Violet was discussing the sermon with the Reverend, and the twins—

Isabella and Catherine—were hounding Cassian for stories about his latest travels to Russia. That left her and Kitto to bring up the rear of their little procession. It was the last arrangement she wanted to be in. Rosenwyn sent a final pleading look in Ayleth's direction for some relief, but Ayleth was oblivious to her distress.

'Is there something in your eye again, Miss Treleven?' Kitto enquired as they began to walk, his neutral tone of concern a thin mask for the teasing beneath. He'd caught her once more.

'I'm quite fine. Thank you. I was just wondering, how you are enjoying being back in Porth Karrek, Mr Kitto?' She could play the politeness game, too.

'I've only been back a few hours,' he answered with a polite smile to match her polite, cursory answer. At this rate they would exhaust her store of small talk before they reached Treleven House. 'However, Porth Karrek is much as I remember it.' The mask slipped for just a moment and in that moment, Rosenwyn glimpsed disappointment again in his eyes. That was when she knew. The great Cador Kitto had a secret: he didn't want to be here, in Porth Karrek. Why would a man not want to be in a place that lauded him? That considered him famous? How interesting.

No. Not interesting, she corrected herself. Men weren't allowed to be interesting, not after the disaster with Dashiell Custis. She was done with handsome faces and fairy-tale fantasies. Mr Kitto could keep his secrets to himself. She absolutely did not want to know them.

Chapter Two

Sunday dinner at the Trelevens' was of good quality, both in terms of food and the company. Well, *most* of the company, Cade reflected, gazing around the long silver-laden table, most of the company being all but Rosenwyn Treleven. She had made it plain on their walk she didn't care for him much, an attitude he felt had to spring from something more deeply seated than smiling at her sister in church. Then again, most of the company didn't have secrets. Miss Treleven did, he'd wager the last of his coin on it. He knew when a woman had a secret. There was no other reason for her instant dislike of him. He didn't take it personally. Her dislike was a defence mechanism. She was hiding something.

Guessing what it might be added an extra dynamic to an already interesting dinner. There was, after all, the usual current that ran underneath these sorts of affairs when there were five unattached gentlemen and, by 'happy coincidence', the host's six pretty, unmarried daughters, four of whom were of an age for consideration. A bachelor intent on survival learned early how to recognise the signs. A composer intent on survival also learned to recognise the potential for future opportunity and this Sunday afternoon dinner was an unlooked-for plum. All four of the gentlemen at Jock Treleven's table were heirs to the various dukedoms that populated this part of Cornwall. Quality company indeed. London mamas would weep if they could see this fine assemblage.

No wonder Treleven had laid out the best china, the best silver, the best wine for this afternoon feast. Marrying off six daughters was a difficult task under the best of circumstances with all the resources of London society on hand to assist. Marrying them off in the wilds of Cornwall was not just difficult, it was daunting. Treleven couldn't afford to squander whatever serendipitous opportunities came his way. And neither could he. These young ducal heirs would have influence they could exert in London on his behalf if they were so inclined.

The composer in Cade thrilled to the opportunity, while the bachelor in him was wary of circumstances that served up dukes and debutantes in the same sitting. Was it expected he would go through Sir Jock Treleven to get to the heirs? After all, Treleven had been the one to introduce them. Cade would rather not be bound in obligation to Treleven, especially if that obligation involved marriage. He could barely support himself, let alone a wife. Sir Jock could offer him nothing but trouble with those six pretty strawberry blondes and their dowries sitting around the table.

True, any one of them could solve his monetary problems, but the price would be too high. He would not live off a wife's largesse. There were names for men like that. Besides, Treleven's daughters weren't his type. They were meant for marriage—to dukes if Treleven had his way. Cador preferred a woman who was able to be freer with herself without requiring any commitment on his part. There were plenty of those women in London. He doubted there were many of that sort out here. His tenure in Porth Karrek would likely be lonely and celibate. He was not willing to sacrifice his pride and his dreams to Cornwall. It had taken too much from him already.

A footman stepped forward to refill Cade's wine glass, another to clear his plate for the next course. Treleven had cut no corners on the meal either: a first course of hare soup, followed by mixed game pie, an entrements of vol-au-vent of pear and now footmen served a delicious-smelling fillet of pheasant with truffles which earned an exclamation from Eaton Falmage, who had taken up truffles as a serious pastime. Falmage lifted his glass to Lady Treleven. 'The white truffles are divine, you must give my compliments to the cook. The flavour permeates the bird perfectly. In fact, I've been working on a new truffle preserve. I should send some of my samples over for your cook. It's the ideal accompaniment when truffles aren't in season.'

Falmage turned his attention in Cade's direction. 'I am interested in the science of food,' he explained with an easy smile. 'I imagine it's much like your appreciation of the science of music. There's no end to the possibility of variations.' That was the hope, Cade thought wryly, although some days he began to doubt music was infinite as he'd once thought, that perhaps he had indeed run out of ways to arrange notes in order to create a unique melody.

'Will you play for us this afternoon, Mr Kitto?' Falmage asked across the table. 'I hope I am not too forward in the asking?'

'Not at all, I would be happy to,' Cade replied. He would play whether he wanted to or not because no one turned down a chance to audition in front of four ducal heirs. This was a prime opportunity to secure his next patron, and his next. The composer's world was a dog-eat-dog existence where one must play the sycophant to navigate the politics of European courts. Commissions did not go to those who were most worthy, but to whomever had the best advocate. Otherwise, he'd never have left Vienna. Even the great Beethoven struggled, especially now that his hearing had failed.

'Rosenwyn, will you play as well?' Falmage turned to her and Cade noted her hesitation.

'I don't think my music is quite at the level of Mr Kitto's,' she prevaricated, but Cade did not miss the sharp look she gave Falmage, encouraging him not to press the matter. Falmage was not daunted.

'I hope you will change your mind. It's just family today, and I've missed hearing you play.' He nodded towards Cade. 'Perhaps you can encourage her, Kitto? Our Rosenwyn was the toast of London drawing rooms when she bothered to grace us with her presence. Musicales last Season felt her absence keenly.'

'Please do not let me intimidate you, Miss Treleven,' Cade coaxed in order to please Falmage and perhaps to provoke her in payback for her cold reception on the walk. He'd chosen his words carefully. One word in particular and it had the desired effect.

Miss Treleven's green eyes flashed and her defiant chin raised just a fraction as if she'd been challenged. 'I am not intimidated by any man, Mr Kitto. If it pleases Falmage that much, I am happy to oblige.'

Falmage smiled and clapped his hands in decisive approval. 'Then, it's settled. We'll have an afternoon musicale. I cannot think of a more pleasant way to spend a Sunday.'

Rosenwyn could think of *several* more pleasant ways to spend an afternoon as they adjourned to the music room with its piano and stringed instruments, and none of them included playing for Kitto, a man who felt he was too good for Cornwall. She wanted to scold Eaton for his part in it, but it was hard to be upset when Kitto sat down at the piano and began to play. He'd chosen a Bach piece she recognised as 'Air on a G String'. He played it to perfection with its plaintive treble and its contrapuntal bass. The music filled the drawing room with a quiet sweetness well suited for a reflective winter afternoon. She closed her eyes and let the music float over her, let it take her worries. It was difficult to dislike a man who could make Bach sound effortless and song-like. Despite Kitto's reputation for courtly affaires, the man was truly a genius. But her adulation needed to stop there, her conscience warned. He was still arrogant. He still had a reputation with the ladies. He still needed to be guarded against. No doubt he used his music to worm his way into a lady's affections along with those good looks and bold smiles.

'That was splendid!' Eaton applauded when the piece concluded. 'You must give a private concert while you're here. Sir Jock can host and I can arrange it, if you'd like.'

'Perhaps, that is most gracious of you.' Kitto rose

from the bench and smiled at Falmage with what was supposed to be gratitude and appreciation, but Rosenwyn noted his eyes didn't dance and his smile was tight, polite, as it had been on the walk. It was not at all the wide, easy smile he'd given Marianne. 'A small concert is not out of the question, although, my priority is the cantata. There is much to be done and only three weeks to do it.'

'Understood. I don't want to steal your attentions. Still, I think there are those who would be eager to meet you in a personal setting.' Falmage pressed his point in a stealthy exercise of his influence. 'Rosenwyn, will you honour us perhaps with Pachelbel's serenade? It's one of my favourites.'

'Of course.' Rosenwyn stood. Resistance would be useless. If Cador Kitto could not refuse Eaton, she surely couldn't. She wondered how Kitto felt about that? All that genius and he had to put himself at the beck and call of the likes of Eaton Falmage. Eaton was an excellent fellow, almost a brother to her and her sisters, but still, she knew what it felt like to be reliant on the good will of others for one's own well-being even when that good will was well intended. Perhaps that was the reason he didn't want to be in Porth Karrek. The effort of being here wasn't commensurate with the gains. What could he gain here that would make it worth his while when he might be in London or in Vienna or Paris? She loved Cornwall, but others did not. In London, society talked of Cornwall as if it were the ends of earth.

It was becoming clear to her that Kitto thought the same. She could almost read his mind as she passed him on the way to the bench. Who could he possibly play for that would be worth spending his talents on? Cap-

tain Penhaligon must be paying him a small fortune for
the cantata in order for him to overlook the issue of his
limited audience—Porth Karrek gentry, miners, merchants, fisherman, smugglers. Hardly the sort that could
give him anything but applause in return. It helped that
Eaton and his friends were here, but their arrival had
been unplanned. Kitto and Penhaligon wouldn't have
known that beforehand.

If the ratio of effort to output was the reason Kitto
didn't want to be here, it invoked the question, why was
he here at all? One more secret to add to the growing
pile of interesting things to know about Cador Kitto.
Rosenwyn sat down and sorted through the music, looking for the serenade. It was one of her favourites, too.
Eaton had chosen well in that regard.

She began to play, losing herself in the easy flow
of the piece, letting herself forget that Eaton had coerced her into this, that Kitto was an inveterate flirt who
likely thought her a prude for rebuking him in church,
that Dashiell Custis had made her into an embarrassment, so that she never dared to show her face in London again for fear of scandal. She loved this piece—it
was even better with a violin. She'd no sooner thought
it than the wistful sound of a bow drawn long over its
strings joined her, raising its melody to hers in poi-
gnant harmony. She opened her eyes to find Cador's
intense blue gaze on her from behind the length of a
violin tucked beneath his chin, his elegant fingers on
the strings, on the bow.

In that moment, she was swept away, elevated. Nothing in the room, no one in the room mattered except
the music, except him, urging her with each measure
he played to let go, to let her soul fly free with him,

and it was intoxicating. She had not been free, not in her heart, for over a year, not since she'd fled London in ignominy. For a few moments, she was alive again. As long as she held his gaze, she was Icarus soaring to the sun.

The room was silent when they finished. She could not look away from him, knowing full well the moment would end when she did. She would be Rosenwyn Treleven again, a woman disgraced because she'd been foolish in love, a woman who could never risk such a thing again. And he would be Cador Kitto, a complicated genius of a man who had landed in the one place he least wanted to be. They had nothing to offer each other beyond this moment. He gave her a slight nod of his head, a warning that the spell would be broken. She braced herself as he set aside the violin, looked away and let her tumble back to earth.

Eaton was on his feet and the others were, too, clapping as if it were a concert hall. Eaton gave her a brotherly hug. 'Thank you, my dear. That was absolutely magical.' He shook Kitto's hand and everyone was exclaiming at once.

'We should play charades next,' Marianne suggested when the excitement ebbed. 'Girls against boys.' It was a suggestion taken up enthusiastically as the sides arranged themselves; the men grouping around Vennor and the ladies flocking to Marianne. 'Come play, Rose.' Marianne patted an empty seat beside her on the sofa.

Rosenwyn shook her head. 'In a minute, let me put the music away.' She wasn't ready to give the moment up just yet. She reached for the violin to put it back in its case.

'Let me do that, I was the one who got it out.' Kitto

took the instrument, his hand brushing hers in the exchange, sending a jolt of awareness rippling up her arm, a reminder that he was charming and seductive even without the music.

'Why did you do it?' She needed to be on her guard. She was weak just now, still reeling from the emotion of the music.

'Falmage coerced you. You didn't want to play.'

'Neither did you.'

He shrugged, managing to look elegant. 'I am used to it, it's a musician's lot in life to always be performing. It didn't have to be yours. I thought it was unfair. Mine, I could do nothing about without offending Falmage. But yours, I could. Perhaps I was sorry for my part in coercing you. At least I could make you glad you chose to play.' He smiled, his voice low and private in contrast to the loud laughter of charades going on behind her. 'So, Miss Treleven, tell me. Was it worth it to play, after all?'

Oh, he was smooth, all elegant soft words and handsome smiles as he flirtingly implied he'd done her a favour. He would want something in return. She needed to be clear with him that she'd not asked for his attentions, nor did she wish to encourage those attentions now that they'd been given in a most spectacular fashion. 'I do thank you, Mr Kitto. I enjoyed our duet, but do not think for a moment that this makes us friends.'

He merely chuckled, unfazed by her bluntness, and, sweet heavens, had he just moved closer to her when she was trying to push him away? The man's audacity knew no bounds. First flirting in church with her sister and now flirting with her with her family just feet away. 'Why so unfriendly, Miss Treleven?'

His voice was an intimate caress, the rest of the company relegated to another world while he seduced her beside the piano. A new thrill of awareness went through her—an awareness that reminded her that for all her protective efforts to shield herself, she was in trouble. This man was a master at breaching walls. Rosenwyn summoned her best defence. 'I know you, Mr Kitto, and I know why you're here. Your reputation precedes you.'

He smiled most wickedly. 'Reputation, Miss Treleven, or rumours?'

'Is there a difference in your case, Mr Kitto?'

Chapter Three

Rosenwyn Treleven didn't back down from a fight, Cade would give her that. She was fierce when another sort of woman would have retreated from her claims. Whatever she was hiding, she was defending it for all it was worth. Did she realise such a strategy only made her more intriguing? That her audacity made her fresh, a welcome change from the worldly women he was used to? Attracting him could hardly be what she wanted. Quite the opposite, in fact.

Beyond her shoulder, the group was fully engaged in charades with Reverend Maddern as mediator. No one was paying them any attention, he could flirt all he liked, draw out her secrets at his leisure. Cade leaned against the piano and looked deep into her eyes, a gesture that worked well with the ladies of the Hapsburg court. 'Then tell me my sins so that I might atone for them.'

Rosenwyn Treleven had apparently never heard of the Hapsburg court. His efforts had no effect. She rolled her eyes. 'Please, do not waste your time. I am not impressed with your lines or practised poses, Mr Kitto. I know exactly the sort of man you are.'

'What a leading statement, Miss Treleven. I have no choice but to ask "what sort of man is that?" as I am sure you know.' He would push her to her limits if she insisted.

'A man who would rather be anywhere than here, who thinks he is above Porth Karrek.' Her words were as frank as her gaze and more than a little startling. He'd not been expecting that answer, especially since he'd gone to great lengths to hide it. Had he not been jovial at the table? Had he not agreed to play for them with pleasant ease? Had he not given them *two* brilliant performances this afternoon? Yet, this impertinent beauty with sharp green eyes had laid him open in the span of a few short hours.

'You're rather bold to have come to such a conclusion on the acquaintance of the dinner table,' Cade replied smoothly, but he was wary now. Perhaps there was a limit to how much he liked her lack of pretence. If she saw that much, what else did she see? 'What would make you think such an uncharitable thing? Porth Karrek is my home.'

'And you've been away for ages.' Her answer came too fast, her gaze spearing him. She was certainly sure of herself. 'You don't want to be here. It was in your eyes at church, just for a moment when you looked out over the congregation, and then again at lunch when Eaton asked you to play.'

'I had no idea I was so transparent,' Cade replied wryly. 'Pray tell, if you know so me well, where *do* I want to be?'

She did not even hesitate. 'In London, moving from party to party. I'm sure even out of Season, London is more entertaining than Porth Karrek.'

'Is that what the rumours tell you? Tsk, tsk, Miss

Treleven, for listening to gossip. I am well aware of the reputation the society columns cultivate for me.' He leaned close. At this distance he could breathe her in, the scent of cinnamon and vanilla, the smells of a warm winter kitchen, a scent at odds with her sharpness. 'The truth is, London is too expensive.' He'd been forced to leave just when London was getting interesting with the founding of the Royal Academy of Music.

'Is that the only reason you're here? Money? Or is there something more?' Good Lord, the woman didn't stop. The picture she painted made him out to be a mercenary or a coward.

He did not like the other implication, which hit too close to home. The Landgraf's wife had ruined Vienna for him. 'If you're suggesting I'm running from a jealous husband's temper, you'd be entirely in the wrong.' He might dally with married women, but he was careful not to let things go too far and he was scrupulous in his choices. He stayed away from the wives of jealous husbands. But he did worry—had word of the debacle in Vienna reached as far as Cornwall? That would be surprising indeed, even after the months that had passed. But he had to know. 'Whatever gives you the idea that something sordid is involved? Moreover, why do you care?' The last was meant to throw her off balance, to remind her they were flirting here, not conducting the Spanish inquisition, that perhaps her interest in his proclivities signalled her own interest in him. But she did not take the reminder.

'I have five sisters, sir. I wouldn't want you to lead them astray.' Ah, so this was about her sisters and not Vienna. Thank goodness. He couldn't manage another disaster.

'Could I?' He challenged her with his eyes. He was on more comfortable ground now. This was the type of conversation he was used to navigating.

'You know you could. You're that sort.'

'*That sort?* And what sort is that?' If she wanted to call him a rake, he would make her spell it out. He deserved that courtesy at least.

'The handsome sort.'

'You think I'm handsome? I am surprised. Something complimentary from you at last, Miss Treleven. I will consider it progress.' Although, progress with her was irrelevant. Miss Rosenwyn Treleven and her opinions did not signify. He was not here for romance or for dalliance. Even if he was, he would not pursue such things with her. For one, she saw too much of him. Honesty made for a crowded bed. Bodies should be naked in bed, not souls.

Green eyes flashed. 'Consider it nothing at all, sir. Just an observation.'

'Like the dust in your eye this morning?' He chuckled. 'Perhaps there's another reason you're so unfriendly other than on your sisters' behalf?' Not that he cared, he reminded himself. Still, it was galling to his pride to think there was a woman he couldn't charm. He'd charmed the most beautiful women in Vienna and Paris, women lovelier than Rosenwyn Treleven and far more worldly. Of course, he wasn't *trying* to charm her. Perhaps he should? It would certainly serve her right to fall victim to the charms she railed against. But that would only prove her point—that he *was* a superficial flirt. Best to stay away from her and her assumptions, yet he found himself awaiting her answer, wondering what uncomfortable truths might fall from those pink lips next.

'Besides, I'm not suggesting you're running. I'm suggesting you're hiding.' That did *not* make it better.

Cade gave a derisive chuckle. This time she was wrong. How little she knew! 'If I was hiding, I assure you I certainly wouldn't come here.' His demons could find him too easily. Here, every nerve was exposed. Everywhere he'd looked today in church the past was on display, and his shell was so very fragile even after all these years if a mere church service could get to him.

It was time he went on the offensive. Perhaps she saw something of herself in him? 'May I assume the blade cuts both ways? What are you hiding from in Porth Karrek? You're a woman of status and a bit of fortune. Surely you can do better than Porth Karrek. You needn't be here.' From Falmage's comments at dinner, she hadn't been here. She'd had Seasons, but those had come to an end a year ago. By necessity or by choice? It was hard to tell. Miss Treleven looked to be in her early twenties. She had reached that dangerous age of possibly 'having outgrown London', if one was being delicate. On the shelf, if one was not. Had Miss Treleven with the fiery hair and sharp tongue not taken? Was that her secret?

'Unlike yourself, *I* happen to like it here.' Her chin took on its defiant tilt, her smile smug as if she'd won some victory. Cade didn't think. He just responded, his temper overriding the last of his patience. He'd done her a favour this afternoon and she was repaying him poorly.

'That's convenient for you then, since you don't seem to be going anywhere else.' He shouldn't have said it. The implications were mean, cruel even, but he'd had enough of her conjectures and judgements. She froze, her face becoming stone-hard and just as expression-less. Her dancing eyes shuttered and he felt the loss of their keen vitality. They weren't playing at a war of words any more. Although she stood beside him, she had withdrawn from him completely. There was no scold, no rebuttal, just silence where sharp repartee had been moments before.

He ought to fill that silence with an apology. No gentleman called attention to a woman's lack of success on the marriage mart to her face no matter how sharp-tongued she was. It was poorly done and all because the truth of her darts had stung him. But in his newly pricked anger, he couldn't bring himself to do it.

Laughter went up from the charades game and Miss Treleven made a show of turning her attentions towards the noise with exaggerated interest. 'I do believe I'll join them. If you'll excuse me, Mr Kitto?'

The opportunity to apologise slipped away with her. He'd bungled that entirely. Bungling things with women was certainly new for him. He hadn't charmed her. He'd insulted her. And for what reason? Because *she'd* insulted *him*? With the truth? Was that why he felt so wounded? Or was there another reason? Surely it couldn't be that he'd wanted her to think better of him when he didn't care about her opinion. To prove it, he'd return to the party and show her how much he didn't care by enjoying himself. Then she could revisit just how much he didn't want to be here.

The best revenge would be to enjoy herself and show Cador Kitto his insinuation that she was somehow socially undesirable, a spinster in the making, had no effect on her. Determined to have her revenge, Rosenwyn sat on the sofa, surrounded by her sisters, and threw herself into the game. But revenge was only revenge if the other party was aware and it seemed Cador Kitto wasn't. Either that or he'd had the same idea as she in proving the other wrong.

Instinct told her it might be the latter. She rather thought in hindsight that he hadn't been trying to hurt her with his words as much as he'd been trying to protect himself. She'd got to him, been too bold with comments she should have kept to herself. Then again, she'd been doing a fair bit of protecting, too. Not only of her sisters, but of herself. Cador Kitto was good-looking with classic, dramatic features, blue eyes that gazed right through a woman as if he could—as if he *wanted*—to see into her heart; a look he'd no doubt cultivated to much success in the European courts.

He was certainly a test to the protections she'd put up in the year since the incident with Dashiell Custis. How strong *was* her resolve? It seemed she was not immune to a bit of curiosity where their visitor was concerned. Her mind was intrigued by him. What was his story? What had happened to him after he'd left Cornwall? What had shaped him? Did he still have family here? If so, wouldn't he be happy to see them? Happy to be back at last? She couldn't imagine not wanting to see her family. Why was he so reluctant to be back? Although he didn't seem too reluctant at the moment. In fact, he seemed right at home.

On the other team, Kitto was standing shoulder to shoulder with Cassian and Inigo, all golden and laughing as they called out guesses to Eaton's mime. Rosenwyn looked away. It had been a mistake to look at his mouth, to think about his mouth. It was a mouth made for the taking and giving of kisses with its firm upper line and its slightly softer lip below. It was a commanding but generous mouth. Objectively speaking, that was. Not that she wanted to try out the hypothesis. Kisses always led to other things, to other troubles. Kisses were dangerous that way.

Ayleth nudged her. 'He's not an easy man to look away from, is he?'

She flushed, embarrassed over being caught. 'I was merely looking in that general direction, not necessarily *his* direction.'

Ayleth laughed, unconvinced. 'It's all right to look, you know. It doesn't mean you have to marry him. Besides, you aren't going to let Dashiell Custis prevent you from falling in love again, are you? What does that prove? Or change? He was rotten and you were lucky to find it out before it was too late.' 'Too late' in Ayleth's mind meant before giving in to Dashiell's rather persuasive appeals to elope and live a romantic happy ever after.

'This isn't about Dashiell,' Rosenwyn said firmly. While it hadn't been too late for avoiding the public debacle of an elopement, it had been too late to avoid other, more private aspects that not even Ayleth was aware of. Rosenwyn had kept those to herself and thankfully been spared the need to make those aspects known to her family. She'd been lucky in that regard but she was still embarrassed to think how close she'd come to playing Dashiell's lovesick fool. She'd thought herself smarter than that. 'I just happen to think Mr Kitto and I would not have much in common.' Around them, the charades game finished.

'Certainly not your love of music or your accomplishment in that regard,' Ayleth replied with soft sarcasm. 'It didn't look that way to me.' Her sister elbowed her with a sly smile. 'The two of you appeared engrossed in conversation.'

'We were having a disagreement, that was all.' She refused to disclose she'd all but called him a rake and that he thought her a missish spinster with no prospects. Was that how others saw her these days since her return from London? As someone who had *failed*? Who was destined for the shelf?

'You know what they say: the line between love and hate is a thin one,' Ayleth chided her encouragingly. 'Perhaps you and Mr Kitto are merely testing one another.'

Rosenwyn dismissed the idea with a shake of her head. 'Don't be silly. Why would I invest time in Mr Kitto when he'll be gone after Christmas? A girl can have no expectations there.' He was hardly the sort she was looking for: stable, honest, homegrown, committed to Porth Karrek.

'You don't have to marry him.' Ayleth laughed. 'The very reason that he'll leave makes him safe, perfect in fact. Just a few stolen kisses under the kissing bough and nothing more. He might be what you need to put Dashiell Custis behind you. We could call him a transition.' Ayleth rose and shook out her skirts. 'I think I'll go talk to Eaton, he's planning a truffle-hunting expedition to Italy next summer. Do you want to come?'

'To Italy?'

'No, silly goose. To talk with Eaton.'

Rosenwyn waved her sister off, seeing the simple ploy. She didn't want to talk to Eaton as long as Cador Kitto was standing next to him. Certainly, Mr Kitto was intriguing both in looks and background, but there were other ways to assuage her curiosity without associating with him directly. He was Porth Karrek born. If she cared enough to solve the mystery of him, she could check the church records at St Piran's. Sometimes the best way to manage curiosity was to appease it. Once she knew his secrets, Cade Kitto would no longer be interesting. That was the theory at least. Christmas was her favourite time of year. She would not let a newcomer who would be gone by New Year's blight it.

Chapter Four

Cador Kitto's presence wasn't easily banished, however. The memory of him lingered long after the gentlemen had departed. It didn't help that Marianne wanted to dissect the afternoon in detail while they sewed in the evening. 'What do you think of our composer?' Marianne asked the girls at large.

Rosenwyn raised her gaze from her embroidery hoop to study her sister in all her youthful enthusiasm. She'd been like that once—looking forward to her first London Season. That seemed years ago. Marianne was set to come out in London this spring. Gentlemen and dresses were all she talked about these days. She'd fit right in with London in a way Rosenwyn never had. 'Don't flirt with him, Marianne. He's far too worldly for you to cut your teeth on,' Rosenwyn counselled sharply, the words as much for herself as for her sister. There'd been moments today when those blue eyes had threatened her own good sense, when it would have been too easy to abandon her defences and give in to Kitto's flirting. She could see all too well where Marianne was headed with her question. In her sister's cloistered world, Cador Kitto would be an exciting visitor, fresh come from London, the embodiment of all she thought she held dear. But in the end, a man like Kitto would laugh at her.

'I liked him,' Marianne argued. 'He was so stylish. His boots were from Hoby. Did you notice? He's not so big, not like Eaton. Falmage intimidates simply by walking into a room. But Mr Kitto was just the right height. A girl could rest her head on his shoulder or look in his eyes as they danced without getting a kink in her neck, didn't you think so, Rosie? You were right across from him at dinner and had the best view.'

The best view of those teasing blue eyes that provoked and pleased by turn.

What Rosenwyn thought was that she'd seen men like him in London, men who only acted like gentlemen at Almack's. Men like Dashiell Custis who had nearly broken her country girl's heart. Just nearly, though. Rosenwyn was smarter now and she would not let such a cad loose on her sister, on *any* of her sisters. 'I think he's not for you, dear.'

'Why ever not?' Marianne protested with a pretty pout bound to drive the London dandies mad in a few months. Rosenwyn almost pitied the gentlemen this Season.

Rosenwyn set down her embroidery and gave Marianne a stern look. 'Because he has more sophisticated tastes.' She could not be more delicate than that. The man fairly reeked of that 'sophistication', in his well-tailored clothes, the gold waves of his hair skimming his shoulders with dramatic elegance. At the dinner table, he'd looked the complete artiste. He would be devastating beneath the chandeliers of a London ballroom.

'Oh, pooh, by that you mean he's had mistresses and

opera singers. You can say it, I'm grown up now.' Marianne tossed her red-gold curls.

The argument sat poorly with Rosenwyn. She was heartily tired of everyone championing Cador Kitto. Her father had invited him home, Eaton had fussed over him, Marianne had flirted with him. Didn't they see the danger he posed? She fixed Marianne with a strong stare. 'Very well, what I *meant* to say is that aside from his reputation, which, by the way, you should know nothing about, he's arrogant. He thinks Porth Karrek is beneath him and yet he has you trailing after him like he's the Pied Piper.' There. She could not be plainer than that. Her sisters stared at her, glances sliding between one another, unsure how to respond to her outburst. They thought she was out of line. Well, she wasn't going to apologise. Rosenwyn stood. 'Excuse me, I seem to be ruining your talk of daydreams.'

She pressed her forehead to the cold pane of the drawing-room window and looked out into the night. There was nothing to see but it was better than answering to her sisters. They meant well, but they didn't understand. They couldn't. She hadn't told them everything that had happened in London. She couldn't save herself, but she could save them from making the same mistake, and she would. It's what she did. She was a fixer, a saver. She saw problems and she solved them. She was known for it, in fact. When the Cardy children had needed new shoes, she'd seen that they had them. When the grammar school had needed a new bell, she'd organised the raising of the funds. When the graves at the churchyard needed upkeep, she'd arranged for a groundskeeper by recommending young Edward Bolitho, the candlemaker's son, for the position.

But you couldn't save yourself... whispered the irony. She did not need to be reminded of that. She'd spent the last year in Porth Karrek throwing herself into charity work trying to forget, trying to atone, trying to prove to herself she belonged here, that the life she wanted was here. She didn't need London—not its ballrooms full of glittering diamonds and silks, not the applause at the musicales or the flattering whispers that her piano playing rivalled the professionals in the Academy.

She heard the rustle of skirts behind her, felt her sister's soft touch at her sleeve. Ayleth, the peacemaker, the counsellor. 'You probably think I am out of line.' Rosenwyn sighed.

'No, not at all. I was wondering what Mr Kitto said today that has upset you. It must have been terrible.' Sweet Ayleth always took her side.

'He called me a spinster,' Rosenwyn confessed.

'He did?' Ayleth queried. 'He said those *exact* words?'

Rosenwyn shook her head. She had to be honest. 'Not exactly. He said it was good I was happy here because I don't seem to be going anywhere else.' His comment today had certainly pricked. It implied she was someone to be pitied and she was definitely *not* that. What did he know about her? If he knew anything, he'd know she was an essential part of the Porth Karrek community. People depended on her. She had purpose here. She was *needed*. Wasn't she? That was her fear rising. She turned to face Ayleth. 'He's not right, is he? Is that what people think of me now?'

'No, my dear, of course not,' Ayleth was swift to assure her. 'But you are changed, Rosenwyn. Bolder, sharper.'

'I've never been one to guard my tongue,' Rosenwyn was quick to argue.

'It is different, though. The sense of fun has gone out of your wit. It's a cutting wit now. A man dare not look cross-eyed at you for fear of it,' Ayleth cautioned. 'You have become a beautiful rock men break themselves against, lured in by your loveliness, but wrecked by the sharpness of your tongue when they get too close, like The Beasts in the harbour.'

Rosenwyn stared out into the night, her sister's revelation hitting her hard. 'I didn't know. I didn't realise…' Her voice trailed off. 'But is it so wrong to want to protect myself? I do not want to leave myself open to another Dashiell.'

'And in doing so, you've left yourself open to no one,' Ayleth rebuked gently, taking her hand. 'Not even me. You used to tell me everything, but I think there was more to London than what you've shared. Maybe some day you'll tell me?'

'Maybe.' Rosenwyn was non-committal. She wasn't sure she'd ever share what had happened. It would only deepen her shame and there was plenty of it to go around at the moment. She'd behaved awfully with Mr Kitto today. Her sharp tongue had flayed him mercilessly with her accusations—accusations she should have kept to herself. He did not have to answer to her. 'I fear I provoked Mr Kitto today. I owe him an apology.' She became serious, 'But that doesn't change the fact that he's too dangerous to be let loose with Marianne.'

She squeezed her sister's hand, silently thanking her for her patience and understanding. She had been difficult, a trial to the family and she hadn't meant to be. She could do better and she'd start tomorrow with a visit to Mr Kitto. She'd stop by Karrek House in the morning on her way to town for the annual gin and cake progression. After all, an apology was not capitulation or acceptance. It was merely good manners. She could hardly demand good manners from Kitto if she didn't exhibit them herself. This was something she could fix and fixing was something she was good at. That was the theory at least.

In theory, removing to Cornwall was supposed to lower his financial concerns while raising his creativity with a change of scenery. Cade put his head in his hands and blew out a breath, frustrated. His excellent accommodations, provided by his still-unseen patron, Captain Penhaligon, in the Karrek House gatehouse certainly satisfied the former, but the latter hadn't quite worked out that way when it came to his creativity. So far this bright Monday morning, all Cade had managed was to rearrange snippets of ideas he'd hoped to piece together for the cantata, but no inspiration had struck.

The snippets remained as unconnected as they had been in London and just as incoherent. No matter how many times he rewrote them or transposed them, nothing pleasing emerged. The proof was in the untidy state of the parlour where sheets of music lay strewn about on every available surface and books lay open where he'd sought inspiration. Cantatas needed stories and he had four weeks to produce one. Not even that. It also had to be rehearsed. He needed to have these pieces and parts strung together within two weeks in order to give the choir and the little orchestra time to practise.

But today was the day, Cade told himself optimistically as he surveyed the messy parlour. He was *not* leaving the house until he had a page of music worthy of him. Then, perhaps, he'd treat himself to a nice long walk out of doors if the weather held. If there was one good thing about being in Porth Karrek, it was that he didn't miss the soot of London. The air here was cleaner, sharper. A man could hike and truly stretch his legs along the cliffs. Too bad he couldn't compose a symphony to the Cornish weather. Such a symphony would use all the stylistic trends so popular now in music: the chromatic harmony, the free form of the movements evoking emotions. Bach, with his love of format and patterns, would have hated it, of course. This new music was sweeping and emotional, valued for its dramatism as opposed to its mastery of format. If only he had such an inspiration for Christmas, but the images of a Cornish Christmas had been lost to him for years and he was in no hurry to find them.

A knock at the door interrupted his musings. Cade levered forward on his chair, his back to the door, and called out, 'Come!' He was expecting the maid, who brought down his luncheon and came to clean, not that there was much to clean. He didn't want her to touch the parlour or the study. Nor did he want anyone else to visit—on his orders to Captain Penhaligon. He must be allowed to concentrate. Time was of the essence.

Cool air blew in through the open door, teasing the flames in the parlour's fireplace and rustling his papers. He could feel its bite at his back. 'You can set the basket in there. I'll lay the food out later when I'm ready,' he instructed, waving a hand in the kitchen's general direction, not looking up from the papers at his desk. Perhaps if he moved this stanza to later in the piece, he might make a better beginning? 'I've set out my laundry for you to take.'

'I'm not here for the laundry, Mr Kitto.' Firm, clipped

female tones brought him to his feet, with no small amount of surprise. What was she doing here? After yesterday, Rosenwyn Treleven was the last person he'd expected to interrupt him. Yet here she was, smiling, rosy cheeked from the cold and looking entirely too attractive in a long coat of blue wool trimmed in dark fur at cuffs and collar. It was hard to remember what a shrewish tongue she had when she looked like the personification of fresh air. 'I had business up at Karrek House and took the liberty of bringing your lunch basket and your patron, Captain Penhaligon.'

A tall, broad-shouldered man with windblown hair dressed in boots and greatcoat stepped forward with an air of confident self-possession, his hand extended. 'Mr Kitto, it's a pleasure to meet you at last. I must apologise for being the most distracted of hosts. It's been an intense few days with the storm and the wreck.'

Cade nodded, taking the Captain's hand with a firm grip of his own. He'd have to take the Captain's word for it. 'I certainly understand.' He rather thought there was more to the Captain's distraction than bad weather and a boat wreck, both of which Porth Karrek was used to. The Captain had the look of a man who'd just come straight from bed and meant to be back there soon.

Penhaligon cleared his throat, trying to look as if there was no other place he'd rather be. A clear lie. 'How was the carriage? The inns? Everything was satisfactory? The gatehouse is up to your expectations? The piano?' Penhaligon enquired, his eye drifting over the disarray that populated the parlour with a faint air of disapproval. A military man would not appreciate the mess that often accompanied creativity.

'Everything is ideal. Thank you.' Cade's first thought

upon arrival two nights ago had been that the place was marvellous—a whole house to himself. He couldn't dream of affording such space in London. 'The piano is exceptional.' It sat at an angle in the far corner, a grand piano in elegantly carved rosewood done in the recently revived late rococo style, far too elegant for a mere gatehouse parlour.

'I had it sent down from the main house for you. Reverend Maddern assures me it's in tune, but you must tell me otherwise. My brother purchased the instrument for his wife last December, right before the accident.' His voice faltered over the last. He cleared his throat again and crossed the room to the decanter, suddenly eager to keep busy. 'We're both prodigal sons, aren't we? Perhaps a small toast is in order, if Miss Treleven doesn't mind?' He poured them each a drink and handed a tumbler to Cade. 'Here's to our first Christmas back in Cornwall, Mr Kitto. May it be merry and bright.'

Cade drank to the toast out of politeness. He didn't care whether Christmas was merry *or* bright. He cared only about getting through it, surviving intact with his bank balance in the black on the other side of the year and his demons thrust securely back into their cages.

Pleasantries observed, Penhaligon was distracted once more. 'I do apologise again for being a poor host, but I must excuse myself. Miss Treleven, Kitto, good day.'

Just like that Cade was alone with a woman who had given him the impression yesterday she'd wanted nothing to do with him. Yet she was here, of her own accord it seemed. It certainly made a man suspicious.

Chapter Five

Miss Treleven trailed her fingers over the keys, experimenting with the release. 'This piano is a Sébastien Érard, it has the double escapement action.' It was something Cade liked in an instrument, although it was a technique currently much debated among musicians.

'I'm impressed. You know something of music and its instruments, Miss Treleven.' She'd played expertly yesterday, but it was an interesting surprise to see that her knowledge extended beyond playing.

'Yes.' She looked over her shoulder at him. 'I had the chance to play a prototype in London. To have such an instrument at your disposal is almost worth the journey, is it not?'

'Almost,' Cade said tightly, resisting the temptation to engage in conversation. The instrument had pleased him greatly, but he didn't have time to discuss its merits today. 'I am not prepared to receive.' He made no excuse for his dishabille. He was dressed only in trousers, shirt and waistcoat, his shirt open at the neck, his waistcoat unbuttoned. He'd not bothered with a cravat or any of the usual ornamentation—no fobs, no watch chains. At home, working, there was no need to play the well-dressed gentlemen. He'd not been expecting visitors. Certainly not visitors dressed in expensive blue coats that showed off their complexion. 'Was there something else you needed, Miss Treleven? I apologise, but I have work to do.'

Miss Treleven's sharp eyes narrowed contemplatively. Her shoulders straightened as if she were gathering herself. Cade braced himself. 'There *is* something else, Mr Kitto. I came down here to do some apologising of my own. We parted on poor terms yesterday and that was my fault. I said things that were out of line.'

'No offense taken. You are free to speak your mind.' He would give her polite absolution, but nothing more. He knew how these conversations went. She'd apologised to set the tone, perhaps to give *him* the chance to reciprocate. He would not. There were consequences if he did apologise. She would feel the scales had now been rebalanced and they could now 'start again', on fresh ground, or some such nonsense women liked to believe. He did not need to start again or to start anything with Miss Rosenwyn Treleven. She wasn't good for a man's equilibrium, one moment a vision in blue, the next a probing harpy calling out one's secrets.

She drifted from the piano to the table where his papers were spread out. 'How is the cantata going, Mr Kitto? I admit to being curious.' She studied the pages of half-written stanzas and he hoped she wouldn't see right through the lie he was about to tell.

'It's going well enough. It will be ready for Christmas Eve.' He offered her nothing more. Perhaps now she'd take the hint of dismissal.

She looked up from the pages with an arched brow that called him to account. 'Don't lie to me, Mr Kitto.

Remember, I know something of music. The choir is set to begin rehearsals in two weeks and you have nothing of substance here.'

'How kind of you to point that out,' Cade drawled, on the defensive. The parlour suddenly seemed smaller with her in it. She was so…*vibrant*, everything about her carried an edge, not just her tongue, not just her gaze. All of her. She stopped to pick up the pages nearest the piano. 'Please, don't touch those.' He stepped forward to take them from her, but she merely evaded him, sat down at the piano, set the sheets on the music shelf and began to play.

Cade winced as she showed no mercy on the loud, sweeping chords of the opening. He supposed writers must feel like this—hearing their own words read out loud. He felt exposed, naked and in no way erotically so. She came to an abrupt halt where his stanza ran out, unfinished, and pronounced her verdict. 'It's too loud. It batters the soul.'

He knew that already. His cantata was nothing more than sounds that represented nothing but themselves. They didn't tell a story because he didn't have one yet. Every cantata needed a storyline to determine the music. Her comments shouldn't sting. Professional composers were supposed to be immune to criticism. All the same, how dare she criticise his work? What did she know? But it didn't matter what she knew, he already knew she was right. 'I don't believe I asked for your opinion.' Still, he felt compelled on principle to defend his rather mediocre opening. 'Beethoven is loud.'

Miss Treleven gave him a look that said such a thing was irrelevant. 'You are not Beethoven, Mr Kitto. Why be someone you are not? Loud might be the thing in Vienna, but this is Porth Karrek. It won't do.'

'Captain Penhaligon hired me to bring a little sophistication to this part of the world,' Cade argued. This woman was positively infuriating with her honesty and penetrating green eyes. Any more bluntness from her and his pride would be bludgeoned to death.

'Ha, if you believe that, then the Captain has done quite the job fooling you.' She laughed and stood up from the piano. 'The Captain has asked you here to make himself presentable. The whole of Porth Karrek is divided over whether or not to accept him. Jago Bligh and his cronies find the good Captain too much of an outsider, while my father and others see him as a prodigal returned and are willing to give him a chance. I think his rescue efforts on Saturday garnered him a few more followers. Of course, there's still the issue of how he'll line up on smuggling, being Royal Navy and all. If he doesn't make allowances for the smugglers, no cantata in the world will save him,' she said matter-of-factly.

She was patronising him, as if he weren't a man of the world. 'You don't need to condescend, Miss Treleven,' Cade replied tersely. He did not need to be lectured about the petty politics of Porth Karrek. He'd never admit he found her insights on the Captain's motivations useful. He *had* been too caught up in his own situation to fully understand what the Captain had been angling for when he'd hired him. And, in hindsight, he suspected there was more at play than just Penhaligon's desire to bring a bit of culture to Porth Karrek, but to look too deeply into those motivations might be a blow to his pride. His pride had sustained blows enough. 'I know how this part of the world works. I was raised here.'

'I thought you could use the reminder. You might have been raised here, but it's something you work hard to forget. I wager you've been successful at it.' She organised his sheets of music and handed them to him. 'You can't write the cantata because you've forgotten what Cornwall sounds like. You've forgotten its story and perhaps your own.' She strode to the hook by the door where his greatcoat hung with his muffler and took them down. 'Come with me.'

'Where to?' He hadn't time for anything other than composing, as she'd already highlighted. There were fourteen days before the choir was expected to start rehearsal. Every hour was precious.

'To remember Porth Karrek and I won't take no for an answer, Mr Kitto.' She probably wouldn't. If he refused, she might stand in his parlour arguing all day and then where would he be? Another day lost. There was always the chance she might have a point and *that* was the only reason he was going on a walk with her. He needed inspiration and he couldn't afford to overlook any opportunity to find it. Walking with her had absolutely nothing to do with wanting to match the challenge in her green eyes, or curiosity as to what those pink lips might say next. This had nothing to do with the fact that she seemed inordinately capable of getting a rise out of him. He had no time for an infuriating woman…unless, of course, she inspired him.

Reluctantly, he took his greatcoat from her. 'Where might we be going, Miss Treleven?'

'To Budoc Lane for the gin and cake progression. It's early this year on account of celebrating the rescue.'

He hesitated, his arm halfway into the sleeve of his greatcoat, but it was too late to withdraw now. He'd already committed. It would be crowded on Budoc Lane. With people, with memories and with ghosts of Christmases long past.

'Stand here, boy.'

His father's grip was hard on his shoulder, his instruction strict as he thrust a parcel of pamphlets into Cador's chilled hands outside the Chegwins' shop.

'When they come out of the store, you give them one of these and what do you say?'

'Gin is a sin, sir.'

Cador shivered. The sky was overcast and it was frightfully cold outside. He could feel every gust of wind through the thin fabric of his breeks. From where he stood, shaking in the December cold, gin didn't look like a sin. It looked warm and fun. People were having a good time. He wanted to argue it wasn't just gin, but cake, too. He'd loved cake, the one time he'd had it. Couldn't they deliver their pamphlets inside?

He knew better than to ask. He'd asked before. One cuffing was enough to learn his lesson. Jesus wanted him to suffer. This life was suffering. That was what his father said.

The door opened, a little bell jingling as a couple came out carrying paper-wrapped packages tied with string. Laughter wafted out behind them, along with the delicious scent of cinnamon and soap, the briefest smell of heaven. Some day, when he was older, when he had money of his own and his father couldn't tell him what to do, or who to believe, he would go inside and buy his mother a bar of French soap.

'Look alive, boy!' his father snapped. 'That be the devil's workshop in there.'

* * *

Cador opened the door to the Chegwins' shop, letting Miss Treleven step over the threshold first before following her into hell. The store was busy. It was a time for shopkeepers to thank their loyal customers with gin and cake, and everyone came out for it, good customer or not. He stood for a moment, eyes closed, and breathed it in. No place in the world smelled liked Chegwins'—tea leaves and spices mixed with candle-wax and soaps and a hundred other fantasies. To a boy of seven, it had smelled like hope.

'It's a good smell, isn't it, Mr Kitto?' Beside him, Rosenwyn Treleven smiled, her eyes dancing as she took in the shelves loaded with goods specially brought in for the holidays; some legal, some likely not. Silk stockings lay side by side with woollen mittens, copper pots beside durable, affordable pewter.

He followed her down a narrow aisle as she selected items for her shopping basket. 'There was a time when I thought this shop was a dream come to life, a place full of anything a person could want. During the Christmas season it was magical.'

She cocked her head to one side, studying him for a moment as she shopped. 'Is that no longer the case?'

'I'm no longer a boy, Miss Treleven. Is it so shocking I no longer have a boy's view of the world?' He'd seen the great shops that lined the Parisian boulevards, where one made private appointments and drank champagne with the shopkeepers eager to curry favour. He'd purchased mere trinkets for lovers that cost a month of his father's income. Chegwins' and its cheap gin was just a small, crowded shop. The bubble was off the wine in that regard, and yet Miss Treleven, a woman of means, who had been to London, who surely knew better, still found pleasure in poring over the shelves.

'It's the ritual that matters, Mr Kitto. Gin and cake is tradition. This is Porth Karrek at its best; the fishing boats are in, the men are gathered around a stove, the women chatting as they browse the festive offerings.' She tossed him a breathtaking smile and he thought perhaps *she* was at her best when she was defending her town. She saw a Porth Karrek he'd never known. Her voice dropped and he had to lean close to hear her, to breathe her in. 'Ezerah Chegwin made me feel special when I was younger and I'd bring my single penny to buy sweets. Now the tables are turned. He is a man bordering on old age, who struggles to keep a shop open when the economy is poor and I am the one who has pennies aplenty. Now, *he* needs *me*. So, I come and I spend them here. I'd far rather give my money to the Chegwins than to a fancy shop on Bond Street.'

They turned down another aisle, this one smelling like springtime. She picked up a bar of soap and breathed deeply. 'When I was little, I could hardly wait until I was old enough to come to the gin and cake progression. I remember the first time I came and bought sweets for my sisters who were too young to attend. How grown up I felt when I made my purchases and Mr Chegwin carefully wrapped them in paper as if I were the grandest customer he'd served all day.'

Cade gripped a nearby shelf to steady himself. Memories threatened, of a boy standing in the cold who'd wished to do just that—buy a simple bar of soap for his mother. How different her memories were than his. How much happier her endings. It was hard to breathe. He had to get out of the store. He was starting to panic. 'Miss Treleven, if you'll excuse me, I'll wait outside.'

He pushed past shoppers to the exit, taking deep gulps of fresh air, and leaned against the windows he'd spent his childhood peeping through. His father was probably laughing at him from the afterlife. He'd waited so long to go into that store, only to rush out, sick and disappointed. His father would think it served him right. Maybe his father was right about other things, too. This life was suffering even though Reverend Maddern argued otherwise. Cade pushed his hands through his hair, steadying himself. This was why he hadn't wanted to come home. Ever. He had not wanted to remember. He had not wanted to walk in the footsteps of his past and face the ghosts of everything that hadn't been.

Chapter Six

Rosenwyn stood at the counter while Ezerah Chegwin tallied her bill. She was impatient to be outside. She hoped Mr Kitto was all right. Inviting him to the gin and cake progression had seemed the right thing to do at the time. He needed inspiration. He needed to remember Porth Karrek. Now Rosenwyn wasn't so sure her efforts to fix his problem hadn't led to other consequences. Something had upset him dreadfully. One moment they'd been chattering about Chegwins' and the next he'd been pale as a ghost. That wasn't the inspiration she'd been hoping for.

'Mr Kitto didn't get any cake. I've had the wife wrap some up for him.' Mr Chegwin winked and added a parcel and a flask to the top of her basket as she handed over her coins. 'He might be hungry later. Let him know we are honoured he is here.'

Outside, she found him leaning against the windows. His colour had returned and he looked once again his elegant, insouciant self, even when she knew better; beneath his greatcoat he was in dishabille. That was Cador Kitto in a nutshell—presentable on the outside, naughty on the inside. 'Why don't we walk on the beach? The fresh air will do you good and there's a path we can take up to Karrek House at the end of it.' Based on his reaction to Chegwins', it would be best if she waited to do the rest of her errands another day.

He took her basket as they walked down the lane. 'What is in here? It weighs a ton.' He laughed, hefting the basket in exaggeration.

'A few things for the church baskets.' There was great need this year. A few more mines had closed and those that were still open relied increasingly on machine power, not manpower. When mines failed in this part of Cornwall, everyone failed.

They reached the beach that marked the boundary between the town and the sea. Behind them, at the other end of Budoc Lane, St Piran's steeple rose white in the clear, cold sky. Before them, the ocean was a foam-crested dark blue. Gulls circled and cried overhead. In the distance to their left were the Karrek headlands. She wouldn't give up. She was determined that Cador Kitto find inspiration. It was a perfect day to show him all Porth Karrek could be, if one knew where to look. Rosenwyn drew a breath. 'Do you hear it, Mr Kitto? Do you hear Cornwall? The gulls, the waves, the cries of the fishermen?'

'There aren't any fishermen out today.'

'No, but I can imagine what they call to each other and so can you,' she persisted. 'Surely you remember the fishermen from your childhood?' She paused, real-ising her mistake. They'd been talking about her child-hood when he'd frozen in Chegwins'. Did he not want to remember his childhood? Was that it? Was there some-thing about growing up here he was so eager to forget that he hadn't been home in two decades?

'Come on, there's a cove just a little way down the beach. It will be warmer and out of the wind.' She started out over the sand, but it was soft and deep here. Her half-boots sank into it, making it hard to walk. She turned to look back at Kitto. 'Are you coming or are you afraid to get your boots dirty?' She'd meant to tease him, but the distraction was a mistake. Her own foot turned in the deep sand. She lost her balance and went down with an undignified yelp. Getting up gracefully from the soft sand proved something of a challenge. But it earned her a smile from Mr Kitto, a real smile.

'Here, Miss Treleven, let me assist you.' Mr Kitto strode towards her, offering her a hand. 'I must insist you take my arm.'

Take his hand? Now it was her turn to be reluctant. It was only a helping hand, but putting her hand into his seemed more intimate when done from the position of looking up into his blue eyes from her seat in the sand.

'Come, Miss Treleven, don't be stubborn. I don't want to explain to your father how you broke your neck on my watch. You'll be in good hands.'

'At least one hand, anyway,' Rosenwyn quipped to cover her embarrassment over being so clumsy. His hand was warm as it closed around hers, his grip firm and confident, strong. It was the grip of a man to whom touching others came easily and it conjured up other images of other touches: those fingers skimming a woman's cheek with the same skill they skimmed the keys of a piano, fingers that played bodies as if they, too, were instruments. Those were images she'd promised herself not to contemplate. She felt like Marianne with her girlish musings. Marianne didn't know better. But she did. Handsome men should be ascribed no more nobility of character than any other man.

They struck out for the shoreline where the waves met the beach and the sand was firmly packed, and turned for the cove. Despite the crisp weather, the cove was sheltered and warmer without the wind. Rosenwyn raised her face to the sun. 'This is lovely. It's a promise that summer will come again. For just a moment, I can imagine that it *is* summer, can't you?' She tossed him a smile and settled on the sand, arms wrapped about her knees, the toes of her walking boots a safe distance from the waves.

'Summer is months away.' Mr Kitto bent and picked up a flat pebble to skip over the waves. The breeze pushed his hair back from his face, putting his sharp features on dramatic display.

'Must you always be a killjoy?' She watched him skip another pebble, covertly indulging in the sight of his body moving through the motions, all fluid, easy grace. What a spectacular dancer he must be with his ease of movement and sense of rhythm. To be his partner on the dance floor would be...nothing she was likely to experience. She had to stop these daydreams. 'Surely you have memories of childhood picnics on the beach, bonfires at sunset.'

'My childhood was much different than yours and much shorter.' He turned from the ocean to look at her, his blue eyes filled with warning that said *this way be monsters*. She would do best to hold her questions.

Rosenwyn did not heed the caution. She patted the sand beside her. 'Come, sit and tell me about it. I would have been barely two years old, so you can't expect me to know your reference. You're a legend in these parts;

a prodigy spirited away when he was eight to train and lead a life of fame. Come tell me what is legend and what is fact?'

'A legend? I don't remember it quite like that.' He did come sit, his legs stretched out before him as he leaned back on his hands. 'There's not much to tell that would be interesting, certainly not the stuff of legends.'

'Let me be the judge of that. Your reluctance only makes me twice as inquisitive and twice as persistent, in case you haven't noticed.' She unwrapped the plum cake from Mrs Chegwin and offered him a piece, a sweet bribe perhaps in exchange for a story.

He took the cake with a wry smile. 'Do you know how often as a boy I yearned for Christmas cake? How many years I looked in the window of Chegwins' and wondered what it would be like to go in, to have the money to purchase something?'

'I did not mean for my story to upset you.' She passed him the flask, but he waved it away.

'I don't drink gin. My father was Methodist. He didn't believe in gin.'

'I think it's hard cider.' She offered it again and took up the slender thread of conversation he'd given her. His father. 'Tell me about your family. Did you have any siblings?'

He took the flask and sipped cautiously, his steely blue eyes warning her, an indecipherable half-smile on his mouth, a mouth she shouldn't be noticing *again*. She apparently hadn't learned her lesson the first time. 'I had nine brothers and sisters. Three plus myself who were alive when I left. The others died young. Robbie was two, Sarah was five, Addie was four, Peter when he was nine, and the baby died at birth.' He rolled out the names and ages without emotion in his voice, but he turned away from her, giving his gaze to the sea instead. 'The winters were too cold. There wasn't enough food. A simple fever could carry them off. A catarrh was fatal. Definitely not the stuff of legends.'

'I'm sorry the doctor couldn't save them, that medicines failed,' Rosenwyn offered softly, feeling her heart go out to him. She loved her large, noisy, often nosy family. She couldn't fathom the concept of losing even one of her sisters, let alone half of them. What would her life be like without Ayleth's companionship or Marianne's giddiness? Violet's quiet bookishness or the twins' boisterous antics?

'Doctor? Medicine?' Kitto shook his head. The harshness of his laugh froze her. 'We didn't have money for food let alone those luxuries. There was no doctor, no medicine. There were cold rags for fevers, tea and broth if we were lucky. Beyond that, the sick in my home were on their own.'

'The church did nothing? Was there no help from charity? I can't believe Reverend Maddern offered nothing.' It sickened her to think of children in such want. She was not naïve. She knew life was hard for many folks. She saw it when she went out with her baskets, but always there was help for the worst cases. 'I can't imagine there was no help at all.'

He laughed again, this time at her and it stung, a reminder that he thought her pampered, she with pennies to put on the counter at Chegwins'. 'My father was a proud man. There was no help from the church since my father had put himself and us beyond it. Even if there had been help, he would have turned it away. "A Kitto helps himself," he liked to say. As for what you can't imagine, Miss Treleven, I am sure there's quite a lot of that. So, forgive me if this attempt at inspiration hasn't succeeded in reminding me of all that is good about Porth Karrek. While you played on the beach, flying kites with your sisters and building bonfires, I was working. The mines, before they shut down, had use for little boys. I could scrabble into small places, I could carry heavy loads. I would sort rock from ore until my hands bled, and for an hour or two a week, I would sing in the vicar's choir, although I had to sneak away to do it because my father disagreed with the Anglicans. But my mother insisted on it and the Reverend was kind.'

Never had it been put to her so bluntly. To have a childhood boiled down to whatever joy could be stolen from singing in the vicar's choir seemed the greatest of tragedies. Childhood should be spent in sunlight and fresh air, taking romps outdoors, yet the man beside her had spent his childhood in the darkness of a mine. 'I am sorry, you deserved better.' What else could she say? She'd meant well today but she'd ended up apologising for those efforts at every turn.

He gave her a piercing look that said her sympathy was not enough. '*Every* child deserves better, Miss Treleven. A man should not bring up a child if he cannot support it. A man should not marry at all if he cannot care for his wife.' The sentiment behind those two simple sentences was rife with open emotion and unescapable conclusions even a stranger like herself could see. He blamed his father for the fate of his siblings. There was guilt there, too, that he had survived, that he'd been given a chance when others he'd loved had not. She was not obtuse. He wasn't merely disclosing, pouring out his soul. He was trying to shock her with his story, a punishment for her probing. This was what she got when she opened the cages of a man's demons. Perhaps she deserved it.

'You see now why I resent being here. This is not a joyous homecoming. There are only reminders of death and guilt here.'

He must truly be desperate for money, then, to come back. Money or work. Maybe both. It prompted another question. How had the great Cador Kitto fallen to such levels of desperation? 'But you *are* here, you've chosen this and you must make the best of it. You need to write the cantata.'

'The past is irrelevant, now? Am I to just forget? I believe I was trying to do just that until you came and dragged me out and started asking your questions.' Argument was his armour. She saw that now. He wasn't attacking her as much as he was defending himself. She must be getting close to the answers if he was fighting this hard, willing to risk rudeness. She did not budge in her pursuit.

'No, you do not get to be victorious, Mr Kitto. You do not get permission to wallow in misery and use it as an excuse for everything negative in your life.'

'And *you* can't have it both ways, Miss Treleven. You cannot tell me to embrace my past and then tell me to wipe it away.' He sighed. 'You see my dilemma now. Why I stayed away. In Vienna, I can ignore it.'

She could imagine how he ignored it: women, parties, balls, drinking, gambling, dissolute living at night, composing by day. Perhaps those choices were also a stab at revenge against the strictness of his Methodist father, but that didn't make the imagining of them any easier. A little sliver of jealousy prodded at her. She didn't like thinking of the man who sat here on the sand beside her with other women; women who let him use them for sport perhaps just to see him smile one more time, to know that for a short while they held the attentions of this handsome, enigmatic man, a slice of the passion that bubbled so near the surface of him, the passion that was evident when he spoke, in his anger, in his laughter, even in his coldness.

'Is your family nearby?' She tried another question, something to take her mind off other thoughts. He'd mentioned his father and that some siblings had been alive when he'd left. Had he made any attempt to contact them since his arrival? There were no Kittos living in Porth Karrek at present, but perhaps they'd moved to another village. She hoped for the best. Perhaps she could encourage a reunion, a chance to heal the past. But he was not done trying to shock her.

'Beyond the churchyard, Miss Treleven? No. They are *all* dead now. My sister lived to adulthood, but died in childbed. My brother joined the army and died in the wars, my other brother embraced a life of crime and met his end in Bodmin Jail.'

He wanted to shock her into silence, shock her into walking away. She would not go. Shocking statements were a defensive strategy. Rosenwyn pressed on, driven in part by her own curiosity to know this man. 'And your parents?'

'My father died last year. The master of their suffering outlived all of them.'

'Your mother?' she asked softly, hesitant to know. There was enormous tragedy behind those blue eyes and golden waves, a tragedy masked by easy smiles and laughter when in the company of others and protected by a sharp-edged tongue when someone poked too close to the truths. A ballroom of two hundred glittering peers would not know the depths of loss Cador Kitto carried. He was not unlike her in that regard—a surprising discovery indeed.

'She died the year I left. If she hadn't, I might not have gone to London at all. It was her dying wish that I go. My father had resisted when Reverend Maddern first asked, but in the end he promised her. It was all she wanted. She saw the potential I had if she could just get me out of Cornwall. Her death saved me.'

'Your talent saved you,' Rosenwyn corrected, instinctively wanting to shield him from such an interpretation of a memory—that his life had been bought at the price of another. It was not the sort of memory a child should carry with them, yet it appeared he had carried it for years. 'If you hadn't gone then, you would have gone later. The Reverend would have seen to it.'

He gave her a dubious shrug, only half-convinced of her argument. 'Regardless, the legend is quite tarnished, after all. Does that disappoint you?'

'Hardly. Yours is a story of resilience—the resilience of a boy who survived against the odds and the resilience of a mother's hope, that despite those odds, her son would do more than survive, that he would somehow change the world despite his humble beginnings.' The waves were edging closer to the tips of their shoes. They would have to go soon and she was reluctant to bring this interlude to an end.

'Music does not change the world.'

'I disagree.'

Cador Kitto sighed. 'Of course you do, Miss Treleven, but that doesn't make you right.'

Chapter Seven

Dear heavens, Miss Treleven would argue with the saints if it suited her. Cade dusted cake crumbs off his hands. 'You see the world differently than I do.' Cade picked up a short stick and began drawing in the sand, trying to ignore the twinge of hope her words had pried open in him. 'I used to believe that, too, back when I was innocent and naïve.'

'You think I'm unworldly, Mr Kitto, because I prefer Porth Karrek to the cities of Europe.' It was always statements with her, never questions. She asserted her beliefs and opinions with confidence. He'd meant to wound her with his comment about naïveté, as if naïveté was something to be ashamed of and he had failed. 'Tell me, what changed your mind?' She had him on the defensive again.

'I looked at what I did, at what I do. I write music for pompous noble men who want to celebrate their birthdays, commemorate their various anniversaries. They pay me to flatter them in song, in symphony, and I do because I cannot afford to live otherwise.' He painted it as bleakly as possible. 'It was easy to lose sight of my hopes when the money started coming in. I'd never had so much money at my disposal before. I flattered myself that it was enough. But when the money stops, one sees there's nothing else left that matters. What did those symphonies, those oratorios signify beyond being a means to the end of keeping me fed and sheltered?'

She was quiet for a while, her gaze on a point near the horizon where sea met sky. Perhaps she was conceding him victory in her silence, at last. The thought disappointed him. Part of him, that hopeful part she'd awakened, didn't want to be victorious. He wanted her to argue, to prove him wrong, because if he *was* wrong, then there was still hope. He did not want to be right on this account.

'Music may not make a difference in a sweeping sense like laws that change an entire nation,' she said thoughtfully. 'But it changes the world one person at a time, it touches people one at a time, it moves us, and not even in the same ways or for the same reasons.' Argument made her magnificent. He could not take his eyes from the curve of her profile, the sweep of her cheek, the slim length of her neck. Want speared him—not just a desire to possess her beauty, but to possess her mind, to think as she thought, to see the world as she saw it. It was a new kind of wanting when it came to women, one that, for a moment, transcended the physical.

She turned her gaze from the sea to him, those green eyes full of her passion. 'Music does make a difference. Music inspires us to greatness, to reflection, to change. The only problem is that the musician doesn't often see the results of his efforts. He can't judge rightly the impact.'

The hope inside him eased, relaxing at her words. It would not die today, not completely. 'The defence rests, then, Miss Treleven?' he said softly, his own gaze dropping to her lips, his body roused by her, by her argument. If he could kiss her, perhaps he could claim some small splendid piece of her.

'Absolutely and irrevocably. You have a great talent. Do not underestimate it.' Her own voice was a mere whisper above the waves. The distance between them on the sand had disappeared over the course of their exchange, both of them too caught up in their arguments to notice. He noticed now. He could see the dark pupils of her eyes, the pulse at the base of her neck, proof that she noticed, too. That she was affected. She had not made her arguments solely out of need to be right. She'd made these arguments for him, because she'd wanted to convince him that he wasn't useless, that his work mattered, his story mattered.

'Rosenwyn.' Her name slipped from his lips before he could rethink it. There was a quiet between them on the beach, a peace that existed nowhere else. Her eyes held his, waiting. 'Do you know what a gift you've given me today?' Even if it wasn't the inspiration he'd been looking for, even if he hadn't discovered the cantata story he so desperately needed, she'd given him something else: optimism, a new lens perhaps through which to view the past. Those were not things to be smirked at. His hand curled around hers, easily, naturally, as if their hands belonged entwined together. 'I haven't spoken of my family for ages.' Most people didn't have the tenacity to keep probing once he made it clear he didn't want to talk. But Rosenwyn had persisted. 'Thank you for making me do it, for not being frightened away.'

She gave a breathless laugh. 'Your secrets are safe. I won't tell anyone.' She wouldn't. He was sure of it. She understood what he'd given to her today were treasures in their own right, things he did not show to the world, but he'd shown her, for whatever reason, even if that reason had been to shock.

'I know.' He brought their hands up, pressing his against hers, palm to palm as he interlaced his fingers through hers. She might be prickly and argumentative, she might be beautiful and stubborn, but she was also trustworthy. One needn't know Rosenwyn Treleven long to know that. Honesty radiated from her along with the goodness that felt honour-bound to shop at Chegwins'. He'd been hard on her with his insinuations that she knew nothing of life. That wasn't true. She just knew life differently than he did.

'What are you doing?' She gave another soft laugh.

'What are you doing, *Cade*,' he corrected with a teasing smile. 'Say my name, Rosenwyn. I want to hear you say it.' He should stop this before it went any further. He was flirting, playing, the way he played with courtly ladies. She deserved better. But he wanted her, wanted to hold her here on the beach before the waves took away the moment. He wanted to feel her pressed up against him, the riot of her curls in his hands as he kissed her, wanted to feel her mouth against his. If he could touch her, hold her, drink from her, perhaps he could take her passion, her optimism away with him to be a light in his darkness.

'*Cade.*' She made his name a caress, an invitation. A single kiss was all he wanted. Surely there was no sin in stealing one kiss. Nothing more. Cade leaned in and captured her lips, his free hand cupping her jaw, his fingers weaving through the depths of her hair, drawing her close until her mouth was entirely his. He could taste the moment she capitulated, the moment she gave over to the press of his lips, all sweet, tentative surrender. He'd surprised her, taken her unawares, although not too unaware. Her breathlessness, the beat of her pulse at the base of her neck, said she'd not been oblivious to the changing tone between them, nor was that change unwelcome. But even now, as she gave over to the curiosity of the kiss, there was a hesitance to her, a holding back, as if she didn't dare trust herself to fully engage. Not because she didn't want to. This was not resistance. It was hesitance. Cade had kissed enough women to respect the difference.

He relinquished the kiss, but not her. He framed her face between his hands, his palms cupping the feminine curve of her jaw. 'It's only a kiss, Rosenwyn,' he whispered.

'Only a kiss? Are kisses so cheap to you, then? A kiss might cost a girl everything if seen by the wrong people, or if it's misunderstood.' Rosenwyn scolded him softly. Only it wasn't a scolding. It was armour. He saw that immediately in her eyes as they rested on him, her gaze so near that he could see the flecks of gold with the green. There was sadness, too, mixed with the pleasure. Why? Because she thought the kisses cheap? Or because they reminded her of other kisses? Was that her secret?

'No, not cheap.' He would not have her thinking he was indiscriminate with his kisses. Such kisses cheapened her as much as they cheapened him. The latter he could live with. He'd done worse than kiss someone for money. But he would not make her complicit to those choices. Rosenwyn Treleven was a woman of virtuous quality, not a worldly woman of the Hapsburg court.

'Then why did you do it?' Rosenwyn prompted,

searching his face. The minx wanted his answer, but she was warning him, too.

He gave a soft chuckle, the kind reserved for the bedroom, for lying in a woman's arms after lovemaking. 'Can't a man ever win with you, my darling? If the kiss is too cheap, I'm a profligate rake. If the kiss is too dear, then I'm warned away from casting pearls before swine. Can't I simply kiss you? Can't I simply express my gratitude for what you've given me today?' he said in earnest.

'A token of your appreciation?' The tip of Rosenwyn's tongue licked at her lips, whetting them in contemplation, the hesitancy, the sadness, lifting in her eyes. She was quite the siren with her lush mouth and searing gaze. 'That has not been my experience.'

He was starting to burn again, or was it more? Perhaps he hadn't stopped burning. He'd not meant to do more than kiss her, but now that he had, a kiss might not be enough. He offered her a wry smile, his hand massaging at the base of her neck. He could not resist the tease. 'Your experience? And what might that be?'

'That kisses don't exist in isolation. They are often beginnings. One kiss leads to another.' Her mouth parted in brave invitation.

Cade leaned in, his mouth hovered above hers. 'It can work that way, Rosenwyn. Would you like it to?' he breathed his challenge. 'If you'd like another, come and claim it.' He'd made his overture, the next kiss had to be hers. That was how the game worked. He didn't pursue where he was not welcome.

What delicious folly this was! Rosenwyn took her kiss, her hands on his hands where they cupped her jaw,

her mouth on his mouth, wide, and open and unyielding
as she drank her pleasure. In this kiss, she allowed herself no quarter and it pleased them both. The kiss might
have been hers, but Cade was a subtle master, leading
her with his tongue, with his body, until he reclined on
the sands, she above him, making it seem as if this was
all her idea, that she was in charge when nothing was
further from the truth. She was on the beach kissing
Cador Kitto, as wildly out of control as a Cornish storm
after all her resolution to the contrary and enjoying it,
wanting it with every fibre of her being.

She nipped at his lip with her teeth and let out a
yelp as Cade flipped her, rolling her beneath him with
a laugh as he reversed their positions. 'Time to give
you a taste of your own medicine, minx!' He kissed
her deeply, then, and she felt the sense of play that had
permeated their kisses dissipating in its wake. Her body
hummed with the thrill of it even as her mind whispered
its last, feeble warning. Glorious, wicked trouble, but
trouble none-the-less.

'Oh! The tide!' Rosenwyn gasped. A dash of cold
water doused her boots, a reminder that they'd lingered
too long in many ways. Cade leapt to his feet and helped
her up, laughing as he grabbed her about the waist and
swung her out of the way of the next wave. The tide
had been rising since they'd come down and now it
had nearly come all the way in. The afternoon was
nearly spent.

'Well, that's one way of knowing when it's time to
go.' Cade was all good humour as he led her to the base
of the cliff path leading up to Karrek House, but there he
stopped and danced her back to the cliff wall, his eyes
on her mouth. 'It's a bit abrupt, though, for my tastes. I

like a more gradual ending to an afternoon. Something like this.' He kissed her again, softly, with promise. A promise of what? Her curiosity piqued against her better judgement. She'd only allowed herself the kiss because there could be no promises and now she was wondering what those elusive promises might be? What form they might take and should she accept? Ayleth's wicked suggestion that she take Cade up on his offer whispered loud in her mind. But Ayleth didn't understand passion, had never experienced how it could sweep someone away, destroy their reason. Rosenwyn knew. She had to stop this.

Rosenwyn pushed gently at his chest. 'It's late. I need to get home. I'm sorry.' Would he understand she was sorry for more than rushing off? That she was sorry she could not give him more?

He kissed her one last time and took her hand, leading them up the path to the headlands. She was thankful for the silence of their walk. It gave her mind time to settle itself around what had happened today. She had not planned any of what had occurred. Everything since the moment she'd stepped into the gatehouse had been a journey into uncharted territory. Did he need the silence as well? Was he thinking of their kiss at all? Was this just another flirtation for him? Perhaps he kissed women daily? His reputation suggested that was a distinct possibility. His skill suggested that reputation was not unearned.

She studied his back with its tapered waist and square shoulders—not as broad as Eaton's, perhaps, but no less impressive. They suited his lithe build. They suited her, too. She'd not felt overpowered by him. She'd welcomed his weight on the beach. Yet, there was a certain strength to him. She'd felt it when he'd lifted her away from the waves, when he'd helped her to her feet. A woman felt safe with him, apparently even when he was seducing her. *Seduction.* That was where this was headed. Could she allow it? Or would it become another mistake like Dashiell?

By the top of the cliff, she'd made her decision. Today could be an isolated incident only. He turned to her and Rosenwyn stuck out her hand. 'This is where we part, Mr Kitto. Thank you for the day.'

Cade laughed. He took her hand, but not to shake. He pulled her forward and she stumbled against him, off balance. 'Is that how it's going to be, Rosenwyn? "Cade" when I'm kissing you on beaches and "Mr Kitto" when we're in public? You need to decide, if we're going to be friends.'

'This is how it *has* to be. It wouldn't be seemly to use your Christian name in public,' Rosenwyn scolded, hating herself for the warmth that rushed through her at his nearness, at his touch, at the caress of his words.

'But in private? Would you use it, then? Would you use it when we are alone as we are now?' He was the very devil with his wickedness and the temptation was real even when she knew better.

'I doubt we will have much opportunity for privacy.' She would make her position clear. There would be no seduction.

'But if we should, I would prefer you use it,' he persisted with a winning smile that threatened to melt her resolve. 'I should escort you home,' Cade said mischievously. 'You could practise using my name on the way.'

She surveyed the darkening sky. She could see already how that walk would go: a few more stolen kisses, a few more stolen promises she shouldn't make. All of it pointless, all of it enough to keep her up at night wondering 'what if'.

'No, there is still plenty of daylight and the walk is short. I shall be quite safe.' Safer than if she was with him.

'I shall watch you until I can't see you any longer, then,' Cade offered gallantly. 'And I shall rush to your aid if needed.'

This was all Ayleth's fault, Rosenwyn thought as she walked home—this idea that she needed a brief romance in order to finally put Dashiell behind her and that a worldly man like Cade Kitto was just the sort to oblige her: attractive, skilled and temporary, a man who lived in the moment and loved in it as well. Cade was not the marrying type. He'd told her. Those remarks about being able to support a family told her as much. When he'd spoken of his father's pride, she'd seen his pride, too. His father wasn't the only stubborn Kitto in the family. Cade would not take charity either. He'd never be content to live off his wife's dowry. He wanted to make his own way. In his profession, that meant living from commission to commission. He was not the fortune hunter Dashiell was. Further reason he was perfect for a brief romance.

Rosenwyn touched her fingers to her lips, still feeling Cade's kisses upon them. Tokens of appreciation, nothing more, nothing less. Well, not quite nothing. They were her souvenirs. When he left in a few weeks, she would have them to remember him by. Her wicked conscience whispered she might have more than kisses. If she were brave, she might have something extraordinary.

Chapter Eight

Cade stood on the cliffs a long while after Rosenwyn had faded from his sight, but not from his mind, or from his body. The day had been extraordinary. His mind still replayed images of her on the beach, his body still burned from the press of her against him. One afternoon had not been enough. He'd not intended or anticipated such a consequence from their kiss. He'd merely intended to satisfy his desire, not create more.

Now, he was left with question upon question. She'd all but admitted she'd been kissed before with her comment about experience and she hadn't kissed like a novice either. Not that he held it against her. He found experience and confidence in a lover a welcome trait. *Lover.* What an interesting, unexpected word when applied to Rosenwyn Treleven and a dangerous one, an arrangement that could see him married and headed down the very path he'd spent his adult life avoiding. Marriage meant responsibility, it meant children. No matter how careful a man was, there was always a chance. Bach had had twenty children, ten who had lived and whom he'd had to support. Cade couldn't imagine supporting a wife and even one child, dragging them all over Europe, chasing commissions or the elusive hope of a permanent post. He also couldn't imagine the alternative: staying in one place, because of what it would entail, living off his wife's dowry and financially contributing to his family's welfare sporadically. He'd become a gentleman composer, a man who composed as a hobby. He'd be no better than his father, another Kitto unable to support his family.

Cade threw a pebble, watching it arc on its way out to sea. The danger was all hypothetical. Rosenwyn was not the sort of woman to be so easily seduced no matter how fine the kisses. No man swayed her from her path. She, and only she, gave herself permission to deviate, which made her kisses, her passion on the beach, all the sweeter. He had not taken those kisses as much as *she* had given them. Of course, heaven help the man who ever truly fell in love with her. She'd lead him around by a ring through the nose with her strong opinions and stronger will. She'd tried to fix *him* today with the walk and all of her questions.

Cade smiled to himself. Rosenwyn had got more than she'd bargained for there. Once he'd started talking, he'd given more and more of himself away: the boy who'd lost his siblings, the boy who'd lost his mother, the boy who'd worked the mines, who found solace in singing in the choir.

There was more he hadn't told her: the boy who'd been the smallest in his class at the conservatory, who was teased and tricked endlessly, who had his pudding stolen by the older boys. The one no one stood up for. He'd worked twice as hard, though. He knew what those pampered boys did not, that life would not be easy and it sure as hell wouldn't be fair. He'd excelled because of it. Resilience, Rosenwyn had called it. He hadn't thought of that boy for a long time. He didn't like to remember himself as weak, helpless, alone.

Those memories were another reason to despise Porth Karrek. His past peered out at him everywhere he looked. And it always would as long as he was here. There would be more incidents like the one today at Chegwins'. Uncomfortable remembrances of the past raised doubts about his present. Was he any different now as a man than he had been as a boy? He was still scraping for money, still worrying about a roof over his head. Those concerns were merely dressed up these days in Hoby boots and greatcoats.

He turned from the cliffs and began the walk back to the gatehouse. The wind had picked up, blowing the skirts of his greatcoat about his legs. He didn't mind, he'd weathered colder nights than this with less protection. It was worth the cold to watch the first evening stars fight their way through the clouds. His mother had told him once that stars were loved ones looking down on their families.

Was she looking down now? What would she think if she saw him? Would she see the flaws in him, the man who did not shirk from using every tool in his arsenal to secure a commission, even dallying with married women who used their influence with their husbands, the man who lived a transient life both physically and emotionally, never staying anywhere or with anyone long enough to develop attachments? The man who hadn't come home when his father had died? Would she understand his choices or would she be ashamed of the man he'd become? His mother had given him everything she had. Was he worth that sacrifice?

Or would she see the best of him? Her precious son well travelled, well educated, well dressed, so no one would ever guess he'd begun life as a miner's son. The last time she'd seen him, he'd stood beside her bed in a second-hand suit of clothes Reverend Maddern had found for him. He had not worn second-hand clothes for a very long time. Would she know every time he composed a lullaby for a noble child's baptism it was for her? Every lullaby a reminder of his mother's wish for her newborn child, every note of it embodying how his mother had found the strength to lift her hand and stroke his cheek, hardly able to speak, but the joy and the hope were there in her eyes even as she faced her own end that he would go on and in that going on, she would go on, too. It was every mother's look when she held her infant son at a baptism. No matter their station in life a mother worried for her child, hoped for that child and all the things he might be. A mother's wish transcended class. The wish was always the same: hope.

What had Rosenwyn said about hope today? Resilience, she'd called it. She'd talked not only of his resilience but the resilience of a mother's hope, that regardless of the odds her son would survive, that he would change the world despite his humble beginnings. It was the eternal hope of mothers from everywhere and from every time.

That was it. Cade froze. A mother's wish. That was Christmas. That was the cantata! Sweet Jesu, he had it! Cade began to run, caging the idea in his mind, holding tight to it lest it slip away before he could capture it. He raced into the gatehouse, fumbling as he lit a lamp, fumbling for the Bible on the bookshelf, the idea in full form now. Christmas was about mothers as much as it was about children. His fingers tore through the pages, searching. What was that verse, the one in Luke? There it was.

Mary pondered all these things and kept them in her heart.

Cade stared at the words, relief surging through him. That was what he'd do. A cantata for Mary, a cantata for mothers. Peace settled on him. He had his story, the cantata would come together now. The wall had been breached.

Despite the late hour, his mind was a hive of excited activity. He could see the notes, hear the sounds of the instruments, the voices, all in his mind. Cade took the Bible to his desk, pulled a fresh sheet forward and began to write, copying verses, composing stanzas. He needed two da capos arias and three recitative pieces, perhaps five if he wanted to open and close with them as well. He would write all night and through the next day and the next night if need be, as long as the words came, as long as the music came. He'd had such bouts of activity before when the music in him would stop for nothing, not for sleep, not for food. When the music had run its course in a few days, he'd visit Reverend Maddern to discuss voices and available instrumentation.

Cade paused from his feverish plans for a moment and smiled. Rosenwyn had inspired him, after all, in the most unusual of ways. He'd not thought to find inspiration in the darkness of his memories and yet he had. He'd have to thank her when he saw her next. But how to thank her? With more kisses, perhaps, although today had shown him how dangerous and complicated those could be. His gaze moved around the room, landing on the piano. An idea came. Yes, that would be better than even kisses. He would send around a note when all was ready.

Chapter Nine

December 8th, 1822, the second Sunday in Advent

Rosenwyn looked down at the note discreetly hidden in the pages of her prayer book as the Reverend preached about peace: peace with the world, peace with one's self. She'd had little of the latter since Monday. The note had arrived last night for her by messenger. After six days of no contact, Cade wanted to see her. She was to wait for him after church.

Rosenwyn wasn't sure what did more to disrupt her peace—the absence of him which had left her spending the week in doubt of their kisses on the beach, or the thought of seeing him again. She ought to tread cautiously. She didn't want him to think she would come running whenever he snapped his fingers. Yet the prospect of seeing him today had stirred up a heady excitement. She had dressed for church carefully in a deep, forest green gown the colour of the season that brought out her eyes and she'd had Ayleth braid her hair into a coronet with a neat bun at her nape.

Rosenwyn slid a glance across the aisle where Cade

sat with Captain Penhaligon, looking immaculate, as he had last Sunday: gold hair brushed to an enviable sheen, his jaw clean-shaven, his dark blue jacket lint-free, the white stock pristine where it rose above the jacket collar. Shoulders straight, eyes forward.

She wished she could see his face. *Turn. See me. Look across the aisle as you did last week.* But Cade was intent on being good. His gaze did not slide her way once. She should be thankful. He was being circumspect, but part of her wanted him to be a little less discreet.

She wanted a sign that he'd missed her this week or at least that he'd thought of her. *She'd* thought of him. What had he been doing? Had he found inspiration for the cantata? Had he forgotten all about their kisses? She was curious and a bit angry all at once. How dare he stir things up again with this request? She'd finally reconciled herself to the fact that the kisses were an isolated incident and that was fine. It was how she'd wanted things between them, after all. She'd been the one to walk away that day on the headlands. His silence was merely him respecting her wishes and now there was this note. What did he want? A church was hardly a clandestine meeting place. She should not be disappointed by that. But she was.

Her questions had to wait. Cade made no move, no glance until after the service when he and Captain Penhaligon crossed the aisle as any neighbour might do to visit. 'Miss Treleven, might I have a moment once the church clears out?' His voice was quiet at her ear, his touch light at her sleeve, all of it proper. No one would ever guess he'd rolled her beneath him in the sand six days ago and kissed her senseless until waves had wet the tips of her boots, not even her. At least not until she looked at his eyes, blue and hot, two banked coals burning just for her. She had not imagined it that day on the beach. He wanted her. The realisation thrummed through her, made her breath catch, made her pulse race, and time stand still. It took an age for the church to clear out.

'Are you ready for your surprise?' Cade asked once the church was empty. His blue eyes danced as he took both of her hands. Whatever he was up to, he was excited about it.

'I wasn't aware I was getting one.' She smiled, finding his mood infectious.

He sat her down in the pew with firm instructions. 'Close your eyes.' For a moment, she thought he was going to kiss her but then he let go of her hands and she felt him move away. Thank goodness she hadn't done anything foolish like part her lips. He was used to more sophisticated women who knew what they wanted from a man.

'Can I look now?' she called to him.

'No, this is not something to see. It's something to hear,' he called back, striking the first gentle chords of her surprise. He'd written her a song! She gasped with the realisation. Cador Kitto had *composed* her a song when he was supposed to be composing a cantata. The song was beautiful, deceptively simple in its arrangement, the music was soft, surging and ebbing like waves against the shore. Her eyes flew open despite his instructions. He'd written the beach! *Their* beach. Where they'd talked and kissed. The music told the story of their words, sometimes sharp, sometimes reluctant, sometimes sweet accord.

Rosenwyn couldn't look away. Her gaze was riveted on Cade's back, on his hands, on his head, bent forward as he played. He was entirely absorbed in the music, turning his soul over to it. The sight was mesmerising and hauntingly erotic. How many women had he teased with such an image, giving them a glimpse of what it would be like if they gave themselves over to him under more intimate circumstances? Although this was intimate enough. He was telling their story in music, binding them together with a song. The piano keys danced, flitting suddenly in a jump and a skip and then surged into strong, loud, crashing chords. She recognised this. The tide had come in. The song was nearly done. He finished with a flourish.

Cade turned from the bench, his eyes moving to where she sat. 'Did my surprise please you?'

'I am stunned.' It was the best way to describe it. 'What did I do to deserve it?'

'You helped me find the cantata.' He beamed at her as he crossed the space between them. 'That day in Budoc Lane and on the beach, you helped me find the story I wanted to tell. I wanted to thank you.' He gave her a long look, a furrow forming between his eyes. 'What's wrong? You did like it, didn't you?'

Did she like it? She liked it and hated it. How dare he play with her emotions? For what purpose did he compose that song when he knew very well there could be *no* consequence? He was not the sort of man she should seek out, but he was the man she wanted. Oh, what foolishness! Why did her heart have to choose a man driven to moods by his passions and his secrets, a man plagued by a dark past, who struggled with ghosts, who was far from perfect and near to flawed? A man who would not stay. A man who would leave after Christmas. It was to have been the perfect scenario. Why now did it seem an impossible one—to only have him for fourteen days and then give him up. The song had been a thank you, but it had also been an invitation to something dangerous, something extraordinary. He wanted her.

'Why did you do it, Cade, when you know very well…?' She couldn't finish the sentence. The words were too risky, they exposed too much of her, what she wanted, what she felt. There was always the chance she was wrong, that she'd read too much into it.

'*What* do I know very well?' he prompted, taking her hands again.

'That flirting with me can lead nowhere,' Rosenwyn said boldly and then the floodgates burst. 'You steal kisses, you write me a song, you are a man of the world. These things mean little to you, but…' Her voice faded and this time he let her cry off.

'But you're afraid those things might mean more to you, that you can't help but ascribe meaning to them. It's the meaning that frightens you, not the passion,' he finished for her. 'Tell me why.'

The church had grown quiet and the silence stretched between them until Cade gave a soft laugh. 'It's harder when the shoe's on the other foot, isn't it? I told you about my ghosts. Why don't you tell me about yours?'

'I don't have ghosts.' She tipped her chin up defiantly.

'Yes, you do.' He laced his fingers through hers. 'Why is it that a woman of your musical talent and good looks has fled London? You were so well thought of,

Sébastien Érard had you try out his prototype and yet you've tucked yourself away in Porth Karrek and dedicated yourself to community work? It doesn't make sense. You should have caught a husband long before now.' He smiled. 'I've had a week to think about you, Rose, and the pieces don't add up. I'm an open book in comparison to you.'

'London was disappointing. I need more from life than being an ornament on a husband's arm.' It wasn't untrue, it just wasn't the reason she'd left. She rose. If she didn't leave now, he would have all her secrets out of her and perhaps more than she was willing to give.

He rose with her, helping her with her coat, his hands lingering at her shoulders in his customary fashion. 'I'll walk you home. There is something I want to ask you.' He was letting her keep her secrets, but there would be a price for that. Perhaps he would stop pursuing her altogether, another week gone until she saw him again in church. This was the second time she'd refused him and they were both aware of the subtle dance between them, he advancing and she retreating when he got too close. Every time she retreated, time slipped away. He would not be here for ever. That was the double bind, the blessing and the curse. If she waited much longer, the decision would be made for her and Cade Kitto would move back into the world and beyond her.

Outside, it was cold, December weather firmly entrenched. She shivered despite the fur at her throat, but Cade seemed at ease in the wind, his greatcoat hanging open, its skirts swirling as they walked. 'I need your help with finishing the cantata. I have a week before rehearsals begin. Would you come to the gatehouse tomorrow? I want to play the cantata for you and you can advise me on a section I'm struggling with.'

It sounded delightful, to use her music skills again, but she needed to point out how inappropriate the invitation was. This was England, not the liberal courts of Europe. 'I am flattered, truly, but an unmarried man doesn't invite an unmarried woman to his home, even in Porth Karrek.'

Cade gave her a sly grin. 'I'm not inviting. You are returning these.' He reached into the pocket of his great-coat and pulled out his gloves. 'You can say I left them at the church. Bring your maid and send her up to the kitchen at Karrek House.'

She smiled at his ingenuity. 'You've done this before,' she teased. But there was truth behind it. How many times had he made such assignations? Did she dare allow herself to be entangled in such an arrangement? The balance between them would always be unequal. His larks were not her larks. Dashiell had taken her virginity, but she still had her heart. She would not part with it lightly. She knew what it would mean if she returned Cade's gloves. There would be no going back. She would need to keep a tight rein on her feelings if she wanted to emerge unscathed. She knew, too, what it meant if she did not return his gloves. He would not enquire again. This was the third ask.

At the drive leading to Treleven House, Cade pulled her aside into the trees. 'There's something else I need before you go,' he whispered. 'This.'

He kissed her long and full, his tongue teasing hers until he wrung a moan of pure pleasure from her. Kissing him was intoxicating, playful and sensual by turn until she was entirely lost in it—in him, in the game—

and overwhelmed by the knowledge that there could be so much more if only she wouldn't hold back. His eyes, his body said as much without words. 'I've wanted this all week, Rose. When I wasn't thinking of the cantata, I was thinking of this, of the beach, of having you beneath me again, your mouth against mine, your body against mine.' He moved, his hips hard against hers, his desire evident in the most physical of ways. 'Do not doubt how much I want you, Rose, secrets and all,' he murmured at her ear. 'Say you'll come tomorrow. You won't regret it. We'll take it slow. Nothing will happen that you don't want.' That was her fear. It would be easy to want to do it all with him. Even now, with her mind conflicted, her body was roused beyond measure. She knew before she reached the front door she would return his gloves in the morning. She had nothing to lose but her heart.

Chapter Ten

The gloves were the first of many reasons Rosenwyn found to visit the gatehouse during the next week. When Ayleth asked where she was going on Tuesday, she claimed a need to visit Emily Faulkner at Karrek House to look over a pair of silver hair clips she'd ordered for Marianne as a Christmas surprise. On Wednesday she brought cakes and biscuits and other Christmas treats from Treleven House, each day staying longer as the cantata took shape until it became clear the cantata would be complete by Friday, right on schedule.

On Thursday, she began to resent Friday. She didn't want this to end. Watching him work was intoxicating, kissing him was addicting and, like any good addict, she knew kissing Cade wouldn't always be enough for her. It was already not enough. Every day she wanted a little more of him, a little more of his mouth, his body, his mind, his soul. But she couldn't have those things for free. She'd have to give a little of herself in exchange and there was no guarantee she'd get that piece back. That frightened her. She might have survived Dashiell Custis, but it had cost her something.

She'd believed him. She'd trusted Dashiell and he had not been worthy of either her belief or her trust.

Cade was struggling too, that became evident as Friday arrived. Each day he'd become a little more withdrawn with his words and more physical with his passion. There was a desperation to his kisses. Perhaps this was what it was like to live with an artist? Mood swings and emotions always on the surface as they created. But Rosenwyn had seen him in Chegwins'. Whatever was driving him was about more than an artistic temperament.

Late Friday afternoon, Cade finished playing the accompaniment for the last aria. The room fell silent. He stretched at the bench, rolling his shoulders to relieve the taut muscles. She rose and went to him, kneading his shoulders with firm, practised hands. This had become another of her self-prescribed duties in assisting. 'You're tight.' She massaged the base of his neck, her hands on bare skin. Even with her present, he didn't wear a cravat when he worked and his shirt was loose affording her access. 'Do you need me to play some of it?' When his shoulders hurt too much to play or his hands cramped from composing, she had played for him, playing back the music he'd written. They'd made a good team.

'I think we're done.' Cade leaned back, his head against her stomach, his eyes closed. *We*. That had become a new addition over the week. We. Our. Us. They were together in this. He reached a hand up and took hers where it worked at his shoulder. 'I should walk you home and then I can tidy the piece up tonight. We can go into Penzance tomorrow and have copies printed.' He sighed. 'Just in time, too. Rehearsals can begin Sunday afternoon.' She knew what that meant. On Sunday, it would be nine days until Christmas Eve. Ten days until Cade was free to go, no longer required to stay in Porth Karrek. They would go into Penzance tomorrow, the nearest town with a printing press, and then their life in the little gatehouse would come to a close. There would be no more reason to visit him, to work with him.

'We should celebrate tomorrow.' Cade craned his neck and looked up at her with those disarming blue eyes. It was the first time he'd shaken off the megrims that had plagued him during the week. As for herself, she'd never felt less like celebrating. This was the part she'd warned herself against, the part where she had to realise this association meant less to him than it did to her. There had been women before her and there would be women after her, women who would massage his neck, bring him food, see to his laundry and in exchange he would shower them with his kisses, his smiles, the gift of watching a genius at work.

'Perhaps we could have a celebratory meal in Penzance, one you didn't have to cook.' His grin faded and he turned around on the bench to face her, to wrap his hands about her waist and draw her on to his lap. 'The cantata is finished on time. Don't you want to celebrate, Rose?'

Rose. She hardly remembered when he'd stopped calling her Rosenwyn and adopted the familiar, so naturally had their intimacy grown. 'I am happy the cantata is done.' She smiled. He'd worked hard. How could she tell him she was unhappy it was finished? Or that she didn't want him to finish it because of what it meant. For a girl who liked Christmas, she was in no hurry for it to arrive this year. 'I will miss this. I enjoyed working with you.' She'd felt useful in a way that transcended assembling charity baskets. She'd used her music this week. She missed that part of her life in London.

His brow furrowed as he studied her. 'This is not the end, Rose. We have time yet. There are rehearsals.'

'And all the festivities.' She smiled again, looking for the silver lining. Maybe if she smiled enough she'd convince herself she was happy. 'We have the bonfire and the Gwav Gool party.' She stopped, getting no response from him. Ah, so it wasn't just the gin and cake progression that prodded his ghosts. It was the whole of Christmas. It hit her in full force how awful that he'd been consigned to write a cantata to celebrate a season he despised in a place that held difficult memories. No wonder it had proved difficult to start.

Her arms went about his neck and she breathed him in, all soap and winter spice. 'Why don't you like Christmas, Cade?'

'It's a busy time of year for composers.' He tried to joke. 'We spend the season putting together your entertainments.' He kissed her lightly at first, his hand threading its way through the careful bun at her nape until he cradled her head in his palm. She felt his mouth smile against hers. 'All those rehearsals and festivities mean I have to share you and maybe I don't want to.' She sensed he was covering something up with his flattering words, but it was easier to believe in it than question it.

Cade did not want to walk her home. He wanted to walk her upstairs to his bedroom, to take down her hair, to undo her gown, to make love to her until her body was imprinted on his so that he'd forget his demons and she might forget hers. He was not the only one with ghosts to lay and hers were in evidence today. The end of the project was forcing her towards a decision; *he* was forcing her towards a decision—to open up to him, body and mind. He wanted to know her, he wanted her to know herself, to stop hiding.

He kissed her, long and slow, his hand sliding up her skirts, along the curve of her calf, over the length of silk-stockinged thigh until he reached the warm core of her, curls already damp. Would she allow him? 'Often pleasure exorcises our ghosts or at least settles them,' he murmured against the shell of her ear. 'Let me give you a little pleasure, Rose.' He touched her then, finding the tiny nucleus at her core. She gave a sharp, sweet gasp of acquiescence to him, to pleasure, encouraging him. Had he ever wanted to give a woman pleasure this badly?

She moaned against his lips, his mouth taking her cry with a kiss. She pressed against his hand, moving against his palm, her body searching for more and even then, he felt the frustrated restraint in her, the restraint that exerted itself even now when her body was on the brink of pleasure, of satisfaction. 'Let go, there is no harm in this pleasure, Rose,' he murmured his encouragement, his own voice husky in anticipation of her fulfilment. 'Let me watch you fly for just a moment, Rose.' Perhaps she would do it for him, if she wouldn't do it for herself. In the next moment the choice was beyond her. Whatever restraint she had lost the battle, overcome at the end by pleasure. She cried out, bucking against his hand, her arms about his neck gripping him tight as if he were her only anchor in a storm and Cade revelled in it. He revelled in her joy, her discovery, the awe in her eyes and the shadow as she breathed, 'I didn't know... I didn't know. Oh, sweet heavens, Cade, I didn't know.'

But he knew. In a blinding strike of insight, Cador Kitto, man of the world, knew. There had been a man before. One who had disappointed her, physically, emotionally. Anger for the unknown cad who'd not shown her pleasure simmered in Cade. Rose deserved the best a man had to offer. Their eyes met, locked. He whispered a single word, 'Who?'

She didn't dissemble, didn't pretend she didn't understand what he was asking. She simply shook her head. 'No one of any consequence. It is in the past.'

That wasn't true. Her ghost was in the present, every time they kissed, every time he touched her, every time desire surged between them, and demanded she acknowledge it—the past was there. 'You are afraid of desire,' Cade pressed her, fearing the worst. What had happened to create that fear? 'Who hurt you?' Whoever it was, Cade would dust off his rapiers and call him out.

'It's not like that, Cade.' Her hand soothed the lines from his brow, understanding what he thought, and she quickly disabused him. 'I hurt myself. He did nothing without my permission, permission I should not have given.' She bit her lip and attempted to move off his lap. He held her tight. If she left him now, he would lose the moment. 'I should not have allowed this.' She tried again to rise.

'I cannot let you go thinking you are to blame. That somehow you are the source of your own hurt.' He certainly didn't want her thinking she'd played the wanton on his lap. Her pleasure had been at *his* invitation, not hers. She had every right to enjoy it. 'Tell me what happened, Rose.' He would, by God, fix it and put her world to rights as she had done for his.

Chapter Eleven

Rosenwyn shifted on his lap. She did not want to tell him. No one liked admitting how foolish they'd been, especially to someone they cared about. It would only prove his belief that she had indeed lived a sheltered and naïve life. 'It's too embarrassing. You will think me the most green of girls.' She'd made one mistake and it had cost her everything a young woman held dear, her one recommending attribute to men of good birth, the sort of men her parents wished her to marry.

Cade bent his forehead to hers with a smile. 'You know my secrets, surely you can give me one of yours in exchange. It is just the two of us here in the gate-house. Your secret will be safe with me, whatever it is.'

'It's not my secret I'm worried about. It's me,' Rosen-wyn confessed. 'You might not look at me the same way.'

'Your resistance makes me all the more curious— isn't that what you said to me on the beach?' Cade gave a soft, encouraging laugh. 'It's not the looking at you differently that worries you. It's that you think I might reject you. Did you reject me after I told you about my family?'

'It's not the same,' Rosenwyn argued.

'I think it is. I risked much in telling you about my family. You are the daughter of a gentleman, a child of privilege and I have some fame, that's true. But at the end of the day I am still a miner's son, a poor boy. I have no rank, only what the notice my talent brings me. To open myself to you was an enormous risk.' He whispered at her ear, 'Trust me, Rose. Tell me who put the hesitance in your kisses, the question in your pleasure?'

There would be no more coaxing. The parlour was silent except for the sound of flames licking logs in the fireplace. He was offering her a bridge, a way to cross over, a way for them to be together. This was about more than sharing an experience, it was about reciprocating his trust in her with her trust in him. He'd trusted her with his story, trusted her with his music. He wanted the same from her. If she could not give him that, they would end right here on the piano bench. He would walk her home because politeness demanded it, but she would not go into Penzance with him tomorrow, would not sit beside him in the family pew at church, would not steal kisses from him beneath the kissing bough. Those were just superficial things she'd lose. The real loss would be in losing *him*, in losing the right to watch him work, the right to watch him struggle, the right to help him in both. She wasn't ready to let go, not yet.

Rosenwyn drew a breath for courage. She could not tell him the sanitised version she'd told her sisters. She would have to tell him all of it. 'His name was Dashiell Custis, the younger son of a viscount. I met him two years ago in London during the Season and we fell madly in love, or so I thought. He flattered me with flowers and gifts and waltzes every night. He made no secret of courting me and I made no secret of liking it. He was fun and reckless. He was handsome and charming and broke. I knew he had no money, only a small property in Hertfordshire that came from an aunt. But one doesn't care about the money when one thinks they're in love. I didn't. I had money enough for both of us.

'He wanted to elope. The Season was coming to a close and he said he didn't want to wait for a long engagement during which we'd be separated most of the time. He had to go to Hertfordshire and, being unmarried, I could hardly accompany him. Why not marry, he argued. We could go there together and put the place to rights. The idea appealed to me.'

Cade laughed softly. 'I'm sure it did, Miss Fix-It. You might be the only woman in England who would delight in renovating a ramshackle estate for her honeymoon.'

'That might be true.' She smiled, delighting in the knowledge that Cade knew her so well. In the months she and Dashiell had been together, he'd never understood her as well as Cade did after only a few weeks. 'I didn't get the chance to find out. Eaton had heard rumours of the elopement at his club and other rumours, too: rumours that Dashiell's property was mortgaged, that his need for money was immediate, so immediate he was willing to marry a Cornish country girl to get his hands on some blunt. He couldn't wait for an engagement. The people who had loaned him money weren't a gentleman's bankers, willing to take an engagement as collateral for later payment.

'Eaton came to me straight away and told me. It stopped the elopement, but…' She paused here as if to warn him of what came next. 'I'd already slept with him. I was that sure of him, that sure we'd be man and wife within the month. There was no reason to wait and I let him talk me into it because I wanted to. He was so earnest in his wanting, so eager. All that was true, just not for the reasons I thought. The sooner he could bed me, the sooner he could ensure his claim to me. If I was pregnant, all the better to bind me to him. There'd be no turning back. I simply wouldn't be able to.' She tried for a smile and a laugh to minimise the desperate straits she'd faced.

'Now you see why I must be so careful. I have a reckless streak that cannot be indulged. I was doing well. I didn't go to London last year and I won't go this year, but then you came along and temptation has found me anyway.' She ran a hand through his hair. 'You with your golden good looks and easy touches, those blue eyes that gaze right through me, *into* me. You remind me of him with your earnestness and enthusiasm and that scares me. I can't afford to make the same mistake twice, Cade.'

She felt his hands tighten against her back, saw his blue eyes cloud as the smile faded from his face. She had insulted him with the truth. 'I am nothing like him, Rose. I have been all that is honest with you.' But he had to end his case there because they both knew it would come out wrong if he made it. He *had* been honest. In some ways he was no better than Dashiell Custis. He had not promised her a future because he didn't have one to offer. He had offered her only friendship because Jock Treleven's daughters were meant for better than a composer of limited celebrity. He'd kissed her because she'd permitted it. He'd shown her pleasure tonight because she'd permitted that, too, knowing full well there were no promises behind it.

'I know, Cade. You *have* been honest and that makes

you far more frightening than Dashiell Custis ever was. With you, I haven't any excuses for my actions. With you, I can't claim I misunderstand the situation.' It was the only excuse she allowed herself about Custis. She had made her decisions with him based on false promises. That was nowhere near the case here.

Cade reached up a hand to tuck a loose strand of hair back behind her ear. 'Everyone makes mistakes, everyone misjudges people at some point and whether it's fair or not, everyone pays. Would it help to know you aren't alone in that regard?' He gave her one of his easy smiles and her worries faded. Cade was as good as his word. He wasn't going to reject her, wasn't going to be disappointed by her brush with disaster.

She smiled back at him, laying her head against his shoulder and snuggling into him, enjoying the comfort of his arm about her. 'Do I sense a confession coming on?'

He kissed the top of her head. 'Yes. You wanted to know why I wasn't in Vienna.'

'You said there was no work to be had. Was that not true?' She hoped it was. She didn't want a lie from him, not even the smallest of lies.

'It is true. But there was a reason for it. I was up for the post of court musician to a prince. He chose someone else. The man who got the post is a talented man, it's not undeserved, but the reason I didn't get it is that a woman spoke poison about me because she wanted more of my attention than I was willing to give her. When she didn't receive it, she whispered horrible things about my character in the Prince's ear. In fact, it wasn't just the Prince's ear she whispered them in. When she was done, no one was interested in hiring a profligate, amoral rake, who spent his money on debauched living, a claim, which I assure you, was grossly exaggerated. I've never been the worst man at anyone's court, although to be fair, I've never been the best either.'

'I appreciate your honesty,' Rosenwyn murmured. So that was the answer as to why he was here. A vicious tongue had cost him his livelihood, although he'd not been an innocent victim. She knew what he meant by not being the 'best man' at any court either. He dallied on occasions with married women and that was always a risky business. She didn't condone it, but that was the cosmopolitan life of the cities. She'd seen it in London, too. At least he'd owned up to it. 'I am sorry...' she drew his mouth down to hers '...but not too sorry. I would not have met you if you'd stayed in Vienna.' She kissed him then, softly and tenderly. 'We're both exiles, but for different reasons. I fled London because the rumours were true. You fled Vienna because the rumours were false.' Both of them had been played by dishonest people. How interesting to discover yet one more thing they had in common, when two weeks ago she'd thought they were nothing alike.

He kissed her in return, hungry and insistent, his desire evident against her thigh, through layers of trousers and skirts. He was the one who drew back this time and set her off his lap. 'I won't pretend I don't want you, Rose. I would claim more than kisses from you if I could. Wolves don't lurk only in the woods.' He was warning her, giving her far more consideration than Dashiell ever had. Dashiell had seen her passion and manipulated it. Cade was giving her a choice because in the end she was the one who risked the most if this went any further. It wasn't only the physical risks, but the emotional ones. Cade had closed himself off years ago. He allowed himself only the indulgence of short physical affairs, which made her gamble all the more mortifying. He might not be capable or willing of giving her anything more even if she chanced it.

At the door, he helped her into her blue coat, his hands lingering at her shoulders. 'Will you come to Penzance tomorrow?'

'I thought it was already decided.' She tied her bonnet on, but her fingers fumbled with the bow, desire and anticipation rising between them once more. He was asking again in the subtle way he'd asked her to come to the gatehouse.

Cade shrugged into his greatcoat and gave her a stern look. 'That was before.' Before he'd pleasured her on a piano bench, before they'd confessed another piece of their souls to one another. Going to Penzance tomorrow was no longer just about printing copies of the cantata. This would be their chance to claim a moment out of time where they could be together, perhaps their only chance. It could be done. The question remained: Should it be?

They did not talk of Penzance as he walked her home along the oft-travelled road that led between Karrek House and the Treleven estate. At the entrance to the drive where the shadows still hid them from view, he simply said, 'I want to leave at eight. Send me a note if you change your mind, Rose.' He bowed over her hand and kissed it. 'I will understand if you do.'

'I won't.' She squeezed his hand in assurance, her gaze steady. 'I'll see you in the morning.' It was tomorrow or not at all.

Chapter Twelve

Penzance, with its population of fifteen hundred, was
by no means a big town, but it was larger than Porth
Karrek and that made all the difference. Penzance
sported a printing press, more than one inn and spe-
cialised shops that allowed a customer more choices.
It was also closer than travelling inland to Truro. Cade
and Rosenwyn's first stop had been the printer's, leaving strict instructions that the copies be ready that afternoon. Then, they took to the streets.

The town boasted a festive air as they enjoyed the
shops before the day turned busy. Merchants' windows were decorated with greenery and crammed full
of Christmas delicacies. They settled at the Turk's Head
inn for an early lunch featuring fish pie with a flaky
crust. They were careful to sit away from the window
where they could be noticed. They were being discreet.
Penzance was close enough to Porth Karrek that one
never knew who one might meet.

'I've reserved a room so that you can refresh yourself
and rest this afternoon while we wait for the printer.'
Cade calmly slid a key towards her and Rosenwyn's
anticipation ratcheted a final notch as she took it. She

hoped she looked as calm as Cade sounded. She'd been on full alert all morning, bristling with awareness of what was to come. There was nothing insinuating in his tone, nothing someone at a nearby table might take as a salacious overture. The implication of his offer was clear to her alone: he would join her shortly.

The room upstairs was small, but clean and bright with whitewashed walls and white curtains at the window overlooking the harbour. The tiny room was dominated by a painted iron bedstead covered in a crisp blue and white counterpane. Other than the bed, the room's only occupants were a washstand and a chair. Rosenwyn hung up her bonnet and coat on a peg. She poured water into the basin and washed her face, took off her half-boots and debated the merits of taking off anything else. Perhaps Cade would like to do that for her? The very thought of being undressed by him, of feeling his long, exquisite fingers on her skin made her shiver in wicked anticipation.

She would like to undress him. She'd start with his cravat, then his jacket. She leaned back against the pillows with a smile. This would be no mercenary wedding night where the bride cowered in a chemise beneath the blankets waiting for the bridegroom to cover her in a perfunctory two-minute ordeal. This was to be lovemaking in the afternoon, a lingering, sensual discovery between two curious and consenting adults. Neither of whom were squeamish virgins. They needn't hurry. They had hours.

A soft rap on the door announced Cade's arrival. He slipped inside and gave a quizzing smile at the sight of her fully clothed. 'Should I come back?'

Rosenwyn got up from the bed and came to him,

hands plucking out his cravat pin and slowly unwinding the length of white cloth from about his neck. 'No, you're just in time.' She gave him a flirty glance, laying aside the pin with the cloth.

'Hmm. In time for what?' He played along, letting her help him out of his jacket.

'For me to undress you.' She worked the buttons of his waistcoat open and then carefully unclipped his watch fob. Rosenwyn pulled his shirttails free of his trouser band and stepped back to admire her work. It was good work, too. 'I like you like this, a little rumpled. You look like a medieval prince who's just come in from swordplay.'

He laughed. 'You have a fantastical imagination.' He closed the distance between them and grabbed her about the waist, dragging her close for a kiss.

'No, no, no!' She pushed at him playfully. 'I am nowhere near done undressing you.' There were cuffs to unfasten and boots to pull off, and then at last she could apply herself to stripping him out of his shirt and trousers. She was a little breathless herself as she divested him of his shirt. Caught up in her own game meant to tease him, she'd ended up teasing herself as well.

Rosenwyn ran her hands up his bare chest, skimming the muscled leanness of him as she discovered him, learned him, all his ridges and planes. She murmured in appreciation, drawing a fingernail across the flat of his nipple as he sucked in his breath. 'You like that.' It was a statement, not a question. She was filing the information away for another time when it might be useful.

'Breeches next, I think.' Her bold hand reached for him, moulding him through his trousers while she teased him with a smile.

'You are a vixen of the first water,' Cade growled, attempting to steal a kiss. 'The moment those trousers are off, it's your turn, minx. Don't think I'll make it easy on you.'

'Oh, I intend to look my fill first.' She laughed and worked open his breeches. Stripping him was erotic, fun. Being in charge had done wonders for settling her nerves or maybe it was the man himself who'd settled them. Being with Cade was easy, comfortable. She pushed his breeches down past lean hips and long thighs, and despite his teasing threats to the contrary, he let her look, let her admire; all of him was unabashedly on display for her. In her admiration, she stepped backwards, knees hitting the bed, and she sat down hard, never once letting her gaze waver. Who knew when she would get to look on such masculine beauty again? Skin like the smoothest alabaster, without a scar, lean strong thighs that framed a large shaft standing at the ready. Those attributes combined with the dramatic angles of his face made him a sculptor's dream, *her* dream.

He came towards her then, all swagger and a wicked light in his blue eyes. 'I take it I pass muster.' He kissed her, covering her with his body until she was pressed back to the bed, her wrists shackled with his hands.

'More than pass.' She was breathless with excitement, with want. They were still teasing, still playing, but there was an edge to that play now that he was revealed in full, a reminder that he was a potent, virile man. The composer, the genius, was set aside, replaced by this intoxicating male. Did his former lovers understand that? In the bedroom he wanted to be loved for himself, not for his talents?

'Now, let us see to you, my dear.' Cade made short

work of her clothes, her undressing taking a different pace than his, and served a different purpose. The quality of their play shifted from foreplay to the mid-game that presaged consummation. Their play was no longer about preparing for passion, but initiating passion's first overtures. He saved her stockings for last, rolling them down bended knees only to reverse the route with his hands moments later, running them up her calves, her thighs, spreading her apart as he came until she was intimately exposed to him.

She closed her eyes, buried her hands in the depths of the bedcovers, ready for his hand, ready for his touch. She knew what this would feel like, the pleasure it would bring. But it was not his hand that touched her, but his mouth, his tongue and, despite her bracing, she gasped her surprise, her eyes flying open. He chuckled, the warmth of his breath feathering her curls. 'You like that.' He borrowed her words. 'I'll make a note of it.'

'Not too many notes just now, I hope?' She nudged him with her leg, encouraging him to go on. Was there anything more erotic than Cade's blue eyes looking up at her from the cradle of her thighs? It was enough to make a girl swoon, but then she'd miss what might very well be one of the best experiences of her life. Rosenwyn had no intention of missing this. She laid back against the pillows and sighed as Cade ran his tongue along the seam of her entrance, up to the nest where her nub lay hidden like a secret treasure, then he licked and teased until the nub throbbed, sending tingling pulses of life shooting from its core. The pleasure wrought by his hand paled in comparison to the pleasure he was extracting now with his tongue and she gave herself over to it, letting it push her towards completion until at last she was there, reeling on pleasure's edge, reaching out and claiming it, bucking hard against Cade lest she be denied any moment of it.

Exquisite. That was the word for it, she thought as awareness returned to her. Cade lay beside her, his blond head propped in his hand, watching her recover, his blue eyes tender in their regard. Never had there been anything like this between her and Dashiell; not in the giving of the pleasure or the aftermath. No. She would not think about that. She would not compare, but how could she not? She might have technical experience, but she was in uncharted waters now. She hadn't known such a thing was possible or that people did such things to one another, derived such pleasure from it. And they weren't even done. There was the joining yet, the end game, and she could hardly wait.

'Cade,' she whispered his name, rolling to her side to face him. 'It's time for your pleasure now. *Our* pleasure. I think this has been one-sided long enough.' Then she made her move.

Good Lord, she was straddling him! She intended to ride him astride and Cade found the prospect entirely compelling. Oh, to hell with delicate words, he found it entirely *erotic*, the sexiest thing a woman had done to him for a long time. Perhaps that was because Rosenwyn was the one doing it. She was a copper-haired Godiva atop him, the long skeins of burnished copper covering her breasts, framing her face while her green eyes burned and her pink mouth smiled like the vixen she was. She rose up and levered herself over him, teasing the tip of him with the merest of contact at her entrance. It seemed to him that his phallus actually strained upwards in its efforts to reach her. He groaned. 'Rose, show mercy.'

She leaned forward and kissed him on the mouth. 'Mercy is granted. All you had to do was ask.' She slid down on him then, taking him inside, struggling at the end to take all of him.

He framed her hips with his hands. 'Rise up a bit, love, and come down again,' he murmured. Ah, that was good. He loved that, loved sheathing and re-sheathing himself in her and her body loved it, too. He felt the residual tightness in her fade, felt her body accommodating him until the fit was perfect. Then came the rhythm—back and forth she moved on him, tossing her hair behind her shoulders, her breasts bared now for him, for his eyes, for his hands. He cupped them, lifting them with his palms, thumbing the pink peaks of her nipples until they were as erect as the rest of him and she moaned, losing herself both in the pleasure she gave and the pleasure she received.

Cade felt his body gather and tighten in the primal sign of impending release. He was about to spend. He would never withdraw in time with her on top. He reached for her, pulling her to him, her breasts pressed to his chest, and rolled. Her jade eyes flashed up at him in surprise, her words lost in a gasp as he thrust once, twice, three times as pleasure took her. Only then did he leave her, making a gentleman's finish in the sheets, but by all the saints, what a ride it had been, right up until the end, both of them panting. It had been safe, too. He knew his responsibility. He was not a rutting stag of a man who'd risk getting a woman with child.

He pulled her into his arms, snuggling her against him as he steadied his breathing. The intensity of their coupling had stunned him. He'd not expected such a visceral response, but truly it had shaken him completely, taken him unawares with its depth, drained him completely and, in its place, left him with a sense of drowsy peace. When was the last time lovemaking had left him too boneless to move, to reach over the side of the bed for his breeches and leave? Had there ever even been such a time?

He must have dozed, something he was usually careful not to do. When he awoke, Rose had moved. She was no longer snuggled against him, but propped on her side, drawing delicate designs on his chest. 'How long have you been staring at me?' Cade ventured goodnaturedly. In truth, the male in him was pleased with the idea that his body appealed to her.

'Not long.' She smiled. 'Although I think I could look at you for hours and never tire of it.'

He drew her to him, wanting her back where she belonged, nestled against him, her head tucked at his shoulder. 'That might be a waste of our time.' He chuckled, but it did prompt a serious concern. The sands in the hourglass were running out. The scores would be ready and they would have to go home. Tomorrow was Rose Sunday, the third Sunday in Advent. They would be busy with other things, other people. Tomorrow, everything would change. With his other lovers, it would have provided a convenient means of backing away from the affair. With Rose, he simply wasn't ready. If one didn't count today, there were nine days until Christmas Eve. He wanted each one of them with her. 'Rose, will you play for me?'

'Play? The piano?' She looked up, confused.

'Yes. For the cantata. I need a pianist. It can't be me. I'll be too busy directing. I have the other instruments accounted for, thanks to your sisters, but I have no one at the piano. Please, say you'll do it.'

We could be at rehearsal every day together. I could bask in your talent, in your company that much longer without contriving excuses to see you.

'Of course I'll do it.' She smiled and he saw how much the idea pleased her. Good. This was his gift to her, a chance for her to reclaim whatever it was she'd lost in London. When that cad had compromised her, he'd taken more than her virginity. He'd take her opportunity to perform, to find fulfilment through her music. She had not said as much. But she didn't need to. He was a musician. He knew. How often did he wonder what he'd be without his music? He'd never had to find out, but she had.

'Cade, where will you go when you're finished in Porth Karrek?' Rose asked casually, but Cade wasn't fooled. It was a serious question even if they hadn't just made love. He needed to contemplate his future.

'Back to London. There's a new Royal Academy of Music that's just opened. It would be good to be part of their pantheon of composers.' It was a pat answer, one that sounded more impressive than it was. In reality, he would have to apply and be accepted as one of their masters. They would have to be impressed with his work. He'd need references. He hoped Falmage might be of use there. Falmage had politely backed off the idea of a private concert. Now, Cade was regretting it from a professional standpoint. He needed all the references he could get.

'You could stay.' Rose looked up at him with those

sharp green eyes of hers, bold as always. 'Why hurry back to London? It's months yet before the Season and you can make enquiries by letter.'

It was the worst, best, most tempting idea he'd heard in a while; to stay meant a chance to steal more afternoons like this, but to what purpose? They would have to end eventually. 'Stay here and throw myself on Captain Penhaligon's charity? How long do you suppose he'll let me stay in the gatehouse once our business is concluded?' Cade chuckled to ease the sting. There were practicalities to consider. 'What would I do with myself all day with no work?' Such things were not part of Rose's world. In the short term, they didn't have to take their differing backgrounds seriously. In the long term, however, they did. He might be famous, but he was a working man. She was a baronet's daughter.

Rose lifted up to face him, warming to her subject. 'We could find you work. Reverend Maddern could have you work with the choir, or you could compose some pieces for Sundays. You could give music lessons to the children. We'd keep you busy.'

'I think you're forgetting something, Rose,' Cade offered gently, not wanting to be the killjoy she accused him of being. 'I need to be paid for those services. I can't perform them for free.' He wasn't like Rosenwyn, who could spend her days assembling baskets for the poor or knitting socks for the needy, or working with children because she *wanted* to. She had no need of money, no need for anything but something to fill her time. He, on the other hand, could not give away his talents for free.

Even then, his valiant Rose wasn't deterred. 'Perhaps that could be arranged, too. You never know until you ask.' She gave him a worrisomely smug smile.

'Rose,' he warned, sensing the direction of her thoughts and plots. Rose was a fixer and, while it was tempting to let her fix him, his pride would never recover. He would not have it said that he used her for her dowry, her connections. Those rumours would make him appear no better than Dashiell Custis. He couldn't subject her to that. Nor could he subject himself to it. If he let her meddle, and if she was successful, one day she would look at him with distaste and she would feel betrayed. 'I do not beg and I do not take charity. I cannot take another handout from Reverend Maddern again. He sent me to school all those years ago and he was the one who put the word in the good Captain's ear about the commission. I am a Kitto and we take care of ourselves.' And he would take care of her, whether she liked his solutions or not. They'd promised themselves this one day, nothing more. He could not let her renegotiate the nature of their agreement.

Rose slid down beside him. 'Understood.' Her hand slipped beneath the covers, seeking until she found him lying in a state of semi-readiness, a state she easily remedied, his shaft jumping to her touch like a well-trained hound to heel. She stroked him until he was hard in her hand and whispered, 'Except perhaps in bed, Cade. You might find begging has its uses.' As long as one of them wasn't begging to stay, he might just survive this.

Chapter Thirteen

December 15th, 1822, Rose Sunday, the third Sunday in Advent

Rosenwyn found the solution to all of Cade's needs in church of all places, in the middle of Reverend Maddern's sermon on joy. She would beg Eaton's empty house for Cade. It wouldn't really even be begging if she framed it right. It would be doing Eaton a favour. The lovely estate stood empty most of the year and Eaton himself had complained about the property going to waste on several occasions. Eaton was always looking for a way to 'improve' Cornwall, as he liked to put it. This just might be the way to keep Cade here while still fulfilling his need for purpose, for work.

If she was being honest, the solution suited her, too. She was loath to part from him and she feared the reason for that. She was falling in love. Perhaps she'd already fallen. It had become clear to her on the way home from Penzance that she hadn't made love with him simply to exorcise the ghost of a lover past. This affair between them had deviated from its original purpose long ago. She kissed him, she made love with him, because she wanted to, because she needed to. Being with him fulfilled something deep at the core of who she was. That fulfilment was joy on the level of which Reverend Maddern addressed today: the deep, abiding joy of being understood by another human being and of being able to understand that person in return. She might not know everything about Cade, but she understood him. She knew what drove his moods. She knew how he thought.

Her gaze overtly watched him in the Penhaligon pew. She didn't bother trying to hide the fact that she was looking at him. When she saw him, she saw his beauty and his flaws. She loved him for both. They were part of who he was. She would lose him over those same qualities, too, if she wasn't careful. He had his father's stubborn pride.

To her surprise, Cade did not come to her after church, perhaps because rehearsals started afterwards. Her sisters had brought their violins and violas. Ayleth had brought her cello. The Treleven girls made up a large part of what passed for an orchestra in Porth Karrek. But he was nowhere he ought to be in preparation for rehearsal. Rosenwyn stepped outside for a breath of air and found him quite by accident in the graveyard, his golden head bare and bowed before a gravestone.

'Cade.' She went to him instinctively, her heartstrings tugged by the sight of him, so alone among the graves. She wasn't certain if he'd heard her. He didn't turn at her approach. She slipped her hand into his and looked down at the gravestone.

Maida Kitto
1 March 1764—24 December 1794
Beloved wife and mother

It was crudely carved, hardly an expensive marker—perhaps it had been painstakingly done by hand. But it was the date that riveted her. His mother had died on Christmas Eve.

Pieces of the stories he'd told her on the beach slipped into place, the picture becoming complete. He'd seen his mother the day before she died. He'd left Porth Karrek on the twenty-third and spent Christmas on the road as an eight-year-old child.

No wonder he hated Christmas...no wonder he hadn't wanted to come home and write a piece to celebrate what must be the darkest time of the year for him. She caught his profile and saw his tears. Cade was crying and she could not ease him, could not take away his pain.

'I don't want to go. Let me stay,' he begged. 'Until you're well, Mama.'

The baby had been born dead in the night. The doctor had carried it away.

It was clearly an effort for her to shake her head. He had never seen her so weak.

'No, you need to go while you have your father's permission.'

He'd heard his father promise when he'd knelt beside the bed. A deathbed promise while his father was in the throes of his own grief.

'I will not last long. A day...perhaps not even that. You needn't worry about me.'

'But it's Christmas Eve tomorrow,' he protested, snuggling up against her. 'No one should die on Christmas Eve, Mama.'

Her hand found the strength to stroke his hair, blond

curls unruly already after the Reverend's effort to slick them down.

'*Why not Christmas Eve, my boy?*' she comforted him. '*I think it would be the very best of nights to come into God's holy kingdom and sing with the hosts of angels. What a wondrous thing that will be.*'

'*I will write you songs, I will have choirs sing, Mama. You don't have to go. I will be the grandest composer of them all. Better than Handel, better than Bach. Just wait and see. Just wait with me, Mama.*'

It was a selfish request. The new baby was already in heaven. The baby would need Mama to look after him and Cade had already had Mama for eight years.

'*Sweet boy, you know I can't. But I will look down on you from the stars and I will hear every note.*' She pressed a kiss to his curls. '*Reverend Maddern is here. He will see you to the London coach. Stand up and let me look at you, my darling Cador, all grown up and off to the big city.*'

'*I'm only eight. I'm not grown up.*'

But he was, deep inside. Childhood had died a long time ago. Maybe it had been when the first baby had died. Maybe it had been when he'd started accompanying his father to the mines to work a man's hours. Or maybe it had been when he'd realised there was no real hope in the world.

If God was taking Mama, it must be true.

He felt Reverend Maddern's kindly hand at his shoulder, helping him to be strong. His mother squeezed his hand one last time.

'*Don't cry. Be happy. This Christmas, Cador, we will both be reborn. You in London and me in heaven.*'

* * *

Why did it still hurt so damn much? Cade didn't want to open his eyes, didn't want to see the tombstone. He was aware of Rosenwyn beside him, her hand in his, lending him strength. He clung to that strength. 'I miss her.'

'These last weeks must have been hell for you,' Rosenwyn said softly.

In her understanding, he found the courage to open his eyes, to set the memory aside. He held her gaze. 'It would have been, if not for you.' Thanks to her, he would now remember Porth Karrek no longer only as the boy who'd lost his mother, but as the man who'd found an extraordinary woman and, for a time, she'd loved him. He would carry the echo of that love with him, a ghost of his present, wherever he went.

Rosenwyn smiled at him and his heart swelled. 'Your mother would be proud of the piece you wrote. Shall we go in? Everyone is waiting.'

Rehearsal ended, marking a full week of practice and progress. The cantata was coming along well, and it needed to with just three days to go before Christmas Eve. Rosenwyn folded up her music and watched as Cade made a point of shaking each choirboy's hand as they filed out. He offered each boy a personal comment as he'd done every day since rehearsals had started. 'That's a very impressive ritual,' she said as the last boy left.

Cade made an excellent teacher. He'd patiently instructed the tenors on a difficult passage. The boys had sung the passage several times, making the same mistake, yet he had not lost his temper although she could see his shoulders tighten each time the passage went awry. He would be good with children. But teaching children would not impress him. He did not want to be a music tutor. He would need to be something more substantial. She might have an answer for that.

Cade smiled at the compliment. 'It teaches them manners without them knowing it. Everyone can be a gentleman whether they are born to it or not and it shows them I appreciate their efforts.' He cocked his arm. 'Shall we go?' The Trelevens were hosting a solstice bonfire on the beach tonight and she was pleased Cade seemed excited about it. With the rigour of rehearsals and his own personal memories of the season, Cade had been under stress this week. He hadn't been himself, but at least she better understood why.

'Are you going to dance with me in the sand?' Rosenwyn slipped her arm through his as they stepped out into the night air. She breathed deeply of the fresh air as they strolled down Budoc Lane with other couples and families to where the street gave out to the beach.

'If you would like.' He smiled and she took it as a good omen. Already she could see the flames from the solstice bonfire. This was one of her favourite nights. It was fun to be out of doors in the winter. She'd been down earlier, helping set up impromptu benches and tables made from planks of lumber on trestles. They were simple arrangements, but in the flame-lit darkness, everything became magical. There was food on the tables now: breads, pastries, a pile of Menhenick buns from the bakery, cakes and pies. Phin Bosanko roasted meat from the butcher's over a spit at the cooking fire and casks of ale stood at the ready.

'Kitto, there you are!' Her father came over and

pressed a pewter tankard into his hand. 'Drink up, the night is young!' He clapped Cade on the shoulder. 'How are rehearsals? Will everything be ready for Christmas Eve?' It was meant as polite small talk—her father didn't know the first thing about music despite his daughters' proclivity for it—and Cade responded, keeping the answer simple and positive.

'You make it sound so easy, but I see those rehearsals. I know otherwise. You are a magician.' Rosenwyn laughed up at him. 'You look very handsome in firelight, did you know that?' The fiddles started up, playing a bright, lively folk dance. 'This is one of my favourites, come on!' Rosenwyn tugged at his hand, giving him only enough time to set down his tankard before they were taken up by a group forming for the set.

Rosenwyn laughed her joy out loud as she passed Cade in the line, moving to a new partner. Oh, this was living! Dancing beneath the stars, the wintry air tinged with the hint of salt and bonfire, the waves just feet away, foamy chaperons to the party, and to be here with Cade, well, that was a wonder beyond all else. She partnered Eaton next, who danced in the sand with surprising dexterity for a big man. 'I must talk to you after this.' She had plans and hopes to set in motion.

'Absolutely, but not for too long.' Eaton winked. 'I've got someone special waiting for me, and you, too, it looks like.' He nodded in Cade's direction. Eaton was in a good mood, that boded well, and Cade would be surrounded by others, he would hardly notice she was gone. But she would notice. Any moment not with Cade seemed wasted with the clock ticking so perilously close to his departure. Unless these moments with Eaton changed that.

* * *

This would have been his life if things had been different. If he'd been born to a normal family. Tonight, everyone mixed, miners with landowners, merchants with the local peers. Tonight, no one cared for rank and class, only for celebrating the season. There'd been bonfires on the beach since Cade could remember, but not for him. His Methodist father had not approved of marking the solstice or of music and dance. Put the two together and it was the devil's own cause, worse even than gin and cake. This was the Cornwall Rosenwyn wanted him to see and it was a better one than the one he'd known.

He knew what she was up to—she wanted him to stay. She thought she could make him love Porth Karrek. But how could he with ghosts around every corner? He'd be walking in the past every day, constantly fighting memories.

Cade let a pretty young girl pull him into another dance, while he waited for Rosenwyn. She'd disappeared after the last set. That was fine. He needn't be possessive, he told himself. Jealousy was not part of their bargain, although much of that bargain was in jeopardy since Penzance. He would be leaving in a few days, there was no other choice. He had to go and he'd always been honest about that. His work was elsewhere. His ghosts were here. Rosenwyn was here.

On the periphery of the dancers, he saw Rosenwyn and Eaton Falmage emerge from the shadows. Falmage made his way towards him and tapped him on the shoulder. 'May I cut in?' His partner blushed, excited to be trading up from the local star to one of the local heirs.

It was well done of Falmage, freeing him up to return to Rosenwyn's side.

'Did you want to dance?' He was a little breathless from the exertion.

'No, I wanted to walk along the beach. Will you come?' She held out a tankard. 'I brought you something to drink since you didn't get to finish the last one.' The spark in her eye suggested she had plans for that walk.

It was quiet further down the beach away from the crowd where it was just them, the moon and the waves and some rocky clefts an intrepid soul might make good use of. Rosenwyn tugged him towards one. 'In here, Cade, it's a cave.' Oh, so not just a cleft, but a whole little room. He heard a match strike and a lantern flared to life, proof it was a room used to being occupied.

Rosenwyn flashed her lantern about the space, showing the empty cave to him. 'It used to be for smuggling, but it's not used much now.'

'Not by smugglers anyway. I am sure every lover in Porth Karrek knows of its existence.' Cade drew her into his arms. 'It's the perfect place for smuggling kisses and there have been far too few of those lately.' Rosenwyn had been right about that. The moment rehearsals had started, he'd been thrust into the public eye, everyone wanting to know how the concert was coming along, people stopping him on the street to talk, people inviting him to dinner, not to forget his meetings with the Reverend to make arrangements for the cantata. His days were full from the moment he got up until he fell into bed. There'd been little time to sneak away with her. She was at rehearsals with her sisters, but there'd been no time to repeat their afternoon in Penzance. He was feeling desperate.

'There isn't enough time, Rose,' he whispered, kissing her fiercely, and she answered him with a hunger of her own. Perhaps she felt it, too, this desperation that made every kiss golden.

'We have time tonight, Cade,' she murmured, her hand dropping between them to find him, to mould him. 'I love touching you.' He loved it, too, the feel of this bold, sensual woman's hand on him, her merest touch driving him to a place beyond reason. This cave might be such a place where no one could reach them, where the world held no sway.

'Not that much time, love,' Cade reminded her with a chuckle. 'Your father gave me a tankard of ale because he wanted me to know he had his eye on me. He wasn't just being friendly.' Still, there might be enough time if he was quick. How might he make love to her here? Would she be amenable to using a wall?

Rosenwyn pulled back and furrowed her brow. 'My father is a very friendly man.'

'I am sure he is, but no father is friendly when it comes to his daughters,' Cade assured her, missing her hand. He was regretting bringing her father up at all now.

'Well, he's not here at the moment and we have plenty of time for this.' Rosenwyn's eyes sparked with mischief as she dropped to her knees in the sand, her hand working his breeches open. 'I've had this idea since Penzance that what's good for the goose is good for the gander, or perhaps it will be the other way around tonight.'

Cade had not thought it possible to get any stiffer. He was quickly revisiting that conclusion now as her words settled in his brain. Sweet heavens, she meant to put her mouth on him, right here in the smugglers' cave. All the while, he'd been thinking about how he might make love to her here and she'd been leaps ahead of him, a plan already in mind. 'I should have known you'd have a plan. You have one for everything, even seduction at a bonfire attended by the whole damned town.'

She laughed up at him, her coppery waves spilling down her back, her green eyes on his face as intensely as her hand was on another part of his anatomy, and his heart lurched. What a sight! How would he ever find the willpower to give her up when the time came? But that time was not tonight. She bent her head to him and took the tip of him in her mouth and such silly considerations like the future fled like the nuisances they were. They had no place here in the cave.

Cade gripped the rocky outcroppings of the wall for stability, for contact with reality as her mouth made its way down the length of him. Nothing he could recall had ever felt this good. Her mouth was a symphony of sensations, licking, nipping, sucking. It was all violins and flutes, staccato bursts and long-held notes, gathering crescendos of tension until he couldn't help but cry out.

Dear heaven, he might die here in this cave from want, from desire, from physically exploding like a shooting star across the night sky. If he lived he might never be the same. His body gathered one last time. Could she tell the end was near? In some remote, practical part of his brain he thought he should caution her. He managed a series of warning grunts, of pleasurable moans and then he gave up and let himself be swept away by the pounding sensations of his release. The wake of his climax swept the beach of his soul clean.

There was no debris from the past, no concerns for the future, only now. Only this beautiful woman. Cade sank down into the sand, reaching for her, pulling her close. He would hold on to this moment as long as he could because when he let it go, the past and future would return.

Chapter Fourteen

'How did you know I'd like that?' Cade asked once sanity reasserted itself and his body had calmed. He liked holding her, liked having her head against his shoulder. No one else's would ever feel quite as right there. He winced at the thought and pushed at it, not wanting it. The future was starting to intrude, taking his thoughts to times and places and people that would come. He didn't want to think of the latter, of Rosenwyn being replaced. Although, logically, she would be, wouldn't she? It was a dismal thought, but a necessary one. It didn't seem realistic, based on his record to date, that he would live a celibate life starting in three days.

'Because I liked it when you did it for me.' Rosenwyn sighed softly against him, her fingers playing at his shirt. 'It stood to reason there must be a counterpart for you.' Her fingers stopped their plucking and Cade sensed she was gathering herself for a question, an important one if she was premeditating it. He braced himself. He didn't need three guesses to know what it was. 'We can have more time, Cade.'

He'd been wrong. Not a question. A statement.

Rosenwyn didn't deal with questions. She dealt with certainties. 'Technically, yes,' he acceded. 'Technically, I am a man responsible for his own time. I need not leave immediately. But to what end, Rose? For another week of sneaking away to caves? Does another week or two matter when eventually the outcome will still be the same?'

He dared not breathe the other end of that equation. *What if he didn't leave at all?* That was fantastical, beyond the realm of possibility. He might want to stay for her, but there was no way to make that happen. He would not take charity, he would not be seen as a man who lived on his wife's dowry. He had no prospects to offer her to compensate for that. He would not come to their marriage as an equal, therefore he could not come at all. A Kitto took care of his own.

'Not if you put it like that. Have I ever told you that you're a killjoy?' She looked up at him, laughing.

'Several times.' He chuckled. It might never be this easy with anyone else again or this honest. He hated how he was already mentally saying goodbye, already forcing himself to think of the future beyond Porth Karrek, beyond Rosenwyn, but he must. It would make leaving easier.

Rosenwyn shifted beside him, straddling his lap, her knees in the sand on either side of his thighs. She looked him in the eye. 'Cade, I am going to ask you a very difficult question and I need you to answer truthfully.' He nodded, his throat dry at the prospect of what she might demand.

'Cade, do you want to leave?'

How to answer? She knew the implications of that answer as well as he did even if she understood them less. 'It's not a question of want, Rose. It's a question of need. My life is out there.' He waved a hand to indicate the world beyond their cave. 'Without my music I have nothing, I am nothing.' He couldn't be nothing in Porth Karrek, not even for Rosenwyn. If he stayed he'd shrivel into nothingness, at best a man who'd once been something for a very short time.

'Let's try the question a different way.' Rose was relentless. 'What if you didn't need to go? What if everything you wanted, *needed*, was right here?' This small space might as well have been Aladdin's cave of wonders the way wishes were coming to life. Of course he'd thought of it, but that wasn't how life worked.

'It's an impossible what if, Rose. There's no sense in playing that game. Everything I need is not here, it's not going to be here and it's not in our interest to pretend otherwise. It will only make parting that much harder.'

Rosenwyn sat back on her haunches, her smile sad. She was disappointed in him and he hated that he'd disappointed her. It seemed either way he was bound to do it, though. Another woman might have argued that *she* should be enough to stay for. Rose did not. She merely leaned forward, kissed him softly and disarmed him entirely with her words. 'I love you, Cade Kitto. I shouldn't, but I do anyway.'

He should have known that wouldn't be the end of it. He should have known Rosenwyn Treleven wasn't the sort to say 'I love you' and just walk away. But it had been easier to let himself believe that than to worry about what she was planning.

Cade fixed his cravat in the mirror of his bedchamber and made his final preparations for the Gwav Gool party Captain Penhaligon was hosting up at the house. He had no excuse not to go. The cantata was a day away and there was nothing more to be done. The choir had got their passage right today, just in time. His two soloists were ready and the little orchestra was passably good, including a few surprises he'd added in private tribute to Rosenwyn's guidance. It would be his Christmas gift to her when she heard it, a token of how much their time together had meant.

Had meant. Past tense. It was all past tense now. The fourth Sunday in Advent was behind him. He'd spent it in church, then at rehearsal, and then the evening at Treleven House making kissing boughs with Rose's family. The cantata performance was ahead of him tomorrow. Then he would leave. Cade considered himself in the mirror. The last party before Christmas. The last party before a lot of things. He wanted to look his best, to have one last memory of Rose, smiling and laughing with him before he disappointed her.

She'd asked him to consider staying. She'd said she loved him. He'd made no adequate response in Penzance and she hadn't brought it up again. It was just as well. That conversation had only one outcome no matter how many times they repeated it. Rosenwyn wanted the impossible. He simply could not give it to her without losing himself and that defeated the whole reason for wanting it in the first place. It would be an impossible conversation. But it would not happen tonight. This evening would be for fun and entertainment, for making memories. He was going to enjoy every moment of it and worry about making decisions later. Cade took a final look in the mirror and set off for the big house.

It was snowing outside; big, fluffy flakes landed on

the shoulders of his greatcoat, a blanket already shrouding the ground in white. Cade smiled and lifted his face to the night sky. Snow was the perfect touch, the pièce de résistance to a night of magic, a night out of time, a night when anything was possible for the moment, like snow off the ocean.

He'd never experienced Gwav Gool from the inside, always from the outside, the grubby-handed little boy peering in through the windows. It had awed him as a small child, the glow of candles, the tables groaning with food, the rich, thick pieces of pies: Pesk Pie with its prawns, Stargazy pie, fish pies of all sorts courtesy of Abel Menhenick's bakery at the centre of it all. Already, as he approached the house, music spilled out, dancing music, another occasion for the villagers and the gentry to mingle. Tonight was a night for remembering the good of the old year and looking forward to the new. Perhaps this year would bring new opportunities for him with the Royal Academy in London, or opportunities he had yet to discover on the Continent. Perhaps those opportunities would at last drown out the ghosts of his past and the ones he was accumulating in the present.

All thoughts of past and present fled, though, at the sight of Rosenwyn on the greenery-draped staircase. She was coming down from the retiring room, surrounded by her sisters, although he hardly noticed them. How had he ever thought they all looked alike? Rose stood out, a flame among them. Tonight, she wore a gown of soft pink silk with rose-gold bobs at her ears, a veritable Christmas rose. His Christmas Rose if he chose. His, not just for the moment or a few days, but his for always. *If* he chose. She smiled when she saw him

and the temptation to throw his fears into the fire and
let them burn surged. What if he was wrong? What if he
could live here? What if she was all he needed? But that
wasn't true, was it? He couldn't stay here or he'd die.

'You look dashing tonight, Mr Kitto.' She took his
arm, her eyes appraising him privately, suggesting
she'd like to peel him out of his carefully assembled
clothes. 'Falmage was looking for you. He said he had
something to discuss. Shall we go find him?' She fairly
glowed.

'First, I want to dance with you.' Cade drew her towards the ballroom. 'I've never been to a Gwav Gool
before. I want to enjoy it. We'll see Falmage later.' If
this was to be the end, he wanted it to be a night to remember. A night of dancing with this woman he loved
but couldn't have.

'Never?' she queried as he led her to an open space
on the dance floor.

'No—remember, my father was a Methodist. Dancing and music were not appropriate.' He swung her
into a polka-like country dance, immediately picking
up the fast tempo. When had it become a simple matter to talk of his childhood? Of his father? Perhaps she
had changed that about him, too. He smiled at her and
tightened his grip about her waist. This was not a proper
ball. No one would care if he held his partner too close.
Tonight he wanted to breathe her in, every vanilla spice,
Christmas-scented breath of her, to store up every sight,
every sound of her against the days to come. When he
left, he wouldn't leave as he'd arrived, resenting Cornwall, resenting the life he'd had here. He might not embrace his Cornish past, but he'd come to terms with it,
thanks to her.

They danced and they ate, and danced some more, no one counting how many times he led her out to the dance floor. Everyone was too busy buzzing about the surprise announcement Captain Penhaligon would make that night. Most of the dances were round dances anyway, but at least he could see her, the light in her eyes, the joy with which she danced and the secret glances she'd send his way. She was in high spirits and they were contagious.

He had nearly forgotten Falmage until Falmage himself sought him out shortly before midnight.

'I have a proposition to discuss, Kitto.' Falmage offered him a glass of champagne from a passing tray. 'I've been hoping to catch you between dances, but your partner has kept you busy.' He took a swallow of the champagne. 'I don't know what your plans are, but I have a property near here that I don't use. It's going to ruin and I've been looking for a way to use it that might enrich the community. I think I've hit upon an idea. A conservatory, a music school, and I'd like you to head it up. You wouldn't just be a schoolmaster, of course. There'd be other obligations, special compositions to compose for holidays and other milestone occasions. Concerts to give throughout the year. We could drive over tomorrow and look the property over and press out the details. What do you say?'

Cade stared at the tall, dark ducal heir in disbelief. When something sounded too good to be true, then it probably was. Then he remembered other things: how Falmage and Rosenwyn had wandered off at the bonfire, how Rosenwyn had been relentless with her 'what if' scenarios in the cave. Had she known Falmage planned to make the offer? Reality hit, like a punch to the gut, so hard that he nearly dropped his champagne. She'd hadn't just known, *she'd* been the one to put the idea to Falmage.

'I don't rightly know *what* to say, my lord,' Cade replied stiffly and truthfully. Anger bubbled up inside. This was exactly what he hadn't wanted to happen *and* what he'd known would happen when two people from different classes acted on their attraction. A footman passed and he placed his untouched champagne on the tray. 'If you will excuse me, my lord.' Not Eaton. Not Falmage. But my lord. He did not hobnob with the mighty the way Rosenwyn did, throwing around their Christian names as if they were brothers. He had been on the brink of forgetting his place after four weeks of too much familiarity.

'Forgive me, Kitto, if I have erred in some way.' Falmage was flummoxed. 'I was under the impression the overture would be welcome. I did not mean…'

'I'm sure you did not. Again, excuse me.' Cade left Falmage standing alone, giving the other man no chance to respond. He needed to find Rosenwyn. They had to discuss this immediately. What other plans had she put into motion without discussing them with him? He found her in the hall, chatting with her sisters. She smiled when she saw him, no doubt expecting good news.

'I've spoken with Falmage.' His tone was terse, he was holding on to civility by a thin thread only for the sake of her sisters. His hand was at her arm. 'If you would come with me, we must talk. Privately.'

Chapter Fifteen

He'd talked to Eaton! There could only be good news that way. The air outdoors was bracing, the snow still coming down. Rosenwyn wrapped her arms about herself. Perhaps Cade would take his jacket off and slide it about her shoulders. Her dress was made for indoors and dancing where it was warm, but of course Cade would want to celebrate and it would be best to do that out here, just the two of them. She would have to act surprised when he told her. Eaton's offer was the perfect Gwav Gool gift, the perfect cap to this wonderful night of dancing with Cade, laughing with Cade. He would see now that he could stay, that they could be together, that there wouldn't be any living off his wife's dowry.

'How dare you go behind my back and beg? I told you explicitly not to do such a thing!' The ferocity of Cade's accusation was stunning and so unexpected that all she could do was stare as she processed the words in confusion.

'What did Falmage say?'

'He offered me a position at his brand-new music

conservatory,' Cade growled, pacing on the front porch of Karrek House. 'So new, in fact, it didn't even exist until two days ago.'

'How is this a problem? I fail to see the source of your anger,' Rosenwyn retorted, her mind having wrapped itself around the words. 'You have been handed a golden opportunity on a silver platter. This is wonderful news, Cade. You can stay, you can have meaningful, music-centred work.'

And you can have me, she almost added. But that was for him to figure out.

'You meddled! Falmage never would have made that offer on his own.'

'Sometimes people need a push to see the vision right in front of them.' She would not apologise for giving Falmage that push, or for giving Cade that push.

'But I told you not to, does that mean nothing?' Cade's anger was morphing into despair. 'You did this without asking me.'

'I did ask you, if you recall, the night of the bonfire. But you gave me no answer. You said you couldn't answer because there was nothing real to consider, only mythical hypotheticals. Well, now, I've given you a real scenario. You have something tangible to weigh against going back to London,' she challenged, hands on her hips, anger coursing through her. 'Stay here, run Falmage's Academy, have a permanent post for life, compose what moves you, pass your love of music on to young children who, like you, might be desperate for such an opportunity. Change lives here, Cade, or go back to London and take your chances.'

Stay here, let yourself love me as I love you.

'You should have discussed this with me,' he ground

out. 'I will not be seen as a weak-minded man who is led about by his wife.'

She couldn't listen to this nonsense any more. All he had to say was 'yes' and he'd managed to bungle that. 'I have laid your dream at your feet and you can't handle it. Instead you will be stubborn, like your father, and doom us to unhappiness and regrets just like he did to your family. You say you hate him, but you are just like him.' The words tumbled out, hot and angry.

Cade blanched as if he'd been slapped. 'If that's what you think, you never knew me at all, never loved me at all, despite what you may think.'

She had never been this mad in her life. She fairly trembled with anger as she spoke. 'What I think, Cade, is that you need to stop running and learn to live with yourself, your past and your present, so that you can have a future. You say you won't marry until you can support a family. But that's just window dressing for the real reason. You are afraid to love.' He made her pay for those words. His eyes went cold, his beautiful, expressive face became stoic. Whatever he was thinking, feeling, was shuttered to her. She was locked out entirely.

He straightened his jacket. 'I feel it's best we end our association now. I will write to Falmage and decline his offer. If you'll excuse me, I have some details to take care of for tomorrow's concert.' He stepped off the porch and walked down the lantern-lit driveway of Karrek House, disappearing into the night as if he'd never been, a ghost of her imagination.

She'd lost him. The realisation was staggering. If her words had slapped him, then his had positively been a blow to her stomach. She couldn't breathe, couldn't think. She reeled, gripping the porch post to stay upright. Should she run after him? Should she go to the gatehouse and make him explain himself? Should she let him go? She didn't know what to do, she didn't know how to fix this.

She didn't know how long she was out there, only that Ayleth was beside her and she was shaking. Ayleth's arms were around her, her sister's soft voice urging her to come in. 'You're cold, Rosie, come inside. Tell me what has happened? Where is Mr Kitto?'

She was cold. Inside and out. She might never be warm again. She collapsed into her sister's arms, sobbing, 'Cade is gone. I've lost him and it's all my fault.' This was how it felt when the world fell apart. She knew, she'd felt this way once before, but that seemed like nothing now compared to the emptiness that swamped her. She just had to get through tomorrow and Cade Kitto would be gone for good and then she could start putting her world back together. Would she never learn? Would she always love the wrong man?

He'd been wrong. He could see that now when it was too late and it had cost him the woman he loved, or rather the woman he'd been afraid to love until she was gone, beyond his reach. She'd been right about that. He was afraid to love, afraid of what loving meant, of how it would change him, of what he'd become if he stayed for her. In the end, he'd chosen fear over love when Falmage had made his offer. He had chosen unwisely. He wanted to tell Rose that.

Cade watched from the side as people filed into the church. The church bristled with a special energy tonight, greenery swagged the centre aisle, extra garlands were tied at each pew courtesy of the Trelevens. Expensive, white-wax candles burned at the front of the church, courtesy of Cloyd Bolitho and his son, the groundskeeper. This service was a joint effort. Everywhere Cade looked there were signs of community donations which had turned the plain little church of St Piran's into a beautiful place for one night. Captain Penhaligon entered with Emily Faulkner, his fiancée of one day, on his arm. They had found the courage to choose love. He envied them. But there was no sign of the person he wanted to see most. Rose.

Reverend Maddern entered, his white half-robe over his darker robe, his purple stole with its gold trim about his neck. He mounted the pulpit and intoned the words that lit the candles: hope, love, joy, peace. All gifts that Rosenwyn had given him, Cade realised. He'd treated her gifts with contempt and not for the first time. He wanted to tell her she was right about so much. He had been too prideful to understand the magnitude of Falmage's offer. He'd been too stubborn to let go of the past and, in doing so, he had become more like his father than he'd ever been. He saw that now. He regretted that now. He could do better and be better. For her. For himself. Cade scanned the congregation for Rosenwyn, looking for her among her sisters. Would she come? Would she play? He couldn't blame her if she didn't. She'd asked so little of him and given him so much in return.

The Reverend's message was short. He gestured to Cade and Cade motioned for everyone to take their places. In the quiet scuttle of the orchestra and choir assembling, he did not see her come in, but when he looked once more at the piano, she was there at the bench, stealing his breath in her green gown, a matching ribbon threaded through her hair. He raised his baton and smiled at her, hoping that one smile would communicate everything his heart felt in that moment; his gratitude that she had come tonight for him, that he loved her. But she did not smile back.

Cade motioned to the orchestra and the sweet notes of a tin whistle, a most uniquely Cornish instrument, filled the church with a plaintive tune. Her stamp was everywhere, her words in his mind as he directed.

'Your cantata needs to sound like Cornwall... You've forgotten what Cornwall sounds like...'

He'd listened. To her. She'd helped him remember. He turned to bring in the piano. Tonight, he would help her remember what she loved about performing. It would be a last gift to her, an apology. But when she began to play, she stole his heart all over again and then she broke it. She lifted her eyes to his, her gaze filled with emotion. She was saying goodbye. She was letting him go.

Chapter Sixteen

Rosenwyn poured herself into the music. Nothing mattered but these moments. Had this church ever heard such beautiful music? Heard such a beautiful message in the lyrics of the arias? Cade had wrought a masterpiece that blended the old traditions of the cantata form with the traditions of his home. Tonight she was part of that. She owed Cade that much at least. He'd given her a chance to perform again. Tonight was a gift given without strings because those strings had already been broken. She'd broken them by tying them too tight.

When the cantata concluded, she was not the only one in tears when the performance ended. The congregation came to their feet, led by Eaton who was the first one to rush to Cade's side in congratulations. 'Not even Handel's *Messiah* is quite as fine as that.'

'I simply must have him,' Eaton vowed when he came to congratulate her at the piano. 'He's splendid, a credit to our part of the country.' But she'd ruined that, too. Cade would never believe Eaton's offer now. Perhaps she shouldn't have pushed. How ironic if it all would have come together on its own if she'd only waited, if she'd only let Cade's music speak for itself. Her stomach lurched, sickened by the thought. The congregation rose, receiving Reverend Maddern's benediction, everyone eager to file out, to wish the Reverend a Happy Christmas and to greet Cade. How would she manage it? How would she face him?

She had plenty of time to think about it. The Trelevens were the last to leave, her sisters surrounded by well-wishers congratulating them on the performance. At this rate, they'd miss the bell ringing at midnight. By the time her family filed out, she'd got her wish. She didn't have to face him. Cade had disappeared from the Reverend's side. There was no relief in the reprieve, though, only disappointment. Reverend Maddern stopped her with a gentle hand as she brought up the end of the line. 'He's in the graveyard. I don't know what happened between the two of you, or why, but you should go to him.'

She shook her head. The older man meant well, but what did he know of affairs of the heart? He would likely be scandalised to know she'd slept with his protégé in the broad light of day in a Penzance inn, or that she'd given him certain pleasures on the beach, or that his darling protégé took these affaires as his due. 'What is wrong cannot be mended, sir.' Besides, if he was in the graveyard, he'd want to be alone with his family.

He gave her a stern look of disagreement. 'Even on Christmas? The one night of the year when all things are possible?'

Perhaps it was the Reverend's words or perhaps it was the sight of Cade's straight back, his gold head bowed as he stood before a tombstone in the graveyard that compelled her to try, against her better judgement—it wouldn't be the first time she'd ignored it. Rosenwyn slipped into the graveyard, shutting the wrought-iron gate behind her silently. She could tell from his posture he was deep in thought. Of course. Tonight was the night. He must have been thinking of his mother all day and tonight as he'd directed. For a moment, she second-guessed herself and nearly turned around. People should not be bothered in cemeteries, but apparently the Reverend felt this would be an exception to the rule.

'Cade.' She came up behind him, her hand at his back. She'd not planned to touch him. 'That was beautiful, the cantata was absolutely perfect. The tin whistle was inspired.' She was babbling, suddenly just another idiot talking to someone famous. 'Your mother would have been proud.' It would be best to step away, to leave him to his grief. She took a step backwards.

'Stay, Rose.'

She stopped, stood where she was and waited. For the first time, she didn't have a plan, didn't know what to expect. Cade turned towards her. 'I'm glad you liked it. It was for you. The tin whistle, the triangle, the drums. You were the one who suggested I give the cantata a Cornish sound. It was a good idea.'

'Thank you. I am honoured.' She hated how awkward everything suddenly was. There was so much unsettled between them. She couldn't pretend there wasn't.

'I should be thanking you. Without you on the piano it would not have been extraordinary. Tonight, you elevated my music. You didn't have to. Why did you come? I was an ass.'

'Love never fails, Cade. I knew what the night meant to you, I knew what you'd poured into the composition.

No matter what is between us, I love you. I can't help it. I couldn't let you down. I'd already done that once.' She couldn't let him go without at least apologising. 'I'm sorry about Falmage. I should have discussed it with you and I should have respected your wishes. You don't want to stay and I forced the issue when you were only trying to be polite. I saw things that weren't there, things between us. You warned me and I didn't listen.'

He stepped towards her, pressing a finger to her lips. 'Shh, Rose, it's I who should be apologising. Christmas has already cost me one woman I love, it will not cost me another.'

'I should not have said what I did about your father.' She could not let him shoulder the blame.

'Yes, you should have. You were right. I don't want to make my father's mistakes. I was being stubborn. You were right. My pride was a smokescreen for my very real fear. I was afraid to love, I was afraid of who I would become if I stayed. Falmage's offer meant I couldn't run away from Porth Karrek, that I had to learn to live with my past. I thought it would be easier to push you away than let the past in. But I was wrong about that, too.'

'What changed your mind?'

'You did, the music did. If you were brave enough to love, if you were brave enough to show up tonight after the things I said, then I needed to be brave enough to let myself love you. When I heard the tin whistle tonight, I realised this is me, all of me. Porth Karrek is about more than the past. It's about the present you and I have made and the future we could build.'

But it was too late for that, Rosenwyn thought sadly.

'I should not have interfered. Eaton would have offered the school without my intervention.'

He nodded. 'Falmage said as much tonight.' He blew out a breath. She could see it in the night air. 'Falmage and I have come to terms. So, all that is left is for you and me to come to our terms. Do you think it's possible for a stubborn Cornish man and a headstrong Cornish woman to do that?'

Hope sparked low in her belly as he reached for her hand. 'I think it depends on what those terms are, Cade Kitto.' Her stomach was a riot of butterflies. He had taken Falmage's offer? What did that mean?

'Those terms, Rose, are marriage.' He knelt in his fine dark trousers on the snow-decked ground of the graveyard, before his mother's gravestone, her hand in his. 'Will you do me the honour of becoming my wife? Of putting up with me for the rest of my days? I promise you nothing except two things: I will no doubt be hard to get along with at times, moody at others, but I will love you, ceaselessly, relentlessly.'

'That's all you ever needed to promise.' She wiped at her tears with her free hand. 'Get off your knees, Cade, and kiss me.'

'Is that how you say yes?' Cade rose and wrapped his arms about her, pressing her close against him as his mouth found hers, both of them crying and laughing, not caring that they'd drawn an audience of those who'd lingered to hear the Porth Karrek tradition of the midnight bells beneath snow-flecked skies.

'I love you, Cade Kitto,' Rosenwyn whispered and it seemed every crack in his heart healed at those words, that her words had made him whole. Ghosts became angels as the snow fell, brushing their clothes with its Christmas offering as it decorated the gravestones in white.

'I love you, Rose,' he murmured, barely getting the words out as the church clock struck midnight and the bells began to peal, echoing in the clear night sky as they rang in Christmas. 'It is true, after all, the Reverend is right. He told me anything was possible tonight.'

Rosenwyn laughed. 'He told me the same thing.' Then she kissed him. 'Nadelik Lowen, Cade.'

'Nadelik Lowen.' Three weeks ago, those words had struck a certain kind of terror in his heart. But not tonight. Cade looked to the sky where a bright star winked among the snowflakes and Christmas was forgiven.

* * * * *

If you enjoyed this story
check out Marguerite Kaye and Bronwyn Scott's
other anthologies together

Scandal at the Midsummer Ball
Scandal at the Christmas Ball